Inked Desires

Hanna Dunn

Contents

Chapter 1

S uzy

The moonlight filtered through the pine trees lining the fields, leaving shadows on the pavement. The crisp air that had been missing for months caressed my skin. Cranking up the radio, I sang along to Justin Timberlake's "Rock Your Body." It was just the cool breeze, JT, and me. I couldn't wait to crawl in my bed and close my eyes, getting lost in a dream world that had nothing to do with my current reality.

The night had been perfect. I'd had dinner and drinks with my best friend, Sophia, and although I was exhausted from a long workday, I felt a sense of serenity. Spending time with Sophia always made me happy. She was like a sister to me, especially when she had lived with me for over a year. I felt like part of me had been missing since the day she moved out, leaving me behind.

Dancing in the seat, screaming out the lyrics, I thought about how I wanted someone that would do everything the song described. No one had ever made me feel the way that JT sang about women. The steering wheel shook in my hands and a screeching sound pulled me out of my JT trance.

"Damn it," I said, hitting the steering wheel with my palm.

The orange flash from my hazards blinked against the dark pavement as I pulled off the road and my car sputtered to a stop. Bad luck seemed to follow me. I squeezed the steering wheel, trying to calm my frazzled nerves. I knew the day would come, the day my car would die, but I prayed it would happen after my next paycheck...no such luck.

Resting my head on the wheel, I closed my eyes, taking a deep breath. "Great, just fucking great." I rocked back and forth, feeling sorry for myself, hitting my head on the cool plastic. I thought about whom to call or where to walk. I hadn't passed a gas station or even a damn streetlight in miles. Without picking up my head, I reached for my phone, bringing it to my eyes.

"Shit." The screen wouldn't power on after I hit every button I could think to press. It was useless. It was dead and now I was totally stranded. What else could possibly go wrong? Sighing, I sat up and glanced in the rearview mirror, but only the shadows from the trees filled my view. No cars, neon signs, or streetlights. Fuck.

I placed my hand on my chest to feel the beat of my heart, which was so hard I swear it was audible. Visions from slasher movies flooded my mind. Girl deserted on the side of the road until she's found by a handsome stranger that ends up being a serial killer.

Should I start walking to God knows where? Do I just sit there and wait for a stranger to offer me help? I never liked feeling helpless—I was too smart to be helpless, but it was the only thing I felt in this moment. It could be hours before someone found me in my car.

I grabbed my purse, dead phone, and keys, and climbed out of the car. My feet ached in the extra-high heels I wore. Leaning against the car, I gave my feet a moment to adjust, as I looked in both directions. Neither of my options were good and I was exhausted. My feet fucking screamed from standing still. Thank God I could sleep in tomorrow after the way this evening was ending. There was a gas station a couple miles back—better to go with what I knew than to walk into an uncertain future. I tapped the lock button on my key chain one more time, helping relieve my OCD need to double-check everything, before I started walking away.

Barely clearing the trunk, a single light came over a small hill in the distance, hurting my eyes with the brightness. The roar of the engine grew louder as the distance closed. I waved my arms as a figure came into view, but the asshole biker drove right passed me as I screamed, "Hey! Hey!" The wind from his bike caused the dust on the road to kick up and fill my mouth.

I turned around, coughing, and screamed toward the bike. I knew it was pointless. There was no way in hell he'd heard me yelling above the roar of his bike, but he had to see me. The red taillight lit up the road as he turned the bike in my direction. I swallowed hard, unsure if this was my best idea of the night—but I'd already made too many mistakes to dwell on that. He was my only hope of getting home.

I stood there like a deer in headlights, unable to move, as I gaped at him. My hands trembled as the figure on the bike came to a stop. The engine was almost deafening, as I took in the sight of him on the machine. The bike was a Harley, a Fat Boy, with no windshield, chrome handlebars, and a dark body. He wore black boots, dark jeans, and a dark t-shirt. He was large and muscular, and I sucked in a breath as my eyes reached his handsome and rugged face. A playful grin danced on his lips as he watched me ogle him. Fucking hell.

"Need some help, lady?" he asked, removing his helmet, running his fingers through his disheveled hair. The dark peaks stood up on the top, the sides were short and clipped, and the color matched the sky—dark. I couldn't see his eyes; a pair of tinted glasses hid them. Could serial killers be so sexy?

"Um, do you have a cell phone I could use to call for a ride?" I asked without taking a step in his direction. Don't get too close—leave room to run. Who the fuck was I kidding? I couldn't make it five feet in these damn shoes.

"Sure." As he leaned back on his bike, I studied his body as he dug in his pocket. The skintight jeans showed his muscles through the denim fabric. Everything clung to him. I wanted to poke him to see if he felt as hard as he looked. What the fuck was wrong with me?

I was too busy staring to notice what he was holding out for me. "Lady, you wanted my phone?"

Snapping back to reality with the sound of his deep voice, I took a step toward him, reaching for the phone. "Oh, sorry."

My fingertips grazed his palm, and a tiny shock passed between us. His fingers closed on my hand as I pulled away. My heartbeat, which had calmed, now began to pound feverishly in my chest. It had to be my hormones. I hadn't had sex in God knows how long—I stopped counting after three months. The man in front of me wasn't my type, but his sex appeal wasn't lost on me. He looked like a whole lot of trouble, and I didn't need that in my life.

I stepped back, keeping my eyes trained on him, as I dialed the only person close enough to help—Sophia. The phone rang and his eyes traveled up and down the length of my body—with each ring, my stomach began to turn. I didn't have anyone else to call.

Tapping the end button, I sighed. "There's no answer. Thanks." I gave him a sheepish smile as I handed him the phone.

"Let me take a look and see if there's anything I can do. Okay?" he asked, as he began angling the bike to shine the headlights on the hood.

"Sure." I hit the unlock button on my car key before climbing in. I put the key in the ignition, but stayed aware of his proximity. No one would hear me scream if he tried to kill me. I couldn't let my guard down.

He put the kickstand down, climbed off the bike, and placed the helmet on the seat. Pulling the hood latch next to my seat, I watched him from the relative darkness of my car, my face hidden by shadows. He was large, larger than he looked sitting on the Harley. He had to be more than a foot taller than me, and looked more solid with the bike illuminating his body. I stared at him, mouth open slightly, my breathing shallow as I looked at him like a piece of meat through the gap between the hood. He oozed masculinity and ruggedness, and I tried to picture him without all the skintight clothes. The muscles in his arm rippled as he touched the parts under the hood.

What would it be like to be with a man like him? Every man I'd dated just didn't work out. They were nice guys, but the spark I wanted was always missing. People think I'm a good girl, and I am, but my mind is filled with dirty thoughts that I could never share with a mate. I'd shared them with Sophia, but she doesn't count. No one had ever done anything fantasy-worthy with me. I can barely speak the words that are needed to describe the things I want done to me, or that I'd want to do to another person in this world.

"Ma'am," he said, snapping me out of the evaluation of my sex life, or lack thereof.

"Sorry, yes?"

"Can you try and start it for me, please?" he said, leaning over the hood, his hands placed on either side of the opening. "Now," he said. The car churned and churned. "Stop," I heard him yell over the screeching noise. He moved methodically around the engine. "Try it again." I turned the key, causing the engine to rattle, but not start.

He stood, rubbing the back of his neck as curses spilled from his lips. The only thing I could see was his crotch. I stared, motionless. His t-shirt covered the belt loops and stopped just above his groin. Damn. He filled out those jeans. He had to be big. Everything about him was big—he couldn't, just couldn't, have a small cock, could he?

The last guy that I'd slept with was more the size of a party pickle. It was the most unsatisfying sexual experience of my life. He was a teacher, and I wanted someone who was educated and self-sufficient, but he was boring in and out of the bedroom. I thought I'd found that with Derek, Mr. Pickle, but I was wrong. He was a wreck, and filled with more mental issues than anyone I'd ever know. He was germophobic, which was problematic when having sex. He'd jump right out of bed immediately after sex to shower and wash the dirty off. I sighed to myself, remembering his need to be clean—never mind that he was an asshole, too.

The hood of my car made a loud thump as the man slammed it. "Your car is a little tricky. Foreign cars can be complicated. I can't seem to get it to start," he said, walking toward the driver-side door.

"It's okay. Thanks for trying." I climbed out, not wanting to be trapped inside. What the hell was I going to do now?

"I was heading to the bar up the road. Want to join me?" He smiled and tilted his head as he studied me. "You can call a tow truck from there. It may take them a while for them to get out here."

I couldn't think of any other option. He was my only hope, my saving grace from the dark roadside, and a means to an end. There were worse things than climbing on the back of his motorcycle and wrapping my arms around him. "Okay, but I've never been on a bike."

"Never? How is that even possible?" he asked, shaking his head, a small laugh escaping his lips. His teeth sparkled in the light, straight and white. His jaw was strong, his cheekbones jutted out more when he smiled, and a small dimple formed on the left side of his face.

I looked down at the ground, my cheeks heated. "I don't know. I just never knew anyone that had one and I find them totally scary."

"It's not far from here and there isn't much traffic. I'll keep you safe," he said, holding out his helmet.

My stomach fluttered as I closed the car door and thought about my first motorcycle ride. The black, round helmet felt cool against my fingers as I took it from him. I scrunched my eyebrows together as I studied it. I didn't know if there was a front or a back, or how to put it on.

"Here, let me help you," he said as he reached for the helmet, removing it from my grip. His hand touched mine and I felt the spark again. Not a real spark, but electricity that I felt with every fiber of my being from the slightest touch. My body wanted his touch, but my mind was throwing up the caution flag.

Placing it gently on my head, he ran his rough fingers down the straps, almost caressing my skin, to adjust it to fit my face. I inhaled deeply, trying to fill all my senses with him. He smelled different than any other man I'd smelled. He didn't smell of cheap cologne, but there was a spicy, woodsy scent that reminded me of home. I closed my eyes and relished the feel of his warm skin against mine.

"All done. Are you ready?" he asked.

I opened my eyes, heat creeping up my neck, as I had been lost in his touch. "Yes." I prayed my voice didn't betray me.

He climbed on the bike, sliding forward, making room for me. "Lift your leg and climb on."

Placing my hand on his shoulder to help balance myself, I followed his instructions; my body slid forward, smashing against him. Rock solid. He turned his head, looking me in the eyes. "Put your feet on the pegs and wrap your arms around me. I don't bite—well, unless you want me to." He smirked, and my heart felt like it was doing the tango in my chest as I pressed against his back. He didn't just say that to me, did he? I lifted my feet off the ground, turning over complete control to the stranger I was entrusting with my life. I locked my hands together, completely wrapped around him.

"Ready?"

"Wait! I don't even know your name. I mean, I'm putting my life in your hands and I don't even know who you are." I gripped his body tighter, clinging to him.

I couldn't hear his laughter, but I felt the rumble of it from deep in his chest. "My friends call me City, sugar." He throttled the engine and my heart skipped a beat. Fear gripped me—there was no turning back now.

My grip became viselike, fear overcoming any need to be cool or seem calm in front of him. He patted my hands before the bike began to move, and I couldn't bear to look. I buried my face in his back, avoiding any chance of seeing the road. The wind caressed my skin, causing it to feel like ice compared to the warmth my palms experienced. Did this man have any soft spots? I flexed my fingers against his chest, wanting to feel his hardness, praying like hell I made it seem natural and not like I was molesting him.

The bike picked up speed, and my heart thundered against his back. I gripped him harder, holding on for dear life, the sound of the engine drowning out everything else around me, except the two of us. He leaned into the bike, his ass moving snugly between my legs. I didn't dare move. He was warm, comfortable, and I enjoyed every minute my body touched his. I closed my eyes, trying to not think about the movement of the bike underneath us—the slight shift and unevenness of the road made me feel off balance.

The noise of the engine changed, and I finally peeked over his shoulder. The parking lot of the Neon Cowboy was packed with bikes and was the brightest thing for miles. I'd driven by it dozens of times, but never thought about stopping. This wasn't the type of bar for kids on speedy, foreign-made bikes, but a place for tough bikers to hang out, drink beer, and pick up chicks.

City backed the bike into an empty spot, and I could feel my body begin to tremble from the fear that finally began to seep through my veins. I did it. I rode on a motorcycle, and with a stranger, no less. My breath was harsh as I blinked slowly and tried to calm myself down.

"You can climb off now, sugar." His legs were straddling the bike and he held the handlebars, securing the bike for me. "Enjoy your first ride?"

I released my hands from the security of his body and hoisted myself off on trembling legs. "It was the single most terrifying thing I've ever experienced," I said, thankful when my feet were firmly on the ground. I stood, trying to get my body to stop shaking and my heart to slow down before walking inside the bar with him at my side.

"If that's the scariest thing you've ever experienced, you need to get out more, sugar. I took it slow with you." He grinned, and my stomach plummeted from his sinful smile. I wanted to see him above me naked and moving in and out of my body slowly, almost at a torturous pace. Everything about him made my body convulse and scream for attention. He wasn't my type. I preferred a bookworm and a man that liked to spend an evening inside watching a movie or playing Scrabble, not riding like a bat out of hell on a Fat Boy to hang out at a bar. I wasn't a barfly and never would be.

The outdoor lights gave me a full view of the man that called himself City. His hair was darker than I originally thought, almost jet black, and an inch long on the top, brushing against his forehead as he shook it out. It was a mess from the wind, with the front hanging over his forehead. I couldn't tell the color of his eyes; they were still hidden behind the tinted lenses of his glasses.

"Yeah, lucky me." I chuckled and tried to play it cool, even though my body shook. If that was slow, I didn't think I wanted to know what his idea of fast and hard were — or did I? Fuck me. He had my brain all jumbled.

After removing the helmet, I ran my fingers through my hair, trying to straighten it after the wild ride. He laughed as he crawled off the bike, taking the helmet from my hands, and placed it on the seat. I watched, mesmerized, as he removed his glasses and put them inside a small bag hanging from the side of the bike. I wanted to see his eyes, and the entire man without a mask or veil.

"Ready, babe?" He motioned toward the door.

I wanted to scream no, but I didn't have a choice. I could never walk into this sort of place on my own.

"Yeah, ready as I'll ever be." I started walking toward the door and felt a hand on my arm, stopping me in my tracks. I looked at his fingers wrapped around my arm and turned toward him. "What are you doing?"

"You can't just walk into a place like this. You're an outsider. They'll eat you alive in there. I don't want anyone giving you shit. We have to make them believe you're with me so they leave you the fuck alone. Unless you want the attention?" he asked with a crooked eyebrow.

"I don't." I didn't mind the idea of making everyone in the bar think we were together. City was hot and seemed like a nice guy; he did stop to help me when he could've driven right by me.

"Just stay by my side and follow my lead. I know these people and I don't want them sniffing around you. They look for easy prey," he said, giving me a smile that made my body tingle and my sex convulse.

"Okay, I'll stick to you like glue and follow your lead." Jesus, I sounded like a dork. I've always been a bookworm. I was national honor society member, and when all my friends were partying, I stayed in my dorm to study.

City nestled me against his side, tucking me between his body and arm. I moved with him, trying to keep up with his fluid movements, but my legs were so short I felt like I almost had to jog to keep time with him. He opened the door and I was immediately hit with a smoky smell, loud, twangy music, and a dozen set of eyes looking directly at us.

Randomly people yelled out "City" throughout the bar, giving me a clue that he was a regular. I felt like I'd entered a seedy version of Cheers and City was Norm, only sexy and muscular. He leaned down, placing his mouth next to my ear. I felt his hot breath before I could hear his words.

"Stick close and show no fear," he whispered, causing goose bumps to break out across my skin. "Let's say hello then we'll call a tow for you."

City looked big enough to handle any man in this place, but I didn't want to take that chance. I concentrated on breathing, keeping my chin up, and watching where I walked. The floor was filled with peanut shells and dust, and it made the walk in the stilettos even more treacherous than normal. I could barely walk when I bought them, but they looked too sexy to pass up.

We walked to a table filled with men all wearing their leather vests, covered in patches. They were unshaven, as dangerously sexy as City, with mischievous smiles on their faces. "Who's this lovely lady, City?" one man asked. His eyes raked up my body, stopping at my breasts before he looked at my face.

"This is Sunshine. Don't even fucking think about it, Tank, she's with me," City said with a smile on his face as he pulled me closer.

Sunshine? I'd never told him my name and he never asked. I didn't like the way Tank looked at me. Thank God he wasn't the one driving by while I was stranded. He looked at me like I was a piece of meat, a meal for his enjoyment.

Tank put his hands up in surrender. "Dude, I'd never. Chill the fuck out. I'm just enjoying the view," he said, his eyes moving from City to me, and not being coy about his visual molestation.

City squeezed my waist. "Sunshine, this is Tank, the asshole. This is Hog, Frisco, and Bear," he said, pointing to each of the men.

The nicknames didn't seem to fit any of the men, except Bear. His arms were hairy and he was big, huge, in fact, with dark hair and a fuzzy face. He looked huggable and kind, with soft hazel eyes.

"Hi," I said, looking at each of them quickly, but I didn't try to memorize their names.

"I didn't know you were bringing a woman tonight, City," Bear said.

"Wilder shit has happened, Bear," City said, pulling me closer, leaving no space between us.

"She doesn't look like your usual taste, my friend." Bear smirked. "I don't mean that shitty, girl, I just mean you're one fine piece of ass and too good for that low-life motherfucker. You should be sitting on my lap." He patted his leg, and I wanted to find an exit. I looked down and studied my clothes. I didn't wear the trashy clothes some of the women in here wore, but I looked classy, sexy even, with not a hint of nerd to be found.

City moved toward Bear, and my heart sank as he began to speak. "Show some respect, you asshole. That's not how you talk to a lady." City stood inches from Bear's face. "Apologize to the lady. Now." City towered over him as Bear stayed rooted in his chair.

Bear looked at me, and I could see him swallow hard before he spoke. "I'm sorry, Sunshine. I was just kidding around. I really am an asshole. Forgive me, please."

"No harm done, Bear," I said with a fake smile, hoping to calm the situation.

"We're going to sit at the bar." City looked at Bear, not moving his eyes.

"Come on, dude, sit with us. Don't mind Bear. He's a total dick. Make his ass go sit at the bar," Frisco said.

"Sunshine and I want to be alone. I'll catch you guys another night," City said, pressing his hand against my back, guiding me away from the table and the large bar area.

"I'm sorry. They can be childish dicks. Bear doesn't have a filter," he said as he pulled out a chair for me. City had manners. Not many of the men I dated did something as simple as pull out a chair for a lady—it was a lost art. "He's a good guy, but sometimes his mouth runs and he doesn't think before he speaks."

"It's okay, really...it is. Thanks for sticking up for me," I said to him as I sat down, pulling my stool closer to the bar. "Why did you call me Sunshine?"

"Well, I don't know your name and you remind me of sunshine—your hair is golden and your smile glows. Just sounded right. I had to come up with something on the fly," he said. "I hope you didn't mind." He shrugged and grabbed the menu lying nearby.

"I didn't mind, but my name is Suzy."

"What would you like, Suzy?"

I wanted to say "you," because somehow this man made me lose my grip on reality. "Virgin daiquiri, please."

"Virgin? Really?" His brows shot up and the corner of his mouth twitched.

"I already had a drink tonight. I just want something sweet, no liquor."

"Do you want something to eat?" he asked. "You a vegetarian too?" He laughed.

"Shut up." I smacked him on the arm. "I'm good. I just want to call a tow truck."

"Gotcha." He pulled out his phone and placed it on the bar. "Hey, darlin', can you put in an order for a cheeseburger, a beer, and a virgin daiquiri?" he asked the bartender.

"Sure thing, handsome," she said, walking away, slowly swaying her hips to grab attention. I turned to City to see if he was watching her, but he was staring at me instead, and my mouth felt dry and scratchy.

"You want to call Triple A or someone else?" he asked without taking his eyes off me. They were an amazing shade of blue, and I couldn't look away. I'd always loved my blue eyes, but his were almost turquoise. I felt like he was staring through me, into me, seeing everything I hid under the surface. I wanted him, but I didn't want to admit my attraction. I couldn't admit it.

"Triple A is good," I said, reaching for my purse to find my membership card. I fumbled with my wallet, finding the card behind everything else inside. I could feel his eyes on me; he studied me and it made me nervous. What was he thinking? I dialed the number as I swiveled away from him, needing to avert his stare.

"Hello, Triple A, how can I help you?"

I could barely hear the tiny female voice above the loud classic rock that pulsed throughout the smoky bar. City chatted with the bartender as I tried to drown them out and give my location and details about my car. They wouldn't be able to make it out to my car until morning. Fuck. I thanked her for helping me before hitting the end button.

"What'd they say?" City asked with a sincere look as the bartender sashayed away from us.

"They won't make it out here until morning because they're busy and we're in the middle of nowhere. I'm to leave it unlocked so they can get in and put it in neutral or something. I don't know how it works. I've never had my car towed before." Now what the hell was I going to do? I was stranded at the Neon Cowboy with Mr. Sexalicious and my dirty thoughts.

"I'll bring you back to your car when I'm done eating. I guess you'll need a lift home too?" he asked, sipping his drink as he eyed me.

I smiled at him. Though I hated the thought of him going out of his way, and I wasn't that comfortable with a stranger knowing where I lived, I couldn't say no. "I'd appreciate it, if you don't mind."

"Not at all, Suzy. I can't just leave you here and walk out the door. I got ya, babe." He turned his stool toward me and leaned into my space. "Where do you want me to take you after we leave? Home?" He quirked an eyebrow, waiting for my response, and held me in place with his hard stare.

Home? Whose home was he referring to? City looked to be the type that had different women falling out of his bed every morning...or maybe he kicked them out before he fell asleep. His fingers brushed against the top of my hand and my internal dialogue evaporated.

"Where. Do. You. Live?" The laughter he tried to hide behind his hand made it clear that I'd sat there longer in thought than I had realized.

I cleared my throat. "I need to unlock my car then I need a lift home. I live about fifteen minutes north. Is that okay? I mean, I don't want to—" He put his finger over my lips and stopped me mid-sentence.

"Doesn't matter, I'll take you anywhere," he said with a sly grin that made my pulse race and my body heat. He licked his lips, and I stared like an idiot. My sex convulsed at the thought of his lips on my skin. What the fuck was wrong with me? Every movement he made and word he spoke turned sexual, as if permeating my brain. I needed to get laid; this man was not hitting on me, was he?

"You want some? I can't eat it all," he said as the plate was placed in front of him.

I shook my head and picked up my drink, trying to cool my body off from the internal fire caused by City. The cool, sweet strawberry slush danced across my tongue and slid down my throat.

I swirled the red straw in my mouth, trying to occupy my mind. His arms flexed as he lifted the burger to his mouth, forearms covered with tattoos. The left arm had various designs woven together—a koi fish, a tiger, and a couple of other nature-themed pieces that seemed to move across his skin, and his right arm had a city skyline. I wanted to touch his arms and run my fingers across his ink. He looked big everywhere, and my gaze drifted down his body and lingered at his crotch. I wondered if his motorcycle and tattoos made up for shortcomings elsewhere, but I couldn't believe a man like him was tiny. There was no way in hell he had a party...

"Pickle?"

I blinked and moved my eyes away from his crotch to his eyes. Pickle? He held it and motioned for me to take it.

"No. Thanks, though. You eat it," I said, feeling like he was reading my mind. God, I hoped he didn't see me staring at his crotch. I sucked down the rest of my drink, wishing now that it did have alcohol in it. Maybe then I wouldn't feel so embarrassed. "I noticed your tattoos. What's the one on your right arm?"

"That's the Chicago skyline," he said, as he took another bite.

"You from there?"

"Born and bred, baby." He grunted and continued to chew. I couldn't take my eyes off his mouth. Watching him eat was erotic to me; his lips moved as he chewed, and he sucked each finger in his mouth to clean off the juices that flowed from the sandwich. Damn. It had been too long since I'd had sex—when eating becomes sexual. Houston, we have a problem.

Chapter 2

City

I could've easily started her car, but I didn't want to. Her beauty caught my eye and I wanted to know more about her. Shit, I wanted to fuck her. I couldn't just drive away and leave her out there to fend for herself. I'm a dick usually, but I couldn't just leave her there.

She looked helpless as I almost drove by her. When the lights of my bike shone on her, dirty thoughts flooded my mind. She had on "fuck me" heels with a short-as-hell skirt and a lacy white tank top that instantly made my dick hard. Her hair fell across the top of her breasts and sparkled in the light. It was golden, and I wanted to pull it while my cock was buried deep inside of her.

I pretended to come to her rescue and try to help, but I wanted to keep her as long as I could. I'd have one of the guys at the bar tow her car back to her place.

I could see fear in her eyes when we walked in tonight. They were large like saucers, her mouth hung open, and she looked around the room like she'd never been in a bar before. The guys here could be assholes, especially when a beautiful woman enters the room. Bear was always a total prick, but he did have a point. I wanted to fuck her and I wanted it dirty.

"How about I buy you a real drink? Just one. You aren't driving tonight, so what's the harm?"

I watched as she chewed her lip. "I guess you're right. My week's been crappy. I could use something...stronger," she said, blowing out a puff of air, causing her hair to move.

"Well, let's change that. Bad date?" I asked. I looked at her shoes before moving up her entire body and stopping at her face. "How can I make it better?"

Her lips parted and her chest heaved as she sucked air in quickly. "It's not so bad anymore. Tonight started out great, I went out with a girlfriend of mine, but it's just my friggin' car that put the icing on the cake."

Friggin'? Did grown women really use that word?

"I'm sure the car is no big deal," I said as I motioned for the bartender. "Know what you want?"

"Martini. A sweet one, please." She polished off her virgin daiquiri. She didn't swear and barely drank liquor; she wasn't like most girls I knew—even her clothes weren't as sexy as I'd expect for a girl her age.

"What can I get you, honey?" Sandy asked.

"Sunshine here will take a sweet martini, Sandy. Anything you can make flavored, preferably." I looked over at Suzy. "Right?"

"Yes, thank you." She looked out of place in a bar like this, but I wanted her at my side. She appeared to be a good girl with a clean mouth, but I could tell her mind was littered with filthy thoughts. She looked at me—no, stared at me—watching every movement and studying my entire body. She wanted me as much as I wanted her, even though she didn't want to admit it or couldn't. "You come here a lot, huh? Everyone seems to know you."

"The guys and I hang out here a couple nights a week after work, and it's close to my house. It's just a place I like to come to relax and unwind a bit after a long day."

She licked her lips, and I swear to fuckin' Christ my cock twitched. I adjusted myself, trying to stop a full-on hard-on from catching her eye. I watched her legs as she shifted in her seat, rubbing them together before crossing them. I had her and I knew it, but the trick was to not scare her off.

"What do you do, City?" She glanced at her hands, trying not to look at me.

"I'm an artist. You?" I left it at that—sounded classier than "I'm a tattoo artist." I was an artist at heart, but my canvas was human skin.

"Teacher. What kind of artist?"

She didn't look like any schoolteacher I'd ever had. I wouldn't have been able to pay attention in class with her walking around in heels and stretching to write on the chalkboard. "Tattoo," I said as I pointed at the artwork on my arm. "You have any?"

"Tattoos?" she asked as her eyebrows rose and her eyes grew wide.

"Yeah, by the look on your face I'd say the answer is 'no.'"

"Oh no." She laughed. "Needles scare the heck out of me." Grabbing her drink, she gulped down half the martini without even blinking.

"Do you swear?" I asked as she set the glass back on the bar.

"What?" She gaped at me.

"Do you swear? Simple question. You've said 'heck' and 'friggin'' so far, but nothing dirty."

"Oh, um, yeah, I swear." Her cheeks turned pink and a small smile spread across her face. "I'm just used to watching my words with the kids around all day."

"Prove it," I said, staring in her sapphire eyes.

"What? Why?"

"'Cause I need to know if it's in you. Are you all good girl? Or is there something more underneath dying to come out?" I hid the smile and laughter that were so close to breaking free from my lips. The pink of her cheeks spread across her face. I knew I'd embarrassed her, but fuck, I needed to know if I stood a chance.

"Yes, I swear. What do you think I am? I'm not a child, City." She glared at me as she raised the drink to her lips and wrapped them around the rim. Fuck. I wanted those lips wrapped around my dick, taking me deep and sucking me off.

"Never said you were, babe. Do you drink besides tonight?" I asked, now smiling because I knew she was upset. I liked the fire I saw in her eyes when I pointed out her good-girl qualities—she obviously didn't like being labeled.

"Sometimes. I'm just responsible. I don't drink and drive. My dad used to be a cop, and it was drilled into my head at an early age." The words she spoke hit me like a ton of bricks. Drunk driving was the one thing in the world that caused my blood to boil.

Good-girl teacher with a cop father? Just my luck. "Nothin' wrong with that. Virgin daiquiris aren't always your thing, then?"

"Why? Do I have to be a drinker? I mean, does it make me less of an adult?"

"No, Suzy. Just trying to get a feel for who you are—what you are."

Her shoulders slumped and she seemed to relax a bit with my words.

"Want another drink? You downed that one quick." She'd surprised me with how fast she polished it off, so my question about her drinking had been answered, but I wanted to watch her get a little pissed.

"One more and then I'm done," she said.

"You order your drink and I'm going to go talk to my friend over there real quick. He's a mechanic. I'll see what he can do with your car tonight." Standing, I motioned to Sandy and pointed to Suzy.

"Okay, don't leave me alone here too long."

"Promise, two minutes, tops." I walked away from Suzy as Sandy approached. The vultures would swoop in soon enough in my absence.

"Bored with Sunshine over there, buddy?" Tank asked as he kicked back in his chair as the others laughed. Tank's smile was wide, and the laughter only encouraged him further. "I can step in if you'd like. I wouldn't mind spending the night with that sweet flower."

I sat down in my usual seat next to Bear. "You can fuck off tonight." I pointed at Tank. "I don't need your shit." Tank just grinned. I knew he was fucking around, but it pissed me the fuck off. I'd known Tank for years, and although he could be a pain in the ass, he had a heart of gold.

"Easy there, City. What the fuck crawled up your ass and died?" Bear said.

"Nothing, man, long day. Sorry, brother."

"Sweet on that girl, huh? Never knew you were such an uptight dick, let alone overprotective of a woman," Bear said.

"I'm not, but fuck, the shit that comes out of your mouth just pisses me off at times."

"Sorry. Just fuckin' with you."

"We're cool." I slapped Bear on the shoulder, hoping to change the mood. No matter what assholes the guys could be, they were still my friends. They always had my back. "I need a favor, Tank."

"Name it."

"Her car's down the road and isn't starting. It's an easy fix to get it moving again, but there's some other issue with it. Think you could take care of it for me and drop it by her place tomorrow?"

"Sure. Whatever you need. You want me to just get it running or fix it for her?"

"Fix it and I'll pay for the repair. Don't let her pay for anything. Just drop it in her driveway."

"Gotcha, kid. I'll need her keys," he said as he popped open a peanut and threw the shell on the floor.

"I'll get them to you before we head out. Thanks, man." I stood quickly, needing to get back to Suzy. I'd already been gone too long.

"Night. Enjoy the Sunshine. Don't get burned," Bear said. Motherfucker.

A man stood over Suzy, invading her personal space, as she backed away as far as possible without falling off the stool. He looked greasy, with long, straggly hair, a dirty top, and stained pants, and he was covered in old, faded tattoos. I'd seen the motherfucker here before, and it never ended well. He always creeped women out, and someone always tossed him on his ass after he had one too many.

"Excuse me," I said as I stood behind him and waited for him to turn his attention toward me.

"What?" he asked without turning around.

"The lady doesn't want to talk to you." I squeezed my hands into fists and tried to keep my temper down for Suzy's sake.

"I didn't ask your opinion."

Her eyes were wide, and she slowly shook her head at me. The anger was clearly evident on my face. I felt like I was breathing fire at this point.

"Get the fuck away from my girl or it won't end well for you." I crossed my arms over my chest and stood there, unmoving. If it weren't for Suzy I would've laid the motherfucker out by now, but she didn't seem like the bar-fight type of girl.

He squinted at her and looked pissed off, but what the fuck did I care? "I don't see your name on her, dick."

"What's going on over here?" Bear said behind me as I grabbed the bastard by the collar, getting ready to pound his fucking face into a bloody mess.

"This asshole is bothering my girl. I think he needs to be taught a lesson." I tightened my grip on the material that hung from his body.

I could see his Adam's apple bob as he swallowed. I knew Bear would seal the deal, and the fucker would move on without me having to punch his fucking lights out. "Sorry, guys. You should be more careful about leaving your property unattended. Next time it may not be here when you get back. Would be a shame for something to happen to this beautiful creature." The fucking bastard smirked.

My fist landed against his face before I realized what I'd done. The fucker deserved far worse than a punch to his jaw. He was a sleazy-ass motherfucker bothering someone that obviously didn't want to be touched. "Get the fuck out of here! Now!" I yelled as he lay on the floor holding his jaw.

"Let's go, asshat. Time for you to leave." Bear picked him up and pulled him toward the door with his feet dragging across the wood planks. "Don't fucking show your face in here again if you know what's good for you."

I shook my hand as pain shot through my fingers. I knew I'd feel that punch for a couple of days, but it was worth it to lay that scumbag out and get him away from Suzy. "Are you okay?" I asked her as I flexed my fingers and studied her face.

"Yeah, I'm fine. Thank you for saving me, again." She smiled at me and looked at my hand. Her smile faded as she saw the way I moved my fingers. "Are you okay?"

"Yeah, bastard had a bony-ass jaw, is all," I said, shaking out the last pain in my knuckles.

She reached out and held my hand. "Sandy, can we get some ice over here?" she asked over her shoulder as she stroked my fingers and rubbed my knuckles with her soft, warm hands. I wanted to close my eyes and relish the feel of her skin against mine. I wanted to touch her. I ached to kiss her, but this wasn't the place.

"Really, that's not necessary. I just want to make sure you're okay, Suzy." I didn't stop her from touching me. I could feel the heat from her skin even after her fingers had moved on to another part of my hand. My hands always hurt from working for hours on designs, so the fist to the jaw didn't help them feel any better. I touched her cheek with my free hand, and she moved into my touch and searched for the contact. "You are okay, right?"

"Yeah, that guy was creepy, but he didn't hurt me. Thank you for coming back when you did."

"Sorry, I should've paid attention and shouldn't have left you. I didn't offend you with being possessive and calling you my girl? "

"Oh, no. I've never had anyone say that about me, ever." Her lips turned down as she concentrated on my hands. How could no one ever call her "my girl"?

"Hey." I held her chin and forced her to look at me. "Every girl should hear those words in her lifetime." I didn't smile. I wanted her to know I was dead serious.

"Yeah, well, I haven't." She let go of my hand and turned away from me, pulling out of my grip.

I didn't think I'd ever used those words when speaking of a woman, except Joni. A sharp pain hit me square in the chest as I thought of my ex, the only woman I'd ever loved. I had a reaction to Suzy like I did when I met Joni, and seeing another man bothering her made me see red. I wanted to protect her, unlike I had with Joni. I cleared my throat and shook my head, trying to rid myself of my lost love. "Well, it's not too late for it to happen. I didn't think I'd be sitting in a bar tonight talking to such a beautiful woman, but here I am. Your story has yet to be written."

"I'll never give up on my fairytale," she said as she let go of my hand and picked up her martini, swallowing the last drops. "Is it hot in here?" She pulled on her tank top, moving it back and forth to cool her skin. Every time the material moved away from her flesh, I'd get a peek of breast, and I had to force myself not to stare.

"Want to take a ride on the bike to cool off?" I asked. I wanted to feel her body against mine again, hugging my hips with her thighs, her arms wrapped around me.

She rubbed her forehead. "I'm feeling a bit lightheaded. I shouldn't have had two drinks."

"I'll make sure you don't fall off the bike. Just hold on tight and I'll get you home safely." I touched her knee, wanting to see if she'd pull away from me, but she didn't. The skin was soft and smooth, and I wanted to run my hands up her thighs and watch her head fall back in ecstasy. I wanted to take her home and have my way with her, but I couldn't just ask her.

"What about my car?" she asked breathily as I pulled my hand away. My touch had an effect on her, based on the tone of her voice. She wasn't good at hiding her feelings.

"I talked to Tank about it. He's going to take care of it tonight and drop it off in the morning. He just needs your keys."

"Really? He'd do that for me?" Her eyebrows shot up and her lips parted.

"Yes, and for me. Keys?" I held out my hand to her, ready to ditch this fucking place.

She dug through her purse, pulled out her keys, and placed them in my hand. She brushed her hair over her shoulder. I wanted to sink my teeth into her. I wanted to hear her moan, breathless underneath me. She truly was beautiful. She had an understated sex appeal to her. She didn't flaunt the beauty of her body, and I didn't think she even had a clue how fuckin' hot I found her. She was the girl next door, the untouched bookworm that every guy wanted to conquer. I wanted to make her dirty. I wanted to make her scream filthy words while I fucked her. I wanted to corrupt this girl in the worst possible way. She would be a challenge, and maybe I'd found someone worthy of my time.

"How will he know where I live?" she asked.

"Registration in the glove box." I twirled the keys in my finger and held my hand out for her to take. "Ready?"

"Duh," she said as she shook her head and grabbed my hand. All I could do was laugh. She wobbled on the high heels as she reached out and grabbed my shirt to steady herself. Sex didn't ooze off of her. There was a quirkiness that I couldn't put my finger on, but the sex kitten was there somewhere underneath the surface.

"Home?" I wanted to ask her "your place or mine," but I didn't think she was that type of girl. My life had become an endless parade of those girls, and there wasn't one thing that said "take me home and fuck me" about Suzy.

"Yes," she said.

I motioned to Tank, and he walked toward us before we made it to the door. "Her car is two miles south, man. Can you have it done by tomorrow?" I asked as I placed the keys in his hand.

"Sure, buddy. I'll have it at her place as early as possible."

"Thanks," I said as I shook his hand.

"Crap," she said.

"What?" I asked as we both looked at her.

"I have to cancel my tow," she said.

"Here." I handed her my phone. "Call them back before we hit the road."

"Thanks." She walked away on shaky legs; the drinks must have had a greater effect on her than I had thought. She leaned on a table with the phone in her ear and her ass sticking out. Her skirt rode up, giving me a view of the back of her legs. The muscles flexed and moved as she swayed back and forth. I couldn't imagine being tipsy and walking in those pointy fucking shoes. Women were insane.

"Make sure her car is running good before you bring it back, got it? No shit-ass job, Tank. I don't want her breaking down on the side of the road again."

"Got it. I don't do half-ass work, City. Got a thing for this girl?"

"I don't have a thing for her—my dick does, but she's just another woman. Stop busting my balls and do me this favor."

Tank laughed. "Sure. I gotcha. I'll take care of the car and you take care of her—get her home safely." He winked at me.

I rolled my eyes and spoke through clenched teeth. "I'm always a gentleman, Tank."

"Like fuck you are, man. Kind, at times, a gentleman, never," I heard him say as he walked away, twirling her keys in his fingers.

"Okay, all done. Let's bounce," she said as she touched my shoulder.

Did she just say bounce? Fuck me runnin'. I was in trouble with this girl. I knew it from the moment I saw her, but my cock didn't want to be the voice of reason. It never did—traitorous fucker. "Let's get you out of here and out of those shoes, Suzy." I wrapped my arms around her waist and helped her to the door.

Chapter 3

S^{uzy}

Did I just say bounce? Hello, the nineties want their phrase back. I'd never been the cool girl, the one that attracted the sexy guy, but hell, tonight I was in rare form. My legs felt like jelly as we walked out of the Neon Cowboy into the parking lot. I was thankful for the coolness of night and the fresh air. City made me nervous, and made every part of my body scream for his touch.

I couldn't take my eyes off his fine ass as he grabbed the helmet and turned toward me. "Can you do the helmet yourself or do you want me to do it for you?" he asked with his head cocked and a smile on his lips.

I just wanted him to touch me. "Can you do it, please? I'm worried I won't do it right."

"No problem, beautiful."

I closed my eyes. I could feel my body sway no matter how hard I tried to stand still. I felt amazing, like I was flying on a cloud. I opened my eyes to peek at him as he adjusted the straps. The world seemed to spin faster every time I closed my eyes. His fingers touched my skin and I swear electricity flowed through his hand. I wanted more—needed more.

"All right, sexy. All ready." Sexy? Oh God, I wanted this man. I watched as he climbed on the bike and held out his hand to me.

"Here goes nothing," I whispered before grabbing him and climbing on the bike.

"Hold on tight." He scooted back into my legs; my entire body felt like it was on fire as I wrapped my arms around his torso and locked my fingers together. His muscles moved underneath my fingertips and I wanted to rub them—no, I wanted to lick them. I squeezed my legs together, leaving no space between us as I leaned forward, resting my breasts against his back.

"Where am I going?" he asked as he started the bike and cranked the engine.

Please don't let me be wrong. "Your place." I held my breath as soon as I said the words and waited for him to laugh.

"You sure?" he asked in an even tone, but didn't turn around.

I'd never been so reckless about anything in my life. "Yes, unless you don't want to..." Did I read the signs wrong? God, what an idiot I am.

"Are you fucking crazy? I've been dying to crawl inside of you since I saw you on the road. Hold on, sugar, you're in for one hell of a ride."

I tried to control my breathing, thinking about his words, but it was useless. Excitement filled me, and thankfully the couple of drinks helped give me courage to go home with this sexy-ass man...or stupidity, but in this moment all I could think of is what the night held.

I held on for dear life as we cruised down the country roads toward his place. I didn't even know where he lived, and I wasn't paying attention to anything but his body and how it felt against me and under my hands. Images of him naked flooded my brain as my heart raced in my chest almost as fast as the bike moved. I got lost in time and didn't seem to worry as much as I concentrated only on his hardness.

I peeled my face from his back as the bike slowed, and I looked around as he backed up. A small white single-story house with green shutters lay before us. His home was on a large plot of land from what I could see. The street was far away from the structure, with a long driveway connecting the two.

"Change your mind, princess?" he asked.

"No, I meant every word." My voice shook and my entire body seemed to quake.

"Climb off first, use my shoulders."

I grabbed his shoulders and could feel the hardness. He was covered in muscle. I hadn't felt one squishy part the entire time I had my hands on him. I'd always describe myself as a tad fluffy. I wasn't lean and muscular, I did have curves and some softness to my body, but not City—he was ripped. I pushed myself off, using his shoulders as leverage, and the gravel driveway made my ability to stand still and straight almost impossible. The drinks didn't help either, and the killer shoes I had on didn't allow me to grip the ground any easier.

I watched as he climbed off the bike, his muscles rippling and shifting with each movement. My mouth watered at the thoughts of touching him and being his for a night. He moved toward me, and I swallowed hard. The closer he moved, the quicker my heart pounded in my chest, and I closed my eyes out of fear and anticipation. I puckered my lips and waited for him to kiss me, but nothing.

"I need to take your helmet off." For the love of God, please help me disappear. I'd forgotten about the helmet, and had to look like a complete idiot standing there with my eyes closed, waiting for a kiss, swaying in the wind, and wearing the damn thing. I'd been so wrapped up in the moment that all I could think about was him—kissing him, seeing him naked, touching him...just him. I smiled and could feel the heat creep into my cheeks. Butterflies filled my stomach, and I closed my eyes, hoping the embarrassing scene that just occurred would be quickly forgotten. I could hear him softly chuckling as he undid the straps and pulled it off my head. "Cute."

I opened my eyes and squinted at him. "Cute? What the heck is cute?"

"You." He tapped my nose, and I rolled my eyes.

"Freaking great."

"Yep, you're cute. Innocent, but fucking dying to be bad." He placed the helmet on the bike, turning his attention back at me. He touched my chin, pulling my face up to look him in the eyes. The rough skin of his thumb glided across my cheek, and I inhaled quickly. "I'm going to make you swear if it's the last thing I do. You're going to be screaming curse words tonight."

Everything in my body ignited at once—my heart pounded, my hands shook, and I stood there on trembling legs, feeling his nearness. The man stole my breath and made me lose all ability to communicate. He wrapped his solid arms around me, pulling my chest against his rock-hard torso, his lips hovering over mine. His hot breath brushed against my mouth as his fingers rested against my throat. My pulse raced under his fingertips, his touch making the rapid beating of my heart increase. Everything ceased to exist as he nipped my bottom lip, sending a jolt of pleasure throughout my body.

An overwhelming craving for more took hold, and I melted into him. A small moan escaped as his lips crushed against mine. Gripping his shoulders, I tipped my head back, giving him deeper access to my mouth. I wanted everything he had to give—all doubts vanished and were replaced by sheer need.

Lust consumed me as he ravaged my mouth and commanded the kiss, deep, warm, and hard. The warmth of his fingers on the back on my neck sent goose bumps across my flesh. Wanting his heat, needing more contact, I lifted the back of his shirt and swept my fingers across his silky skin. There was a cavern near his spine, the outer edges rimmed in hard muscle that flexed underneath my touch. I brushed the edge of his pants with my fingers, sweeping them inside, grazing his skin with my fingernails. His hold on my neck tightened, and he groaned in my mouth. We fed each other air, leaving no room or moment to absorb anything else but each other.

I wanted all this man had to give. I wanted his promise of making me scream words that I didn't use. Bending down and grabbing my ass, he scooped me into his arms, never breaking the contact with my mouth. My stomach flipped like on a rollercoaster, the movement and excitement taking over my senses. The anticipation bubbled inside me as he carried me toward his house, and eventually his bedroom.

I wrapped my legs around his waist, hooking my ankles together, and felt his hardness against my core. With each step it rubbed against my clit, the friction driving me close to the brink of orgasm, until he raised my body to his abdomen. The key scraping against the lock sent a thrill through me—I'm doing this...really doing this. Running my fingers through his hair, I bit his lip before opening my eyes.

"Suzy has claws?" he asked against my lips, his breath warm as it caressed my face. I squeezed my eyes shut, hoping that we wouldn't hold a conversation at this moment. I didn't want to talk or chicken out. City was the most gorgeous man I had ever kissed, let alone slept with. "Want it rough, beautiful, or soft and slow?" he asked with a hard squeeze of my ass, kicking the door closed.

I sucked in a breath, not sure how to respond. No one had ever asked me what I wanted before this moment. "Um," I mumbled into his neck.

Peeling me off his chest, he looked me in the eyes. "No one ever ask you what you wanted before?"

What the fuck? Could he read my mind? "No." I looked down, trying to avoid his gaze. I felt too transparent, and I couldn't stand the thought of being figured out.

He whispered in my ear as he ground his hardness against me: "Tell me what you want and it's yours."

I bit my lip and stared at him. There was no smile or smirk on his face. City looked like a man possessed, and I had no doubts he'd deliver on his offer. I didn't know what I wanted, but I knew I wanted him any way he'd give it to me. What was his idea of rough? Fuck. "Can I have both?"

His eyes sparkled as his smile reached his baby blues. Anxiety filled my body at the thought of him naked and inside me. My breathing became labored with the knowledge that we were inching closer to our final destination. The lights were off as he carried me through the house. He nipped at my neck as I tried to take in my surroundings. His footsteps and our breathing were the only sound as he carried me.

Light filled the room and momentarily blinded me. As my eyes adjusted, I looked around the bedroom before he placed me gently on the bed. The large room had white walls; a large, framed Harley poster hung above the dresser and was the only visible decoration in the room. Dangling my feet over the bed, I noticed that the only color in the room was from the black comforter and the rich auburn wood flooring. City lifted his shirt as he watched me look around, but didn't say a word as he approached. I swallowed hard as I took in his magnificent, tanned torso.

I was speechless, and for me that's a rarity. The six-pack he sported made my mouth water, and my fingers itched to touch it. As he approached, I could clearly see the intricate art on his chest and arms. A black dragon filled his right ribcage, and black tribal designs decorated his right shoulder, looking richer against his dark skin. I never cared much for tattoos, but on him they fit and were freaking amazing.

A twinkle caught my eye, and I leaned forward to get a better view of his chest. There were barbells running through each of his nipples, and I was shell-shocked. Tattoos had become part of the social norm, but piercings still were a bit of a taboo in my mind. Not taboo in that I found them revolting, just the opposite. I wanted to play with them like a new toy at Christmas.

"Still a yes, princess?" he asked as he stood between my legs.

"Yes." My voice was a little stronger now, my resolve more certain than it had been when I'd squeaked out the words before we pulled out of the Neon Cowboy.

He leaned over me, pushing me into the mattress. My face was buried in his chest as he reached toward the nightstand, and I couldn't help myself—I licked the metal around his nipple. As he leaned into my tongue, the sound of his groan filled the room, and the sound of plastic alerted me he'd grabbed a condom. There was no turning back now; I'd be his for the night—at least he was prepared.

"Like what you see?" he asked, his lips twitching at the corners.

He knew he looked good. I was sure he'd never had a moment where he doubted his hotness or sexual prowess.

"Your artwork is amazing and the piercings are just—wow." I didn't know what else to say. I loved everything that I saw and couldn't wait to see the rest.

Hovering over my body, he stared into my eyes and lingered just out of reach of my lips. Placing my hands on his chest, I felt the solidness of his body before digging my fingernails into his flesh. His fingers touched my stomach, and I knew what I wanted. I didn't want slow, but fast and hard...all night long.

The initial softness of his kiss caught me off guard. I expected it to be demanding from the start, but his lips explored mine, testing my resolve to stay the course. He kissed perfectly. A hint of tongue swiped against my bottom lip, looking for entrance, and I willingly granted him access. Our tongues tangled together as his hand explored my body. I wanted him—I craved his touch. I moaned as his hand rubbed against the lacy fabric of my bra. I writhed under his fingers as they skillfully worked my nipple, pulling and twisting.

He broke the kiss, and I felt like I could breathe again. "Sit up," he commanded.

I didn't hesitate. I pushed myself up as he backed away and studied me. His expression made me nervous—but it wasn't critical—as he soaked me in. His lips turned up as his eyes roamed my body, and I could tell that he only had one thing on his mind. He leaned forward, grabbed the bottom of my shirt, and started to lift. "Arms, babe," he said as I sat up in front of him.

I moved quickly as his fingers inched closer to my bra. I couldn't do anything but stare at the cocky grin on his face while he undressed me. He didn't look like any other man I'd ever been with. Having him undress me was the single most erotic moment of my life. His smell surrounded me, a mixture of earth, sweat, and musk. When I thought my heart couldn't beat any faster, his fingertips caressed my collarbone, and it skipped a beat before thundering in an erratic rhythm. I wanted to get down on my knees and pray that I lived through this experience.

"Breathe," he said.

I inhaled quickly, not realizing I'd been holding my breath. I wanted to cover my body, but his lopsided grin made me do the opposite.

He wrapped his hand around my neck and kissed me. My toes curled from the passion in his kiss. I felt a hunger, like I was about to be devoured by him. Pressing my body into his, I became his meal, willingly offering myself.

Our hands and mouths became entwined, and the sound of our hard breath and lips tugging and pulling filled the air. I opened my eyes to look at him, and became entranced by his mouth. I watched as he kissed me, and took in all of his features. His long brown lashes lay against his protruding cheekbones, and were brought out by full, dark eyebrows. A shadow had developed on his jaw line and joined with his sideburns, and I couldn't keep my finger away any longer.

The facial hair tickled my skin as I ran my finger down the roughness to the edge of his mouth. I could feel our lips move under the pads of my fingers. Our hands explored each other feverishly, learning the curves and spots that made one another twitch and shake. There was a delicious torture to the touching and kissing.

My clit ached as his hand inched up my thigh and brushed against my underwear. I gasped in his mouth as his fingers dug into the material and ripped it from my skin. I didn't care that they were my best underwear that I saved for special occasions; I wanted him inside me. He cupped my sex, applying pressure as I moaned and my head fell back. I didn't have the ability to hold it up as he began running his fingers through my wetness.

"Oh God," I said, as my eyes rolled back and my lids fluttered closed.

Warmth surrounded my nipple as his mouth closed around it, and he sucked in a pulsating rhythm. I dug my nails into his skin, needing something to hold. I cried out as his teeth captured the throbbing tip and bit down. Slowly his finger prodded my entrance before slipping inside at an agonizing pace. I needed to be filled and wanted the friction of his palm to relieve the ache between my legs.

I ground my hips into his palm, begging for more, as he pulled his fingers out and thrust them back in. I wanted to palm his cock through his jeans, but his body was too long and his crotch too far away. I grabbed his hair, fisting it in my hand, and he moaned, causing the vibration against my nipple to push me to the edge.

His warm, rough palm stroked my clit as he worked his fingers in and out, massaging my G-spot. Pants and moans fell from my lips as he worked my body like a well-choreographed dance number.

I couldn't stop my body from twitching as my release crashed over me unexpectedly. I screamed his name as the ripples of pleasure cascaded throughout me. I gulped for air, trying to catch my breath as my aftershocks squeezed his finger and tried to suck him deeper.

"Jesus," I muttered, wiping a bit of drool from the corner of my lips. I'd never had an orgasm so intense. No one had ever found my G-spot, let alone touched it with such skill. I lay panting with my skirt on as he climbed off the bed and began unbuckling his belt.

"You ain't seen nothing yet, sugar." His deep laugh filled the room.

"Oh, um." My stomach flipped. I needed to move. "No, let me," I said. He moved his hands away from the metal and closer to the bed. Crawling catlike, I positioned myself right in front of him and tucked my feet underneath my ass. I unbuckled his belt slowly, pulling it out of the loops in a teasing motion. Movement caused my eyes to look downward; straining against the restrictive denim I could see a long, thick bulge.

"Like what ya see?"

Fuck. "Uh huh," I said, swallowing roughly. I touched his stomach and slowly slid my fingers down his skin before grabbing for the button. "You sure about this?" I thought I'd turn the tables a bit. He kept asking me if I was sure, but hell, I knew what I wanted, and it was him.

"Mm hmm," he said with a smile on his face and a twinkle in his eye as he rested his hands on his sides.

He grinned like he knew something I didn't. A small patch of hair lined the top of his jeans—happy trail indeed. I unbuttoned his jeans and slowly unzipped them with fingers more steady than I thought possible. The clicking of the zipper passing by each tooth as I took my time and made my heart race. I savored the moment, freeing his hard-on. I leaned forward and pressed my lips to the soft, dark hair that had been trapped underneath the fabric. His body shook at the contact and his finger tangled in my hair. The denim of his jeans was rough against my palm as I slid up his massive thigh to palm him. A small bump at the tip gave me pause before I looped my fingertips in the sides, licking a path from his belly button to the zipper.

I tugged the material down his skin as I kept my mouth attached to his abdomen. I backed away as the material slid down and his shaft sprang free. My heart stopped and I sucked in a breath, my eyes growing wide.

Jesus. "What the..." What the fuck? I stared in wonderment. Not only was the man blessed with a large member, but also he added to it, decorated it. A large metal loop with a ball hung from the tip. I was eye to eye with it, and couldn't imagine why any man would do that to his body.

"You can touch it." He laughed. "It won't hurt you," he said, moving his abdomen in my direction.

"I've never seen anything like it." I reached out and ran my finger across the shiny metal jutting out. "Will I feel it?" I felt like a complete idiot, but I'd never seen one in person, let alone had sex with someone that had extra parts.

"It will give you a different sensation at first, closest to your opening...some pressure, maybe."

I didn't want to touch it with my finger, so I stuck out my tongue and licked around the cool, sleek hardware. His hips jerked and his shaft lurched from the contact. I reached out and fisted his shaft in my hands, being mindful of the metal protruding from it as I worked it with my hands and mouth in unison. He was rock hard.

"Fuck," he moaned as I slid it out of my mouth and flicked the piercing with my tongue.

I stopped and looked at him, but didn't let go. "Did I hurt you?" His head was tipped back, with his arm outstretched, still with a handful of hair in his grasp.

"Sugar, you can't hurt me. Take all of me."

I smiled at him, and the name "sugar" made me feel all gooey inside. No one had been so forward with me, and it made wetness pool against the fabric of my skirt. I inched closer, stroking him, and held him firm in my grasp. His musky scent was intoxicating.

I knew I couldn't fit the entire thing, but I'd try like hell. I moved forward, allowing more to slide across my tongue, causing his body to tremble and his breathing to turn hard and fast.

"Fuck, baby. That's the spot. Just like that." He fisted my hair roughly, causing my eyes to water.

I moaned against his cock, and he released a shaky breath. I tried to draw him in a little deeper with each stroke of my lips against his warm, smooth skin. I stopped when the metal hit my teeth, flicking it, as his hips shook in my grasp. His hand moved in my hair, pulling and pushing me, controlling the speed as I gagged each time the head hit the back of my throat. I opened my eyes and looked up at him. His mouth was opened slightly, his chest heaved from heavy breath, and goose bumps covered his flesh. Saltiness caressed my tongue as I worked the tip with precision.

"I want to taste you." His words caused warmth to pool between my legs and my core to spasm.

"But I'm not done," I said, looking at him, confused, my hands stroking his shaft. "Don't you want me to finish?" My brows knitted together as I looked at him. He grinned and unclenched his fist from my hair.

"We aren't done. I want to bury my face between your legs and make you scream again."

Well shit, who could say no to that?

"Did I do something wrong?" I shook my head as I looked down at my knees.

His hand gripped my chin, tipping it back, and stared into my eyes. "Suzy, you didn't do anything wrong. Fuck, it was perfect. I want to lick, suck, and then fuck ya, sugar." The words left me breathy and wanton. I felt beautiful and wanted.

He guided my face to his and crushed his lips against mine, sucking my tongue in his mouth as he pulled the skirt down my hips. "Tell me you want me to taste you," he said against my lips.

I swallowed hard; words, again, escaped me.

"Say it, Suzy." With one hand filled with my hair and the other wrapped around my back, he held me in place and left me with nowhere to go. Talking wasn't something that I was used to during sex, and he definitely brought me beyond my comfort zone. "I'm waiting." He bit my lip and brought me back to the moment.

"Taste me," I said, unable to look anywhere but into his dark eyes.

His grip tightened, pulling my head back as he released his hold on my back and began to lay my body back. I felt like a Raggedy

Ann doll; I was putty in his hands. My heart hammered in my chest with anticipation as I waited for his mouth to kiss my flesh. He grabbed my legs underneath my knees and pulled my body to the end of the bed as he knelt on the floor. Gripping the sheets, needing something to hold, I tipped my head back and closed my eyes. Heat flooded my cheeks with the thought of him staring at my pussy. I lifted my head and looked at him as he smiled and ran his hands along my thighs, licking his lips, and absorbed the view in front of him. Not in one spot, but all of me; his eyes roamed over my body before his head leaned forward, and I closed my eyes, unable to look. My body convulsed as his lips touched the delicate skin just to the right of my sex, enough to cause my body to crave more. Suckling the spot where my legs met my core, my body began to tremble. His hands slid down my legs, my entire body was on fire, and I ached for more. I needed more, but this felt more like a tease. He gripped my ankles and lifted my legs, placing each one on his shoulders.

His finger ran through my wetness as his tongue flicked my throbbing clit. My body shot up; I was unable to control the movement caused by the pleasure that shot through my body. His mouth clamped down as his finger slid inside me. His hands were large, but I wanted more of him as my core sucked his fingers inside. He drew me into his mouth and laid his tongue against my flesh, moving it around in circles. My breathing sounded shaky and I tried not to cry out in ecstasy, as I was so close to the tipping point.

Adding a second finger made me feel stretched to the limit, almost to the point of pain. How in the hell would I handle all he had to offer? Swirling his tongue around my clit, his fingers caressing my aching flesh, he slid his hand under my ass, his fingers digging into my skin, as he tilted my hips. My eyes rolled back as his fingers and tongue made all coherent thought disappear. I was so lost in the moment that I didn't notice his mouth leave my body as his fingers stopped.

"Do you want me?" he growled against my clit, and my eyes opened and became drawn to his stare.

I trembled and tried to steady my breath. "Yes."

"Yes, what? What do you want?" he asked, his eyes not moving from mine, his entire body still.

"Have sex with me." I knew what he wanted me to say—he wanted me to use the F word, and I hadn't, couldn't.

"Suzy." He drew out my name and flicked his tongue against me. "You know what I want to hear. Tell me exactly what you want." He withdrew his fingers and tongue, leaving me panting for more.

I closed my eyes and exhaled, needing a moment to gather my thoughts. They were just words, and ones I said every day but never during sex. Drawing in a shaky breath, I said, "I want you. Fuck me, City."

Chapter 4

S uzy

"Never experienced anything like that," I said. How to explain it without sounding pathetic? Damn, nothing in my life had compared to having sex with him. I'd had a few one-night stands in college, but those boys didn't exactly know what they were doing.

City was rough and controlling, and I loved it. I stared at his beautiful body as he knelt before me, his skin glistening with sweat, his muscles moving in unison as he tried to catch his breath. I wanted to take a picture and always remember how he looked—sweaty and sexy as hell.

"That's nothing compared to what I could do to you," he said in a husky tone as he wiped the sweat from his brow. I wanted to lick the sweat off his body. I wanted to do things with him that I normally didn't even think about doing to anyone in my life. He was different.

"Hell," I said, unable to think of anything else. He could do better? Was that even possible?

"Maybe you'll let me show you sometime." A smile crept across his face, but it wasn't a sweet smile. This guy definitely had tricks up his sleeves. My heart raced at the thought of feeling him inside me again.

"You want to see me again?" I asked, unable to believe his words. We were polar opposites, and I didn't know why he'd want to see me again.

"Why wouldn't I?" His eyebrows turned down as his nose wrinkled.

I covered my eyes, feeling like an asshole. "I dunno. I thought this was just a one-night thing."

"I won't lie, I thought it would be just a one-night 'thing.' I wanted you from the moment I blew by you on the road." He moved next to me, wrapping his arm around my body. "You're not like any of my friends or the women I know."

"Well, I've met some of the people you hang out with." I frowned, thinking about some of the guys he'd surrounded himself with. Most of them seemed shady as heck. "They look more like my class full of underachievers or someone I'd see on America's Most Wanted. Not my type."

"They look that bad?" he said in my ear. His low tone made my exhausted body buzz again.

"They're kinda scary, City. They remind me of criminals," I whispered.

He laughed. "Funny shit, sugar. They look scarier than they are." He nuzzled into my shoulder, burying his face in my hair. "I don't hang out with all those guys. Many of them are customers—some of them are my best clients. I stop there on the way home sometimes for a drink. Some of them are friendly and, well, some you've seen are assholes."

"You can say that again."

His body shook and I felt the vibration from his silent laughter. "I spend more time with my family than with those douchebags at the bar." He brushed the hair off my cheek and ran his fingers down my throat before he rested his palm on my chest. I felt exposed. "Are you cold?" he asked as I shivered.

"A bit," I lied. I wanted to cover my body.

"Did you want to leave?" He yawned.

"Um, I'm sure you're tired. I can stay if you want. It's up to you." I didn't want to leave this hot, hunky man and go home to my empty bed. Don't kick me out like a piece of trash.

He grabbed the blankets and covered our bodies. Yes! Inside I was doing cartwheels and screaming with excitement. He pulled me against his side and wrapped me in his arms. His body felt hard and comfortable. I rested my forehead against his jaw and could hear his heart beating in his chest. The sheets were the softest cotton I had ever felt—not really what I had expected. I thought he'd be more of a flannel guy, or those scratchy sheets you find in hotels.

"Comfortable?" he asked with a long, content exhale.

"Very." I hadn't slept in the arms of a man in years. Usually I didn't fit just right, or they were so bony that my head hurt resting against their body, but City was built to sleep on. He was built for anything that involved two bodies.

I didn't quite know where to rest my hand. Did I put it on his chest or leave it at my side? Sophia wasn't going to believe this story when I tell her. She knew me as the good girl that lived in my controlled environment, unable or unwilling to move, but City was like a tsunami that started slowly and built into a giant wrecking ball of sin.

"Hand, babe."

"What?" I mumbled against his chest.

"Gimme your hand."

I moved my hand from my thigh and held it out to him, trying not to touch his skin. Grasping it, he placed my palm on his rock-hard chest, and put his hand on top. "Perfect," he said.

I didn't have any grand illusions, and I wasn't delusional. I knew I'd only have this night with City. We weren't meant to be—he wasn't what I was looking for. He wasn't the type of guy that was part of my master plan. I'd just lie here and enjoy the night in his arms.

I listened as his breathing slowed and changed. His hand twitched against mine as he squeezed my fingers and drifted into a deeper sleep. I felt exhausted, but I almost didn't want to sleep. I didn't want to miss a minute of staring at his body.

Thoughts flooded my mind while I listened to his deep breaths. I wanted to see him again, but would it be a waste of time? Did I want to go down a dead-end street and become attached to him? I knew I could fall for him. Even though I wanted to find someone to spend my life with and have that great happily ever after, I didn't open my heart to just anyone. Heartache was something I avoided at all costs. There wasn't a need to risk my heart if the certain outcome would be disastrous. The war of words continued in my head for a few minutes, until I finally decided to enjoy the moment and worry about the rest tomorrow.

The sound of metal clinking woke me, and I sat up in a panic. I thought someone had broken in while I slept. Looking around the room, I realized I wasn't in my bedroom. Last night hadn't been a dream. Reaching over, I felt the sheet where he had lain, and it was cold to the touch. Sunlight streamed through the sheer white drapes and bounced off the walls, amplifying the light. The room was tidy, except for our clothing from last night strewn about the floor.

My body ached as I stretched, trying to relieve the pain from my muscles being stretched and over the night before. I needed something to wear and had to find a bathroom. I tiptoed out of bed and wrapped the sheet around my body to keep the cold at bay. A flannel shirt hung on the back of his door, and I grabbed it and held it up to my face, burying it in the soft material. The hint of cologne and the muskiness of his skin made my pussy clench. I dropped the sheet, wrapped the flannel around my body, and rubbed my cheek against the wrist cuff. I felt surrounded by City.

Walking to the door that I thought was the bathroom, I opened it and found his closet. Fuck. It was filled with t-shirts, jeans, and hoodies. I studied the contents, running my hand over the soft materials as they hung, before I closed the door. There were only two doors in his room, and neither of them led to a bathroom.

My reflection in the mirror hanging on the back of the door made me cringe. My blonde hair was in tangles and looked a mess, and my eyes looked tired from the night in his bed. A messy ponytail helped to tame my mane, making me feel presentable. Good enough. Opening the door, I peered into the hallway before tiptoeing into the hall. A loud, long creak filled the air as I took my first step.

"You up?" he yelled from the kitchen.

"Yes," I said, trying not to sound annoyed. "Be right there."

"I'm fixing breakfast. Take your time." I could hear dishes, cups, and all kinds of movement in the kitchen. I didn't think I'd ever had anyone besides my mom, Sophia, and Kayden make me breakfast.

The smell of bacon and something sweet drifted down the hall and made my stomach grumble.

An old claw-foot bathtub and white pedestal sink filled the white and black room. He didn't seem too fond of color, which I found odd, since he described himself as an artist. Everything was clean and sparkling. I could tell that he took pride in his home. I searched his bathroom, looking for an extra toothbrush, but tried not to make noise. A knock sounded at the door and I jumped, knocking over some bottles under the sink and smacking my head against something hard. "Shit," I said as I rubbed my head.

"You okay? Did you need something?"

"I'm fine." So not fine. He caught me snooping and probably heard the bang from my head. "I wanted a toothbrush, do you have a spare?" I put my head in my hand, feeling like a fool but thankful that he didn't witness the event.

"There's an extra one in the medicine cabinet. Help yourself." I could hear his footsteps quiet as he walked away.

My face was still red as I left the bathroom and walked into the kitchen, trying to avoid City's eyes.

"Eggs, pancakes, and bacon okay?"

He looked amazing. He wore a pair of black track pants and a smile.

My stomach rumbled over seeing all the food he had prepared. "Did you cook for an army?" I asked.

"Didn't know what you liked, so I made a little bit of everything." He put the spatula on the counter and walked toward me. He was so damn hot. I licked my lips and closed my eyes.

I could feel his hot breath on my lips, and I smelled his scent. "I'm gonna fuck you, right here, right now. Yes or no?"

OMG, OMG, OMG, yes, yes, yes!

I swallowed hard and nodded before I leaned forward.

"Words, Suzy. Now the answer needs to be 'yes, fuck me, City' or 'no, I don't want to.'"

How would I ever say no to this man? I thought about the possibility of never seeing him again, and I wanted one last shot at him.

"Yes, fuck me, City," I whispered against his lips.

His mouth crushed mine and I could taste the coffee and sugar on his tongue. I could only hear our breath as the world around us fell away. His hands trailed up my thighs and cupped my ass. Fuck, this man was pure sin, and I wanted to be his minion.

He broke the kiss and looked in my eyes. I could hear his breathing, fast and hard. "Hands on the counter," he said with a commanding tone. Yes, sir. Gladly.

I turned my back to him and placed my palms on the edge. He pushed down on my back and lifted my hips. I rested my head on the cold tile and waited. Looking behind me, I watched as he pulled down his pants before palming his shaft. I heard a crinkling noise coming from his pocket. He'd planned this—he had a condom ready to go. Lord, help me with this man. Could I resist him?

I started to stand up when I heard, "Back down, sugar." I closed my eyes and followed his command. I felt him stroke my opening, and I sighed. When did I turn into a big ole pile of mush with a guy? He slid inside of me easily; I was slick and ready for him.

He grabbed my hips, holding me tightly as his hardness worked like a machine inside of me. I gripped the counter and my fingers began to tingle from my death grip. He felt amazing, caressing my insides with the metal piercing. My muscles ached as I stood on my tiptoes. He pounded into me, the sound of our skin slapping filling the air, his grunts ringing in my ears. His grip intensified and became almost painful.

"Fuck, your pussy is so damn tight," he growled.

"I love your cock," I moaned. That just slipped out—like it was something I said every day.

"I love being buried in your sweet pussy, sugar."

All the dirty words and the feeling of him stroking my depths pushed me over the edge. My body began to shake, and I moaned, "City."

I heard a loud crack and my ass began to sting. Did he just slap my ass? The pain began to radiate throughout my body and made my orgasm grow and build. My grip began to slip as my insides clenched against his length. Crack. Fucking hell.

"Fuck," he yelled as his stroke became more intense and erratic. I could feel him grow harder inside me as he slammed me against the counter. He rested his head against my back as we both stood there immobile for a moment.

"You got me all kinds of crazy, Suzy," he said through heavy breath.

"Makes two of us." I was thankful the tile was cold. My body was covered in moisture and my skin was hot from the pounding I had just taken. He pulled out, and I instantly felt the loss of him. I waited for my feet to uncramp before trying to stagger to a chair. He removed the condom with a quick snap and tossed it in the trash. I swayed to my seat, thankful that it was only a few steps away. He adjusted himself inside his pants and walked to the stove with a devilish grin on his face.

"Pancake?" His blue eyes stared into mine as he held the pan up, asking permission to slip it on my plate.

I forgot how hungry I'd felt when I walked in. How did the man just fuck me like a maniac and now he was cooking like Guy Fieri?

"Yes. I never met a meal I didn't like." I silently prayed to God the jitters that filled my stomach would subside long enough to eat the giant meal he'd prepared.

"I love hearing shit like that. My sister is so fucking picky it makes me batshit crazy."

I buttered my pancake and watched him out of the corner of my eye as he grabbed the pan of eggs off the stove. An awkward silence filled the room as I looked at my plate. He'd just had his cock in me as the food sat on the stove, and now what? I wanted to keep the conversation flowing, and figured I'd follow his lead.

"Just one sister?" I asked.

"Just the one, but I have three brothers too. Eggs?"

"Everything," I said, moving my pancake to make room for the eggs and bacon. "Five kids, wow, your mother must be an amazing woman."

"Yeah, I think we caused most of the gray hair on her head, which she now dyes to keep her youthful appearance. We aren't the traditional Italian family. You have any brothers or sisters?" he asked, plopping the eggs on his plate and then putting the pan back on the stove.

"A sister, she doesn't live here. She's still up north, where we grew up." I poured the syrup on my single golden pancake before cutting a chunk.

I envied City. He had a big family and they had a bond that I'd never had with mine. He had something I always wanted.

"Ah, I can't imagine only having one. We're kinda a gang. We do everything together." He stuffed the eggs in his mouth and grabbed a piece of bacon. "You've missed out."

I loved that it seemed easy between us; we were comfortable, and he made me feel that way. "I guess so, but I have some friends that I'm closer to than any of my family." I placed the forkful of buttery goodness in my mouth and let it sit on my tongue a minute before I chewed it. "My mom's kinda a flake, and my dad works all the time, so I just have my friends."

"Damn, that fucking sucks. My family gets together every Sunday for dinner, and it's usually a bit loud."

"Every Sunday?" I saw my parents every week, but sometimes it was only for an hour, and dinners only happened on holidays.

I tried to go slow, not wanting to eat everything on my plate. I didn't want to look like a pig, but I was starving.

"Every Sunday. It's required, or my parents think something is wrong. Sometimes my grandparents come over and it turns into an all-day affair. Mom usually wakes up early to make the sauce and meatballs. We're required to be there at one for an early dinner."

It sounded nice. I'd never had anything like that in my life—never knew families did that kind of thing, besides in the movies.

"Hmm, that sounds like fun." I ate my breakfast and thought about all the family things I'd missed out in my life. My parents seemed too busy to deal with us at times, let alone have me over for dinner every Sunday. I knew they loved my sister and me, but we didn't have the close-knit family that City had described.

"It is, but I work with my brothers and sister and sometimes it gets to be too much. So, babe, do I get to take you on a proper date?"

"Oh, sorry," I said. "I'd love to go on a date with you. I mean, we already..." I moved my hand around, lost for the right word to describe what we did the night before.

"Fucked." He laughed. "I don't know if I will ever get over your good-girl thing you have going on."

"I'm not a good girl, City." I wasn't, and I knew it. Good girls didn't think about the things I did. They didn't want the things I wanted, and they sure as hell didn't go home with strangers. "What we did last night wouldn't have happened if I was a good girl." I smiled at him.

"You're a woman, Suzy. Sex doesn't make you a bad girl; it makes you human. That shit was explosive last night, and this morning I needed to be in you again. I wouldn't change a goddamn thing." He must have sensed I was uncomfortable with the entire conversation. "I don't think you're bad. If someone does, then fuck them. I don't give a shit what anyone thinks about me."

"I know. It's not always so easy." I wanted to change the subject. "Do you want me to call my friend to pick me up?" I didn't want to dissect my qualities at the moment.

"I'll take you home after you're done, okay?"

"Thank you. I have a ton of things to do today." I had to grade papers—it was the end of the grading period, and grades were due on Monday morning. I had to make lesson plans and pay the bills before the weekend ended. My work never ended, not even on the weekends. Teachers don't walk out the door on Friday and leave it all behind—we work on the weekends and walk through the door on Monday prepared to teach the budding students not always so interested in learning. I sighed, thinking about all the work I had to do, but I was the only one that could get it done.

"No problem. I have to get to work by noon, so no rush."

I wiped my mouth unable to consume another morsel. "Where do you tattoo?"

"Inked. Ever hear of it?"

"I drive by it every day on the way to work, I think." I remembered seeing the sign, but had never set foot inside. "Looks like a nice place."

"Ever been?"

"Oh, no. I meant from the street. Doesn't look like the other shops in the area. Yours is pretty. How long have you worked there?"

"I don't think I've ever heard it described that way. My sister does all the decorating. We own the shop and opened it about five years ago."

Well, maybe he wasn't the starving artist I thought he was.

"Why don't you stop by sometime? I'd love to pop your cherry." I started choking. "Ink, babe, I'd love to give you your first tattoo." He laughed.

I patted my chest and coughed. "Maybe someday I'll let you. My parents are just anti-tattoo, and I never found anything I'd want to look at for a lifetime. How'd you pick yours?"

"Each one signifies something in my life." He pointed to the city skyline on his arm. "This is a reminder of where my family comes from, Chicago. It's where I grew up, and I go back every summer to visit my friends. It's part of me in more ways than one." He laughed and rubbed the tattoo on his arm.

"And the fish?"

"Ah, the koi. Well, that one I had my brother, Anthony, do when we opened the shop. It's a symbol of determination and power to achieve goals. We always talked about opening our own shop, and we'd finally achieved it. Plus, I fucking love the color orange."

"Looking at your house, I'd think you loved white."

He picked up my plate and laughed. "This place is only temporary. I don't see a point in splashing color on the walls. I'm surrounded by color all day at work. It's calming to come home to an empty canvas." Artists—complex creatures.

"I understand. My walls are actually white except for one blue wall in my bedroom. I'm not the typical bubblegum-pink girl."

He began to clean the kitchen and put the dishes in the dishwasher. His muscles rippled and flexed with each movement. My mouth watered as I remembered what it felt like for him to be above me and in me—I wanted more of him.

"I'll finish cleaning up. You go get ready to hit the road, okay?"

I could get used to being waited on. Mind-blowing sex? Check. Good cook? Check. Sexy as hell? Check. Manly, yet nice? Check. He had all the right qualities and kind of reminded me of Kayden. I didn't want Kayden, but I wanted someone that cared enough to take care of me.

"I'll just be a minute," I said as I stood from the table. "I don't want to take up any more of your time."

"Take all the time you want. I can't get fired if I'm late." He laughed as he kicked the dishwasher closed. "By the way, is Suzy your full name?"

I hated my full name. It sounded stuffy and old. "No."

"Spill."

"It's Suzette."

"Now that's sexy as fuck. Suzette." It rolled off his tongue, and I felt the moisture from my core begin to pool. Fuck, he'd made me a total cock-loving whore, and I wanted to hear him scream my name.

"Right." Looking over at his beautiful skin and taut muscles, I drank him in—memorized the picture before I walked out the door, leaving him to finish and to get the hell out of here. He could definitely become a weak spot if I didn't put distance between us. That yin and yang bullshit didn't really work in real life.

Chapter 5

City

I shut the bike off and waited for her to climb down. She tried to remove the helmet on her own and stood there looking as drop-dead fucking gorgeous as she did last night. She fumbled with the straps, trying to pull it off, but she frowned and her fingers began to move frantically. "Lemme get that for you," I said as I motioned for her to move closer.

"Sorry," she said, blowing a puff of air out.

"It's my pleasure, trust me." I winked and watched her cheeks pinken. I worked the straps apart slowly, trying to prolong the ending to our time together. I felt like she was going to give me the brush off. Her body language didn't match the last twelve hours. I needed to set another date with her and dig deeper into the woman she was instead of who she pretended to be.

"Thanks," she said, trying to look me in the eyes.

"There. So, about the real date. How about tonight?" I asked. I didn't see a point in wasting time. I wanted her in my bed again—or against the counter.

"Um, I guess tonight is good." She looked at me and then to her feet.

"Sugar, it's just a date. A real date—no strings attached." I grabbed her chin to look into her sky-blue eyes. "We kinda missed that part of getting to know each other before I took you. I'll pick you up at nine. Wear something warm."

"Okay, I'll be ready. Want me to drive?" She looked at my bike, wrinkling her nose, and then noticed her car. "Wait, how did my car get here already? I totally forgot about it breaking down. What the heck?"

"Tank fixed it for you and delivered it about an hour ago. It's all ready, but to answer your question, no. We're taking the bike."

"Oh. Do you have his number so I can pay him?" she asked, her eyes wide as she chewed her lip.

"I got it. He did it as a favor to me."

"Oh, I couldn't. Let me pay you for it, then."

"Suzy, let me do something nice for you. Really, it wasn't a problem. Tank and I worked it out. I don't want you broken down again on a dark country road."

"I know. I just try and watch my money. I was going to get it fixed."

"Well, now it is. Nine tonight, and warm clothes." I leaned forward and kissed her lips. I grabbed the back of her neck and drew her closer. The light, sweet scent of her perfume filled my nostrils, as I tasted her lips. Everything about her was fucking sweet, and I wanted more. I consumed her mouth and commanded her body with my kiss. I wanted to leave her weak in the knees and wanting more when I drove away. I broke the kiss, but kept my hand in place and watched her as she stood there with puckered lips and her eyes closed. Exactly the response I wanted.

"Sugar," I said, smiling at her as her eyes fluttered open.

"Oh, sorry. I say that a lot around you." Her cheeks turned pink as she bit her lip.

"We'll finish that kiss later. I can't wait to crawl back inside that delicious pussy of yours tonight. Digits," I said before she had a chance to walk away. I programmed her number in my phone and sent her a text as she walked in her house. She'd be back for more.

I started the engine, revving it a couple times before pushing backwards and down the drive. She waved with a sweet smile on her face. My cock ached as I thought about all the dirty shit I wanted to do to her. I watched her in my side mirror as she watched me drive away. I had her.

"Where the fuck you been, Joey?" Mikey said as I walked through the door of Inked.

We opened Inked about five years ago. Everyone in my family has an artistic streak, and we didn't trust outsiders with our money. Growing up, my father had drilled that mantra in our heads. Don't trust others when you can do it yourself. We agreed that there would be no outsiders unless absolutely necessary. Problem with it, though, was that you could never fire family, especially when they're part-owners. Mike had the spaz gene. He was known for overreacting.

"I had to drop someone off, shithead. Who made you boss?" I asked as I set my stuff down at my workstation.

"You're typically here early. I started to get worried. You could've called or something, asshole."

"Don't get your panties in a bunch, Mom. I'm here now, so shut the fuck up."

Mikey threw his hands in the air—showing his surrender or disgust, I couldn't tell. He was the shop manager since he had absolutely no artistic talent, but he was one hell of a piercer. His real passion was fighting. He had joined the circuit years ago and often traveled out of town for a fight. Fighting with your hands and tattooing do not mix. My hands were precious to me. I needed them to work my magic and see the smiles on the faces of my customers.

"Mom called to remind us about tomorrow," Anthony said as he walked out of the employee-only area. Anthony is my oldest brother and probably the most unsettled. He's an amazing tattooist, but he's a musician. He dreamed of hitting it big, but for now he was ours.

"What the fuck?" Mikey said.

"How could we forget? It's only been the same day for thirty years," Izzy said as she unpacked her machine.

Izzy's the youngest and the only girl beside my mom. My parents kept trying until finally they had the little princess they always dreamed about, after having four boys climbing the walls and roughhousing. She was girly and kind, but if you crossed Izzy, she'd kick your ass. We were all overprotective of her, but we were scared of her too. In my family, the ladies ruled the roost and weren't to be crossed. She got that commanding personality from my mom, and led with an iron fist.

"Let's run down the schedule before I open the doors," Mikey said, leaning over the counter, looking toward the work area.

I listened to Mikey babble on about the clients of the day. I already knew my lineup. I had to finish a back tat I'd been working on for months, and a girl wanted me to fix her bad choice in a tramp stamp.

My mind kept wandering to Suzette. My mom would be happy if I brought a good girl home for once—someone that could give her grandchildren someday. I was not ready for that. My dick was doing the thinking instead of my head. Get your head on straight, man—too much pussy out there to settle. I was getting a little ahead of myself, but Suzy may have been the first respectable girl I'd met in a long time. I never brought women I'd dated or slept with around my family. None of them had a future with me, and I didn't feel the need to subject my family to an intruder or an outsider.

"Joey." My sister stood, her face invading my personal space.

"What, Iz?" I looked up and noticed her squinty eyes as she studied me.

"What are you grinning about?"

"Nothing."

"Oh, bullshit." She pointed at me and tapped me on the forehead. "You've met someone. Spill it, brother."

"There's nothing to tell. You think you're a mind reader, but you aren't, sis."

"I've known you my entire life. You walk around here all moody and serious, but today I'd say you're almost glowing, ya big pansy ass."

"Fuck off, love."

"Ooooh, jackpot. Who is she?" A giant smile crept across her face as she leaned forward and stared in my eyes. She wasn't going to let it go. Everyone stopped what they were doing to listen to what I had to say, and Izzy's impending inquisition.

"Fine, Iz. I met her last night and I'm taking her out tonight. Happy?"

Iz twirled around and giggled like a schoolgirl. "Extremely, big brother." She kissed me on the cheek. I leaned back in my chair and watched as my sister celebrated like I was about to walk down the aisle.

"Don't get ahead of yourself, Iz. It's just a date."

"Oh, now come on. I can tell by the look on your face that she's a little bit more than just a simple date. I want the deets."

Grunting, I crossed my arms over my chest. "She was stranded and I stopped to help her. I brought her home and I'm taking her out tonight, simple as that."

"Hmmm."

She came closer, not believing a word that I spoke.

"Izzy, leave it at that."

"Who is she?"

"She's a school teacher, but I don't know much about her."

"You've had sex with this girl. I can tell." Izzy poked me in the chest. "You can't hide anything from me."

"Well, shit, Iz. That's none of your business, really." The door chimed as my client walked through the door. I was thankful that I had a reason to end the conversation and save the grilling for another day. But I wouldn't get too comfortable. I knew my sister's interrogation would happen sooner rather than later.

The shop had a buzz today. Everyone had smiles on their faces. The fall weather always made people happy. I had been coloring in a beautiful flower that I had inked on a client, Michelle, a week ago, but she couldn't take any more pain to finish it that day.

"It's healing nice, darlin'." I wiped the blood and ink off her skin.

"Yeah, I can't wait to see it finished. Sorry I pussied out the other day, City." She closed her eyes as the needle poked the still-healing skin.

"Hey, it's cool. I've seen huge men in tears getting a tattoo. I rather you walk away than pass the fuck out."

Her eyes opened and she started to laugh. "Really? Guys have actually cried?"

"Yes, like little babies. So no worries. Now hold still so I don't fuck this up." I patted her leg with my rubber gloves and set out to finish the beautiful tattoo.

I loved working with color. Flowers weren't normally my thing; I loved animals and intricate designs, but flowers were a challenge and were laced with bold colors.

My phone vibrated on the table and I glanced at it as I dabbed the needle in the pink liquid.

Suzy: I can't make it tonight. Sorry, City.

Fuck, she was brushing me off. I couldn't stop and text her back. Little Ms. Suzy would have to wait. I'd have to remind her of how good it felt inside her and how fucking hard she milked me.

"Something wrong, City?" Michelle asked.

"Nah, darlin'. Just thinking about something."

"Didn't mess up my tattoo, did you?"

"Hell no. I don't fuck up."

"Thinking about a girl?" Her eyebrows wiggled up and down.

"A woman." I didn't look up as I spoke to her, and I kept my eyes glued to her tattoo so I didn't have to eat my fucking words.

"Lucky cunt," she muttered.

"What?" I'd heard her loud and clear, but just wanted to see if she'd 'fess up.

"Oh, nothing. Wanna talk about her?"

"Nope. I'm good. Shit's between her and I, Michelle."

I had to get in that pretty little head of Suzy's. I knew I scared the fuck out of her and I should. I wasn't her type or some clean-cut cocksucker. I knew how to please a woman, take care of myself, and have a good time. I just couldn't give her a chance to run away like a scared little princess.

Time felt like it stood still as I colored in the same area over and over again to get the shade just right. A small hint of gray near the pistil and I had finished this flower of torture. I wiped off the ink and patted her calf. "All done. Take a look."

She glided her hands down her legs in a seductive manner, but I didn't take the bait. "It's beautiful. You're fucking amazing." Not going there—not with this one.

I grabbed my phone, needing to change Suzy's mind about tonight.

Me: Come on, it's Saturday night. Live a little, sugar.

I washed my hands as Michelle sat back down and stared at the finished masterpiece.

"You remember what I said last time about taking care of the tattoo? Stay out of the sun, don't go in the pool or ocean until it heals, and keep it clean. Let me cover it for your trip home first. You can pay up front. Iz can check you out." After grabbing a new pair of gloves, I covered the area with a dressing.

"Don't you want to check me out?"

I could hear the hurt in her voice, but fuck no, I didn't want to check her out. I only had one person on my mind, and it was Suzy Goodie Two-shoes.

"Pfft, fine." Michelle stomped off as I grabbed my phone and typed another message.

Suzy: I don't think it's a good idea. I had a great time with you. Thanks for your help.

Like hell I'd let her off that easy. She was going to be mine again.

Me: I'll be there at nine—be ready. No ifs, ands, or buts.

Suzy: City—No.

Me: Boyfriend?

Suzy: No. I'm not a cheater. I don't think we'd work out—we're just not right.

Me: Sugar, it felt right this morning when my cock was buried inside of you and you screamed my name. Nine. No strings—just FUN. You know the word, right?

I cleaned my workstation and prepped for my next willing victim. I wouldn't let her weasel out of a night of fun. She didn't respond right away, but I knew that she would. She had to be thinking about the way she looked at me when I was buried inside her. I knew I had her. I just had to get beyond all her brains and rules. I had to reel her in. I knew my last sentence would agitate the hell out of her. I didn't think people besides the fuckheads in her class challenged her very often. I wasn't a boy and didn't know how to take no for an answer.

Suzy: Nine.

Gotcha.

Suzy opened the door with a smile on her face and a killer outfit. "Hey. You look amazing." She had on furry boots, skintight jeans, and a fluffy, oversized sweater.

She eyed me up and down, studying my outfit. "I guess I'm dressed okay."

"I'm not a fancy guy. I wear my jeans, t-shirt, and boots or sandals."

She made a face at me—what the fuck was that about?

"You never dress up?" she asked, as she locked the front door and turned to face me.

"Only when necessary. Tonight it isn't." I sat on the bike and held out the helmet. "Want to do it yourself?"

She plopped it on her head. I laughed as she fiddled with the straps. "Want help?"

"No...I'm perfectly capable of doing it myself." She fastened the buckle under her chin. "See?" The helmet slid forward, covering her eyes. "Damn it."

I couldn't help myself; I burst into laughter. "Come here, lemme help."

Her lips pursed with annoyance.

"Don't worry, sugar, you'll get the hang of it."

"I'm not used to all this..." She motioned to the bike, her eyes still hidden as I pulled her toward me.

"Live a little. Learn to let go."

Her lips turned up in a smile. "Not that you know, but I'm a total control freak."

"We'll work on that." I pushed the helmet on top of her head and grabbed the straps.

"I'm perfect just the way I am." She squinted at me, which made it harder for me to stop laughing. The pissed-off-teacher look made my dick rock hard and my balls ache.

"I didn't mean it that way. I mean you need to learn to have some fun," I said, grabbing her chin after fixing the fasteners.

"I have plenty of fun, for your information."

"Climb on, sugar." I patted the seat. "What do you like to do for fun?"

Her hand touched my shoulder as she hoisted her leg over the bike. "Well, I like to read. I go out with my friends sometimes. Um, I like to hang out at the pool. I like to play games. I do plenty of fun things." Her body rested against mine and I closed my eyes. Down, boy—not tonight. She didn't mention one thing that resembled fun in my book.

"What about a club? Concerts? Parties?" A girl her age should've experienced a couple things in her life. She went to college and had to live a little...I mean, fuck. "I know you've never ridden a bike before."

"I don't dance. Concerts, a couple of times in college, and parties? Do work parties count?" She clasped her hands around my chest and sealed the gap between our bodies.

"Everyone can dance. I saw how your body moved last night, babe. You can dance." I turned the key and throttled the engine.

She swatted my chest. "Hush."

I'd embarrassed her. Good—I needed to push her. I wanted to learn what she was really all about. The good-girl bullshit worked for me, but I needed to know there was a sinner underneath that polished veneer.

"Well, tonight we're going to add a few check marks to your life." I moved my body, leaving no space between us.

"What are we doing?" she asked against my back, already hiding her face.

"Heading to the beach."

"It's dark, though."

"Exactly."

I drove slowly through her neighborhood, waiting for the right moment to pay her back for the smack on my chest. I hit the open country road at the end of her development and gunned the bike. Glancing in the side mirror, I could only see her blonde hair blowing in the wind.

I sped up, and she pinched my pec and yelled, "Stop!"

I didn't listen, pretending the wind made it impossible to hear. I pointed at my ear and shook my head. "I can't hear you."

"Slow down," she yelped.

Stopping at the red light, I turned to look at her. "There's no one around. We're safe—I promise."

"I don't know if I can ever get used to riding on this dang thing."

"Do you trust me?"

"What?"

"Trust, sugar. Simple question."

She sighed. "I do."

"Then enjoy the ride. It's freeing and there's nothing like it in the world. Ready? Hold on." I gunned the bike, but not enough to lose control, as she screamed in my ear. I couldn't stop myself from laughing.

She still had a stranglehold on my chest as we rolled into the beachfront bar. I squeezed the bike into the only single space available. Charlie's was the place to be seen on a Saturday night, and by the looks of it, half of the town was there.

"Can I open my eyes now?" she asked, her voice muffled from my jacket.

"We're here. Off you go." I pried her fingers apart and patted them.

"Charlie's?" She climbed off the bike and unlatched the helmet quicker than I thought possible.

"Yes. Have you been?"

"No." She looked around the parking lot.

"Hey," I said as I grabbed her chin. "It's okay. I'll give you plenty of firsts." I smiled at her. "I like the idea of showing you new things." There were so many things I wanted to do to her. I wanted to ruin her in every possible way. Fuck the lawyers and the boring motherfuckers.

"I rarely come down to the beach, let alone at night."

"Well, tonight there's a DJ, and I want to dance with you."

"Oh," she said, her eyes wide in shock. "I told you, I can't dance."

"You can and you will. Might take a couple of those sweet drinks you like, but you'll do it."

"Oh, suck it."

"I plan on it." I smirked at her and grabbed her hand.

Chapter 6

Suzy

Did I know what a good time was anymore? I went to college and knew how to live it up and let go. My life had become so wrapped up in work and finishing my master's degree that I kind of forgot what it meant to let go and unwind. I'd always put more pressure on myself, wanting to get ahead in life, not wanting to worry about paying the next bill. I lived comfortably and I was happy with that. I enjoyed staying home and reading a good book. Hell, it was cheaper than going out to a bar and drinking. I needed to watch my pennies, and drinking them just felt silly.

"I'll take a margarita," I said to the bartender, reaching in my purse, but City put his hand over mine.

"I'll take a Yuengling, please," he said to the bartender, and then he looked at me and said, "I got this, Suzy."

"I can pay for myself."

"We're on a date, sugar. I pay when we're on a date. Put your money away—I'll find another way for you to pay me back." Butterflies filled my stomach as he said the last word in my ear close enough that I felt the vibration.

I grabbed my drink, letting the cool liquid slide down my throat. I needed liquid courage if he thought I would dance with him tonight. Dancing and me didn't mix, never had. I never knew what to do with my hands, and I always felt like everyone watched me—it freaked me the hell out. If he wanted to dance, I'd give him exactly what he asked, and make an ass of myself to prove him wrong.

City picked up his beer and studied me. Why did he have to be so damn sexy? I didn't want to like him, but I did. His cockiness wasn't like the other men I'd dated; it had nothing to do with his career or his material possessions. No, his was natural and sexual.

"I'd like to say you should slow down, but fuck it, I like when you're tipsy." He sipped his beer and leaned against the bar.

"I don't see you tearing it up."

"I can't, I'm driving and I don't drive drunk. Have to keep a clear head when you're on a bike." He ran his finger over the rim of the bottle, and all I could do was stare at him.

The band took the stage, and everyone clapped as the lead singer began to speak. "Thank you. Thank you," he said as he motioned for the crowd to quiet down. The guitarist began to play, and the crowd grew quiet. A soulful melody filled the air as the lead singer began to sway. The rhythm was intoxicating, and if I were home, I'd be dancing around my living room making a total ass of myself without any witnesses.

"Finish your drink." City's lips were set in a hard line, and I knew what he wanted.

"Think you can handle all this?" I motioned up and down my body. Fuck, how else could I stall?

"I know I can." He licked his lips, and I didn't want it to affect me, but he got to me. "I remember the way you moved against my cock, sugar." He brushed the hair off my shoulder, and my spine tingled.

My face grew flush as images of last night flashed in my mind. I didn't respond to him as I polished off the last sip of my margarita. "I warned you." I shrugged and smiled. Here goes nothin'—let's show this big boy whatcha got.

Holding hands, we walked to the middle of the dance floor. The music wasn't the right tempo for a slow dance or to shake my booty, as Sophia used to call it. I didn't really know what to do as I stood there and looked around. He wrapped his arm around my back and pulled me close. "Feel the music. Follow my body."

Every inch of his front touched mine as he began to move with the music. Wrapping my arms around his neck, letting his body guide mine to the beat, it struck me how well the man could move. His body rubbing against mine caused my nipples to harden, and a familiar ache between my legs returned. The memory of how he felt inside me, moving in the same rhythm, made my knees feel weak as he held me against his torso. I let him move my body—I became pliable in his hands.

"See? You got moves," he said in my ear as I buried my face in his chest.

I didn't know if the liquor had given me the ability to move with the music or if it was the man holding me, but I'd never moved this gracefully in my life. I looked up into his eyes, and he stared at me with the side of his mouth turned up in a grin. Why did this sexy-ass man, who lived life totally opposite of me, want me? We didn't fit—we didn't make sense on paper, but that didn't stop my body from reacting to him, no matter how hard my mind said to ignore his charms.

"You think too much. Stop making a list of why you shouldn't be here. Feel the reasons you should," he said, and kissed my lips, distracting me as he pressed his erection into my stomach. My doubts vanished. I leaned into his body and grabbed his pecs, toying with the piercings underneath his shirt. "Don't start something you don't want to finish, Suzette," he whispered against my lips.

"I always follow through, City." I smirked and winked before pressing my lips against his. I couldn't resist him, at least not in person. I'd live for tonight and deal with the fallout tomorrow. Our bodies slowed as we kissed. He ran his fingers through my hair and then fisted it, tipping my head back to give him deeper access.

I breathed his air, no room left between us, as he held my body to his. He pulled back and left only a small gap between us, not releasing his hold on me entirely. "I want to taste you."

Fuck me. Every bit of my body felt hot and damp. I wanted City more than I had last night. "You do?" No one had ever talked to me like he did.

"I will." I could see his eyes change with his words, his pupils fully dilated. "I don't make false promises."

I swallowed hard, unable to stop the barrage of sexy images from invading my thoughts. Why can't he be a lawyer or something other than a biker tattoo guy? He probably wouldn't have this effect on me if he was anything other than who he was —City.

"Stop thinking and dance." He released his hold on my hair and swung me out, pulling me back against his body with a thump. Christ have mercy on my soul.

For once in my life, I felt like I could actually dance. The music was slow and sensual, and let me move without feeling like an idiot. We touched each other constantly and didn't lose eye contact.

The music slowed and everyone began to clap. "For our next song..." the lead singer said.

"Want another drink, sugar?"

"Yes, I'm parched." City had me all kinds of crazy. I felt like I was drooling, but my mouth screamed for something cool, and my body needed a break from the foreplay on the dance floor.

City motioned to the bartender, snapped his fingers, and pointed at me. "Aren't you getting one?" I asked.

"Just a water. I'm driving, remember." I respected him for sticking to his original plan. "Plus, I'd rather get you a little liquored up. We have an appointment down on that swing." He pointed in the distance to a dark object.

"What's out there?" I asked, squinting and trying to get a better look, but the beach was shrouded in darkness except for the glimmer of the moon on the ocean.

"Darkness."

"And?"

"You. Me. Darkness." The corner of his mouth tipped up, and I swear to God his eyes almost twinkled.

The bartender placed the margarita in front of me and I picked it up, needing a diversion. I ran my tongue along the salt before taking a mouthful of the cool, sweet liquid in my mouth. I swallowed fast, and the alcohol burned my throat on the way down. I looked at City, and he was watching me intently, curiously. I licked the rim again, letting the salt dance on my tongue, and saw his chest expand as he breathed in quickly.

"Keep doing that, sugar, and I won't let you take another sip."

"What? This?" I licked the rim again, keeping my eyes trained on him, and let my tongue drift as far as I could.

"Fuck," he muttered, running his hand across his face.

Two can play a naughty game, City. I may not be the hussy he was used to being with, but I knew how to get a man's attention.

Smiling against the glass as I took another sip and looked away, I pretended to be uninterested. The salt tasted good, mixed with the sweet, tangy drink as I let the liquid linger on my tongue before swallowing it. My legs felt tingly as the liquor spread throughout my system.

"Damn," I said, my face becoming flushed.

"What's wrong?" He raised an eyebrow, cocking his head.

"Strong drink. Guess the first one never left my system," I said, tipping it back again and sucking down the last bit of liquid.

"That's it. Come on, Suzy. I got something for you to lick." He grabbed my hand and started to tug me away from the bar.

"I can't," I protested as I set the glass on the bar.

"Oh, yes you can. You said you always follow through, and I'm cashing in on that promise, sugar." Butterflies filled my stomach with the knowledge that we were not going to be watching the waves. City had plans for me, and I couldn't back out now.

We reached the last step on the deck, and I stopped before my feet hit the sand. "Wait." My hand fell from his. "My boots. I don't want them to get ruined." I tried to give an innocent smile. I really didn't want to ruin them. They cost me more money than I wanted to admit.

He grunted and moved closer to me. We were eye to eye, with him flat on the beach and me perched on the step. He didn't say a word as he reached down and picked me up. I laughed as he pulled me against his chest. "Wrap your arms around me."

My laughter stopped as I wrapped my arms around his neck and stared at his face. City was beautiful; his dark features and ice-blue eyes that looked clear in the moonlight stole my breath. His jaw had a shadow from the stubble, and I ran my fingertips across it, remembering the night before. His lips were full and beautiful and screamed to be kissed. His eyebrows were manly, yet neat—no waxing, but he groomed them. His dark hair flopped with each step, and I couldn't help but smile. He was everything I wanted and exactly the type I ran away from.

City sat down on the swing, still holding me in his arms. "Straddle me," he growled in my ear as the swing moved back and forth.

"But people can see us." I looked around as my heart thumped in my chest.

"Could you see the swing from up there?" He smirked.

"No, I couldn't, but if someone catches us we could get in trouble."

"Sugar, we won't get in trouble and no one's going to find us. Trust me. Now straddle me."

I scanned the deck area, and he was right—no one was looking for us, or even seemed to notice that there was anyone on the beach.

"You a regular here, big boy?" I said as I adjusted my body.

"I only come out here to be alone. You're the first girl I've ever brought here."

"Hard to believe that I could be your first in anything."

"Sugar, no bullshit. You gonna kiss me or what?" he asked, grabbing my chin.

"Depends on the what," I said giggling, as he squeezed my waist, pulling me close, our noses touching.

"You talk big, little girl. I'm going to get that taste I've been looking forward to."

Chapter 7

I couldn't stop the thought of Suzy moaning on my lap, facing away from me last night as I finger-fucked her. She was hesitant at first, nervous someone would see us, as I unzipped her pants enough to slide my fingertips inside. I wiped any thoughts out of her mind with a few strokes of my fingers. I watched her face as she rested her head against my shoulder—I watched her eyes roll back, and a small sound escaped her lips. "Quiet, sugar," I whispered in her ear, and she obeyed. Stroking her insides, circling her clit until her body shook and her pussy clamped down on my fingers.

She didn't move at first as I withdrew my fingers from her lace panties and brought them to my lips, wrapping my lips around them as I sucked her juices, and she stared at me with an open mouth and wide eyes.

"Mm. Taste yourself on me." I bent down and pressed my lips to hers, dragging my tongue across her bottom lip.

"City." She moaned in my mouth.

Reaching up and pulling her face to mine, I crushed my lips to hers.

"Joey. What the fuck?" Something hit my shoulder, and I blinked.

"What the fuck, Iz."

"Your dopey ass has been sitting there in fucking La-La Land for ten minutes grinning like a fucking mental patient. Snap. The. Fuck. Out."

"Couldn't just leave me there?" I asked. "And Iz, stop fucking hitting me. You're the only person that I let get away with that shit. You're always poking me with those bony-ass fingers."

"It's time to eat. Mama's been calling for everyone to come to the table." She rolled her eyes at me before walking away.

"I'm coming, Ma." I adjusted my dick in my jeans. My mind had become a little too engrossed in my fantasy, and the relief I needed would have to wait. I climbed off the couch and slid my hand in my pocket, looking for the phone that vibrated against my dick.

Suzy: I love your idea of or what.

Based on her message, I could tell I wasn't the only one thinking about our time on the beach.

"Iz, what the hell do you call the what, where, when, why, and how in English?"

She looked at me confused as I sat down at the table. "Trying to impress the teacher?" She giggled.

"Just answer the question, please." I sighed and stared at her, placing the phone on the table.

"What teacher?" Ma asked.

"Iz, what's it called? Throw me a bone."

"Interrogatives." My sister rolled her eyes before turning to face our mother. "He's schtuppin' a teacher, Ma."

"Isabella! That's not appropriate at the dinner table." My mom set the lasagna on the table. "I want details, Joseph." Ma winked at me.

Me: Wait until you feel the rest of my interrogatives.

I placed the phone on the table and looked around the room. Everyone had their eyes glued on me instead of the meal, as they usually were. "What?"

"You're smiling as you type—who is she, Joseph?" Ma said as she dished out the first steaming slice of heaven to my father.

"Just a woman, Ma." I held up my plate as I waited to be served. My mother was traditional in many ways, refusing to let us serve ourselves. She was the one to dish out the food and to sit last.

She held the lasagna over my plate. "I've never seen you like this. You want your piece, baby? You hungry?"

"Hell yes." I licked my lips and moved my plate closer to the piece hovering just out of reach.

"Then you're going to tell me about her, yes? No information means no food." She held the slice of lasagna to her nose and inhaled it. "Mm, it would be a shame for you to miss out on this meal."

I sighed. Women—the root of the evil in this world. If pussy wasn't so fucking perfect I'd swear off them for eternity.

"Fine, Ma. I'll tell you about her after we eat. Can I please have a piece now?"

"Sure, baby. You can help me wash the dishes and tell me all about her."

Fuck. "You're an asshole, Iz." Throwing me under the bus with my mother was a skill, and kept the heat off her. "What about Dean? Still seeing him?"

"Bella, you better not still be seeing that man. He's nothing but trouble," my mother said.

Iz glared at me across the table. Served her little gossipy ass right for airing my shit at the dinner table.

The conversation turned to sports and football, as it always did on Sunday. My grilling was soon forgotten as my brothers and Dad stuffed their faces and rubbed their stomachs. I finished my lasagna, wiping my plate clean with a piece of garlic bread, before picking up my phone again.

Suzy: WTF. I teach math—no clue what an interrogative is. Hello—I don't get your angle.

Me: At the end of my linear path I have a point for you.

Did that make sense or did I just make a complete ass of myself? Fuck. This girl had me all fucked up. My parents always wanted their children to "settle down" and make babies, but I'd always been more interested in perfecting my skills and not wanting to get tied down, at least not after Joni. We didn't marry young and follow their path in life, and I thought my parents were secretly proud of us for waiting. They were happily married and have been for over forty years—they tied the knot right out of high school. Times were different.

Suzy: Oooh, you know just the right things to say to a girl.

Me: Tuesday night = (dinner) + my linear path + your diameter

"Joey, grab your plate. We have a date with a sink and some dishes," Ma said from behind me. I looked up at her and saw her smiling and reading over my shoulder. Fuck.

Suzy: No can do—grad classes. I'll take a rain check.

I turned off my screen and placed it in my pocket. Nothing was secret or sacred in this fucking house.

"Everybody bring your plates in the kitchen. Come on. Clear off the table," Ma said. The room filled with grumbles, but we all knew the drill. Thirty years later we didn't need to be told what our roles were in this family. My father was the figurehead, my mother told everyone what to do, and we did as told without giving lip.

Ma waited for me by the sink as I set my plate on the counter. "Did you find someone?" She was beaming.

"I just met her, Ma," I shooed her to the side so I could start tackling the dishes.

She threw the dishrag over her shoulder and eyed me. "Baby, the heart knows what the heart wants. Your sister told me you've been acting differently. It's written all over your face. Sometimes fate steps in and throws you off the course we've set in life."

"Don't go crocheting baby blankets yet, Ma."

She placed her hand on my shoulder as I scrubbed and avoided eye contact. "Joseph, I know the man you are. I know you're guarded with your heart after Joni, but you have to open again sometime. You need to find someone to trust in life. Is this girl worthy of that trust? Is she worth the risk?"

"Ma, I barely know the chick."

"Tsk, tsk. Someone doth protest too much." She kissed my cheek, ruffling my hair. That shit made me crazy, but with my hands full of soap I had no other option but to let her do as she wished.

"I can see you're not going to stop. She seems like a good person. She's different, Ma. She seems genuine, but I'm not rushing into anything."

"What about her? Is she madly in love with my baby boy?"

"Ma." I should hate her calling me her baby boy, but my mother could call me anything in the world. I adored the woman. "She isn't jumping on the Joey train. I don't think she really wants to see me."

"What? Why not?" She leaned against the counter, crossing her arms. "You're perfect."

"That's 'cause I'm your kid. I'm hardly perfect, Ma." I cleaned the last dish and placed it in the rack to dry. "You don't really know everything about me, no matter what you think."

"I know more than you think, sweetheart. Iz has loose lips, you know." I could beat my little sister's ass. I'm sure she doesn't tell my ma about all her love affairs. "I know you're quite the ladies' man. I'm not judging you, Joey. You never bring any girls around, but I know you."

Fucking Iz. "When and if I find the one, Ma, you'll be the first to know." I kissed her cheek, and her radiant smile lit up the room. "Suzy sees me as a tattoo artist that rides a motorcycle and hangs out in shithole bars. I don't exactly rank up there on her boyfriend material checklist."

"I kinda like this girl already." She giggled. I loved hearing the sound of her laughter. "She doesn't know everything about you and our family?" She raised her eyebrow.

"No, I don't tell anyone about us, Ma."

"Checklists are made to be changed. She needs to know the Joey I do. Are you going to ask her out? Makes her yours?"

"That's what I was trying to do at the table, but she has class."

"Ah, a smart girl too. Joey, don't ask a girl out through text message. That's what's wrong with you kids today. She needs to hear your voice when you ask. Texting is too impersonal, and I'll never understand it. Call the girl."

"I will. I'll call her later. Happy?"

My ma wrapped her arms around me and said, "Very."

Chapter 8

S uzy

I couldn't get him out of my mind, and it had been less than twenty-four hours since he dropped me off with a soul-stealing kiss. His cocky smile, his muscles, the way he touched me stayed with me long after he left. No one had made me want to break a rule more than he did. No matter how hard I tried to concentrate on my lesson plans for the upcoming quarter, my mind drifted to him.

Trying to quiet my brain, I flipped on Catfish as I crawled in bed. It had been my guilty pleasure since this show began. I loved watching the train wrecks and the broken hearts of those that thought they fell in love with someone, only to find out that they weren't who they pretended to be.

I used to tease Sophia and Kayden, my old roommates, mercilessly about how different their little tryst in New Orleans could've turned out. Their situation was different; they had mutual friends and had checked each other out, so they felt it was a sure thing.

On paper, Kayden and Sophia didn't work—it wasn't a match made in heaven—but their love was undeniable. It was electric. Sophia followed her heart, and his pull was inescapable for her. She fell for him hook, line, and sinker. I never understood it until I got to know Kayden. He wasn't anything like I thought—his heart was pure, but his path in life had been different than mine. I'd never believe Sophia would find a guy without a college education and a criminal record to fall in love with, but they were the happiest couple I knew, and I wanted that kind of love.

My checklist had been realistic in theory, but City had me questioning my method and requirements. I'd dated men that fit on paper, but the chemistry lacked. City was just so City. I was approaching the end of my twenties, sitting in bed, eating bonbons, and watching Catfish alone.

I am happy, aren't I?

My phone began to move across my nightstand. I popped the last morsel of chocolaty goodness in my mouth. "Herlo?"

"Hey, Suzette." The vibration of his voice through the phone made my heart skip a beat as I swallowed the chocolate slowly. Damn, why did I have to eat that last piece before I answered? Herlo? I sounded like I had a speech problem.

"Oh, hey. How are you?" I grabbed the water on my nightstand and washed down the last bit of candy.

"I'm well, sugar. Whatcha doin'?" I heard rustling in the background. Were those his sheets? Was he naked?

"Just watching television, and I'm about to go to sleep, you?" I wiped the chocolate from my lips and licked my finger. These little bitches were so damn tasty.

"I just crawled in bed. What are you wearing?" he asked in a smooth timbre.

OMG, he didn't just ask me that. I looked down. I had my ratty go-to clothes for when I lounged around the house. "Um, a tank top and flannel pajama pants."

I could hear him laughing. "Really?"

"Yeah, why? What are you wearing?" Please don't say you're naked.

"Nothing, sugar." Damn it all to hell. "You still there?"

"Yeah." I knew he could hear the change in my tone, as it came out all breathy and quiet.

"When can I see you again?" he asked.

"I don't know, City." I wanted, God how I wanted to scream now, but I needed to think about him—us.

"Don't deny you want me, Suzy. I can hear it in your voice. You're thinking of my cock inside you and your lips on mine."

My breath hitched as the images played like a movie in my mind. "I won't deny it, but that doesn't make it right," I said, moving down in the sheets and turning off the television.

"I'm not asking you to be my girlfriend, Suzette. I remember you having an earth-shattering time yesterday. I can still hear the sound you made when I made you come against my fingers." A small moan escaped his lips.

My heart ached when he said he didn't want me to be his girlfriend. What the hell? Stay on course—do not waiver from the list.

"It was the sexiest fucking sound I've ever heard, sugar. The way your eyes rolled back and your body rocked into my hand. Fuck."

I squeaked. OMG, lemme die. "City."

"The taste of you on my tongue after. Fucking perfect. I'm rock hard thinking about you."

"You are?" I whispered.

"Rock fucking hard." His breathing changed like it had when he fucked me. I could never forget the sounds the man made when he came. "Friday night, Suzy. No excuses this time."

"Okay. Friday."

"Good. I'll be thinking about that sweet pussy all week, sugar. Sweet dreams." His words were drawn out and his tone was sexy as hell.

"Night," I whispered back before the phone went quiet and his harsh breath disappeared. Listening to the man turned me on, and I wanted to run to his house and have sex with him, but I didn't. Reaching into my nightstand, I grabbed my trusty battery-operated boyfriend of the last five years and thought of City as I climaxed. The orgasm didn't compare to the one I'd had under his deft fingers. He fucking ruined one of my simple pleasures.

Fuck Monday mornings. I never wanted to get out of bed. I pulled in the school parking lot five minutes late before throwing my bags down in my classroom, and I headed to the copier to be prepped for class that started in ten minutes. Damn. I hated being rushed.

I tapped my finger against the copy machine as it slowly churned out each piece of paper. People walked in and out of the teacher work area with quick hellos and "happy Mondays."

"What are you grinning about? It's Monday and you never smile, bitch," Sophia said behind me.

"I wasn't smiling." I turned around to see her grinning like a loon that had just escaped the funny farm.

"Oh, you were, sister. What happened?" Sophia always looked so put together and breathtaking.

"I have so much to tell you. I'll come see you during my planning period."

"By the look on your face I'd think you got laid this weekend. I'm not talking about a boring bullshit fucking either. You got fucked," she whispered in my face. I felt my face flush. "You did, don't lie, and I want every last detail."

The homeroom warning bell blared, and I started to panic, grabbing my papers in a crazy heap. "I'll be up third period. I'm going to be late, Sophia. I gotta run, babe."

"I'll hunt your ass down if you don't show up," Sophia said as I reached the door.

"I'll be there, whore. Shut it."

She smiled at me like a proud mama.

Sophia shut the door to her office. "Tell me, and I mean all of it."

Sitting on the comfy old couch in her office, I rested my head against the wall. "What do you want to know?"

"Don't play coy with me. You know more about my sex life than anyone else in the world. I want all the information, starting with who and when."

Sophia sat at her desk and rested her head on her hand. "I met him Friday night."

"Friday night? I don't remember you meeting someone," she said, her eyes looking upward as she replayed our time at the martini bar.

"After I left you. My car crapped out and this drop-dead gorgeous man stopped to help me."

"Helped you out of your panties too, I presume?" She giggled and slapped the desk.

"Eventually." I laughed. "I called you, but you didn't answer. I went with him on his bike to call a tow, and ended up having a drink or two."

"Bike? Like the ones the drunks ride around here with the electric motors, or are we talking smokin' hot Harley action?"

"Smokin' hot."

"His name?"

"City, but it's a nickname. When we left he asked where I wanted to go, and I told him I wanted him to take me to his house. I'd had too much to drink, because you know that just isn't me."

"Whatever. You're dying to be naughty but those uptight pricks you date are missionary men. Bleh. Keep talking," she commanded.

"Pushy wench, aren't you? When he undresses, girl..." I sighed. "Oh. My. God. His body is covered in tattoos, his nipples are pierced, and he, and he..." I covered my mouth and tried to hide my grin.

"Breathe, Suzy. He what?"

"His penis was pierced too." I swallowed, remembering how it looked.

"Oh, now I'm enthralled. So your ass breaks down, is rescued by a sexy-ass biker with tats and piercings, and..."

"I slept with him. More than once. I stayed the night, and he had me before breakfast too."

"Have you talked to him since?"

"Yes, we went on a date Saturday night, and he wants to take me out again on Friday."

"I know that look. What's the problem?"

"He's just not...isn't what I'm looking for." I frowned.

"Suzy, baby, listen to me. Do you like this man?"

"Yes."

"As you would say, did he make your body tingle and make you scream?"

"Yes, more times than I can count."

"Do you want to see him again?"

"I do, but—"

"Fuck buts, girl."

"He's a tattoo artist and lives in an old house. He just doesn't fit my checklist. He's a biker, Sophia. What could we possibly have in common?"

"You and your damn lists. If I had a list I wouldn't have Kayden and Jett. I can't imagine my life without them. We can't always control everything in life; sometimes life jumps up and smacks us in the face."

"I know, Soph. He scares me," I whispered.

"Has he hurt you?" She stood and walked toward me with her eyebrows drawn together and her mouth set in a hard line.

"No. I mean, I'm scared I could fall for him. I've never been with anyone like him, and I want to see him again. I've never had that spark, and with him it's like lightning."

Sophia sat down next to me and grabbed my face. "You listen to me, Suzy. You're young and have your whole life ahead of you. If you want to be with him, then do it. Stop trying to fit everyone in your mold. Rules are made to be broken. Give the guy a chance, babe. He's not asking you to marry him, is he?"

"No, he said he's not asking me to be his girlfriend either."

"Kayden wasn't looking for a girlfriend, but here we are, engaged with a baby. Sometimes life doesn't give us what we're looking for, but it gives us what is supposed to be. We just have to be willing to take the plunge. Live a little. Take a risk for once."

I smiled and hugged her. "You're right, Sophia, but I need some time and distance. So, Kayden still makes you happy even after everything?"

"I wouldn't trade a moment I've had with him. He's everything to me. My life's complete, Suzy. You need to find that guy that makes you feel whole. The one that gives you a reason to wake up each morning."

"So I should just enjoy the ride?" I wiggled my eyebrows at Sophia and laughed.

"In a matter of speaking, yes. Was it beautiful?"

"What?"

"His dick, Suzy. I've never seen a pierced one in person."

"Oh my God, it was the most beautiful thing I'd ever seen."

"I'm so excited for you, Suz." She bounced on the cushion, causing both of our bodies to shake. "When are you seeing him again?"

"Friday night. He didn't give me an option to say no."

"Smart man. You're such a pussy at times—listen to your heart and not your mind for once, got me?"

"Yes, Mom. I understand."

"Oh, and Suzy?"

"Yes?" I turned and looked at the grinning Sophia.

"I want pictures."

"You're such a whore." I laughed as I walked out the door.

Chapter 9

C ity

Me: Are you in bed?

Suzy: Yes, you?

Me: Yep, just lying here thinking about you. 24 hours until I hear you scream my name again.

We'd been texting all day. I never looked forward to a simple phone call or text from any chick. I ached for her. I lived with a perpetual boner now. We didn't have an exclusive deal, but the other girls didn't seem to do it for me anymore. My dick didn't ache for them. It wanted Suzy and her tight, sweet pussy.

Suzy: What's your real name?

I thought I told her my name, but maybe I hadn't.

Me: Joseph.

Suzy: Can I call you Joe or Joey?

Me: You can call me anything you want, sugar.

Suzy: Joey. It suits you.

I never felt like a Joey—it seemed childish, and the nickname City seemed to fit me better.

Me: Tank top and PJ pants?

Suzy: Yes. Y?

Me: Just want to know how to picture you as I stroke myself.

Craving the release, I stroked quicker, gripping it in my hand. I didn't want to come too quickly tomorrow night—I wanted to savor her and feast on her body.

Me: I'm going to picture you with your legs on my shoulders and your beautiful tits bouncing from my dick, slamming into you.

I stroked myself as I waited for her reply, caressing the tip, toying with the ring, giving it a tug.

Suzy: That's sexy. I can't wait to suck on you. Feel your velvety hardness in my mouth.

Oh, the little girl could be dirty. Time to push the envelope.

Me: Tell me one of your fantasies.

I wanted there to be a bad girl underneath—someone that wanted to get dirty with me. I stroked my shaft slowly and pictured her tight cunt milking me.

Suzy: Really?

Nothing was easy with this one.

Me: Yes, pick one.

Suzy: I always wanted someone to take me from behind and for him to hold my wrists at my side so I can't move.

Fuck me, it was a start at least. I wanted to pound her into next week. I wanted her so bad I thought my dick would break in my hand.

Me: What else? More.

Suzy: I always heard choking was amazing.

I stroked my cock faster and harder than I had before. I pictured my hands wrapped around her throat, watching her face turn pink, and feeling her clawing my chest as I rammed my cock into her. The warm liquid spurted, landing on my abdomen before I could stop.

Me: Fuck, sugar. You just made me come so fuckin' hard.

Suzy: OMG.

Me: Are you touching yourself?

I grabbed my shirt off the floor and wiped up the mess that I created lost in my mental fuckfest.

Suzy: Yes! You do things to me, Joey, things I've never felt before.

Me: Wait till tomorrow, sugar. Put a finger inside yourself.

No reply. She must be following my command. Fucking perfect.

Me: Don't type; just watch the screen, Suzette.

Me: I'm going to fuck you from behind and hold your wrists so tight in my grip that your fingers will go numb. My cock's going to throb inside of you—hit every spot that makes you scream, sugar.

How in the fuck was I getting a boner already?

Me: When I see your body grow flush and dew on your skin, I'm going to wrap my hands around your throat from behind and apply pressure until you're gasping for air and milking my cock for more.

Me: Come for me, sugar.

I lay in bed and pictured her touching herself. Down, boy—fuck.

Suzy: You're bad for me, Joey.

Me: Who the fuck wants to be good? Sweet dreams, beautiful.

Suzy: Night, Joey. I'm looking forward to the ride tomorrow night bahaha

I turned off my ringer and stared at the ceiling. I planned to give her more than she could handle and make all of her fantasies come true. Suzy was getting to me and cracking the well-built wall around my heart I'd created after Joni's death. Air—I need air. I jumped out of bed and put on a t-shirt and jeans. I needed to think, and I did that best on the open road.

I revved the engine a couple of times, put on my riding glasses, and cracked my neck. The roads were clear. The cold weather kept most of the snowbirds that traveled south off the roads, especially at night. I kicked the bike in top speed and felt the wind lash my exposed skin and blow through my hair.

I rode for over an hour, winding through the country roads before pulling in my driveway after midnight. My muscles vibrated and I felt exhausted. My mind was too tired to think of anything but my bed.

After grabbing my keys and jacket off the couch, I headed out-side. Even though the calendar read October, the air was sticky and the sun made my skin burn—but I knew there would be a chill in the air tonight. Florida's winters were bipolar. Sometimes hot, sometimes cold—a totally fucking guessing game to keep you on your toes.

I tried to use Suzy's crazy-ass fucking method—I made a mental checklist while I drove. She had pros—fucking beauty, smart as hell, kick-ass career, independent, kind, innocent—but she also had cons. She was too fucking innocent and she could crush my heart into a million fucking pieces. Think, man. She has to have other fucking flaws. I liked the geeky girl underneath the hot, beautiful body. She wasn't used up and bitter from her experiences.

I walked in the shop early to find Mikey sitting at the front desk, rifling through the papers. "Morning, Mikey."

"Hey, bro, how's it hanging?"

"Little to the left," I said, adjusting myself.

"Never pegged you for a lefty. Thought maybe down the middle."

"Fucker, how could it hang down the middle? You need your head checked or some shit?"

"You know, maybe you weren't blessed with the Gallo family genes. Just sayin.'"

"Dumb fuck. You've seen my dick—you pierced the motherfucker for me."

Mikey chuckled. "I know, fucker. Just yanking your fucking chain. Touchy this morning, aren't we?"

I threw my bag next to my chair and walked up to the desk.

"Not touchy, Mike. This fuckin' girl is stuck in my head."

Mikey shook his head and started to laugh. "Ah, she's cracking that cold, dead heart of yours?"

"Fuck, I don't know. I'm seeing her again tonight. What the fuck am I doing, man?"

"Pussy. She got good shit, huh?" He grinned.

"Platinum pussy. Has my brain all fuckin' jumbled up, man."

"Never thought I'd see the day."

"Makes two of us," I mumbled.

"Listen, you want anyone else fucking her?" he asked as he placed his hand on my shoulder. He was always into love and touching, and it made me batshit crazy.

The thought of anyone else touching Suzy made me want to fucking vomit, or beat the shit out of the bastard. "Fuck no, I want to be the only one inside her. I don't like sloppy seconds."

"Well, there's your answer."

"Fucking hell." I shook my head and stared at the floor.

"Doesn't mean you have to marry her, Joey. Just make sure she doesn't want to fuck anyone else. Make her yours—take the leap."

"For once, Mikey, you're right. Fucking miracle." I couldn't deny it anymore. I wanted her and couldn't stand the thought of anyone else touching her or kissing her beautiful lips.

"You know I always got your back. It's been years, man. Joni would want you to be happy." He grabbed the schedule off the counter as the door chimed and the rest of the Gallo pack walked through the doors. "Would they have been friends—Joni and this girl?"

They had some similarities. Joni would think Suzy was funny as hell and sweet. "Yeah, they probably would have liked each other."

"She doesn't want you alone, wherever she is."

"Thanks, Mikey." Waiting for everyone to get settled, I grabbed my phone and sent Suzy a message about tonight.

Me: You're mine tonight, Suzette.

Chapter 10

S uzy

The day dragged on, and the students were in a foul mood. I needed the weekend to start. When the lunchtime bell rang, I walked in my office, plopping in my chair as I let my head fall back. "Jesus," I muttered. I closed my eyes for a moment and listened to the stillness in the air, since the kids had cleared the building. Two more class periods—I could do it.

I opened my drawer, grabbed my container of leftover pasta, and searched for my phone. I hoped City messaged me—I needed something to brighten up this shit day. I looked at the screen and my stomach fluttered. I was "his" tonight. What did he mean? Sexually?

I never liked to be called Suzette, but the way it sounded coming out of his mouth made my breath hitch. He always seemed to whisper it in my ear or say it against my lips, and it drove me crazy. I wanted to hear him say my name tonight.

Me: Only tonight?

Hell, did I just sound needy?

City: All things are possible.

What the hell did that mean?

"Hello. Suzy, you in here?" I heard Sophia calling from the door.

"In my office," I yelled, grabbing a forkful of noodles.

Sophia stood in the doorway and made a sound of disgust. "I don't know how you eat that Ragu shit cold. Bleh." She scrunched her nose, opened her mouth, and stuck her finger inside, pretending to gag.

"Hey, Mama Guido, what are you doing slumming it down here?" I stuck the noodle in my mouth and made a face at her.

"Kayden and I were talking, and we wanted to know if you and the cock piercing wanted to come over for a barbecue tonight?"

"You just want to molest him with your eyes."

"No, I don't. I have my hunk. Kayden still makes me tingle thinking about him." She made a silly face and shook her body like just the thought of him brought her pleasure. "I want to meet this guy and see if he's worthy of my little Suzy. Plus, Kayden could use a little pick-me-up. Maybe they can be friends and we can double date." She rested her body against the door with her leg crossed in front of the other and her arms folded. I always had a hard time saying no to Sophia.

"Well, I'd have to ask him. I don't know what he had planned."

"Send me an email after you ask him. It'll be fun. Don't take no for an answer. You've piqued my curiosity about this man that has you all types of insane. I mean, sweetie, I've always known you were crazy, but he has you questioning everything in your perfect little mapped out life. I must meet him."

"Fine, Soph. Let me ask him."

Me: BBQ at my friends' place tonight. You game?

"There, I asked. It's up to him now. Happy?" I grabbed a huge forkful and slowly placed it in my mouth—anything to gross Sophia out. She was the queen of sauce and meatballs. I missed when the house used to fill with the smell of her cooking. I'd come home after a long day and Kayden would have something divine on the stove. Now it was Ragu and me against the world.

"Ugh, I can't stand here and watch you eat that shit."

My phone chirped. "Wait," I said as she walked away from my office. "Incoming."

"So?"

City: Sounds fanfuckingtastic. What time shall I give you a "ride"?

"Um," I said as I felt the heat creep into my cheeks. "He wants to know what time we should arrive."

"He talks all proper like that?"

"Nope, but that's all you're getting. Time, please?"

She sighed. "Eight, okay? If you're gonna be late just let me know, whoreface. Bye," she said as the door closed behind her.

Me: Sophia said to be there at eight. Pick me up around ten till to be there on time—Sophia doesn't do late.

I knew that Sophia would take one look at City and practically be doing cartwheels. She'd never liked any man I had seen since we became friends. I flipped through the paperwork from my mailbox this morning as I waited for City to respond.

City: I'll be there at six thirty. Be ready for me, because I'm hard as a fuckin' rock. I have plans for that pussy before we go to the BBQ.

OMG, OMG, OMG.

Me: I'll be waiting with bells on.

Five minutes left before the next barrage of hooligans walked through the door. My afternoon classes were murder. They weren't bad kids, but they were challenging and mentally draining.

City: Naked—no fucking bells.

A fire ignited in my body as I read the screen. It's on like Donkey Kong.

Chapter 11

City

"Coming," a female voice from inside yelled.

"I remember you saying those very words twenty minutes ago," I growled in Suzy's ear.

Her cheeks turned a rosy shade of pink as she bit her lip, trying to hide her smile. Suzy pushed her hair off her shoulders and fixed her shirt, as though she wanted everything perfect and in place.

"Stop fidgeting, sugar."

"Oh my God, I can't. Sophia is going to take one look at me and know what we did," she said, dabbing her fingers at the corner of her lips.

"If she doesn't, then I didn't do it right."

A beautiful brunette opened the door with a smile. She looked me over, starting at my face, and then her eyes raked over my body. I felt almost violated by the way she appraised me. She looked at Suzy with a devilish grin and opened her arms. The girls exchanged hugs and whispered words that I couldn't hear, but Sophia's eyes didn't leave mine.

"Sophia, this is City."

"Nice to meet you, Sophia." I extended my hand to her. Sophia's hair was pulled back in a sloppy bun that sat on top of her head. She had a bright white smile and kind eyes.

She placed her hand in mine. "Nice to finally meet you, City. I've heard all about you." She winked.

A grin crept across my face—I guessed I got the thumbs-up from her friend. "Nice things, I hope."

"She spoke very big of you." She giggled, and I felt my cheeks heat. I could tell these girls together were going to be a handful. "Come on in. Kayden and Jett are out on the patio starting the grill."

I extended my arm for Suzy to walk in front of me, and I watched both girls walk inside as I stayed close behind. They lived in a small apartment that was decorated with mismatched pieces that all worked. SportsCenter was on the television, and baby things were scattered everywhere.

"Don't mind the mess. Children have a way of overtaking every-thing, no matter how small." Sophia waved her hands around and picked up small toys off the floor before tossing them in a basket near the television stand.

The door to the patio opened and a tall, muscular man holding a baby walked into the living room. His head was clean-shaven, and he looked like someone that I'd find down at the Neon Cowboy—or a guy who would walk in my shop for some work.

"Kayden, baby, Suzy brought her new beau, City."

Kayden eyed me warily. I held out my hand to him. "Nice to meet you, Kayden. Suzy talks very highly of you and Sophia."

Kayden placed the baby in the crook of his left arm before ex-tending his right hand to me. "Glad to meet you, City." He squeezed my hand tightly, almost to the point of pain, but I didn't dare pull away. I knew the fuckin' macho bullshit. He was staking his claim on Sophia and giving me a silent warning with Suzy.

"Oh, Jett, come here, baby." Reaching for Jett, Suzy plucked him from Kayden's arms.

"No hello, Suzy? How are you, Kayden? I've missed you, Kayden. Just oooh, Jett." Kayden laughed.

"Oh now, Kayden, you know I love you. Gimme a kiss," she said, puckering her lips and closing her eyes.

My heart raced with the thought of Kayden placing his lips on hers. I squeezed my hands into fists. They were just friends. Kayden planted a kiss on her cheek as he rubbed the head of his child before walking into the kitchen and wrapping his arms around his wife.

"He's gotten so big," Suzy said as she bounced the baby in her arms, patting his butt. She looked natural with a child in her arms, like it was something she did every day. Her eyes lit up as Jett gripped her thumb.

"He's growing like a weed," Sophia said from the kitchen. "What do you guys want to drink? City, what can I get you?"

"I'll take a beer if you got one."

Suzy's eyes grew wide and her nostrils flared, and I didn't know what I said, but obviously I'd fucked up somehow. "But it's okay if you don't. I'll really drink anything."

"Coming right up. Suzy? Virgin daiquiri, babe?" Sophia snickered as she opened the fridge and began to dig around.

"What did I say wrong?" I whispered in her ear.

"Kayden doesn't drink. He's an alcoholic and has been clean for about a year now." She looked at Kayden and Sophia before returning her attention on the cooing baby in her arms.

"I didn't know. Shit, you should've given me a heads-up, sugar."

"I'm sorry. It just slipped my mind."

"It's okay, City. It's not something the ladies like to talk about. It's always the giant elephant in the room," Kayden said as he handed me the beer. "I can be around alcohol and not drink." He sat down on the couch and put his feet up on the coffee table. "Sit down; let the ladies work their magic in the kitchen. We'll take care of the meat, like God intended."

"I don't want to hear about your meat, Kayden." Suzy snickered.

"Kitchen, Suzy, but let Sophia cook." He pointed at her then toward the kitchen, and snapped his fingers.

"I can cook, Kayden," she said as she rubbed her nose against the baby's face before handing the baby to Kayden and walking away.

"City, Suzy can't cook a lick. She's the queen of pre-made. Just an FYI," he said as he cradled the baby and ran his finger along the chubby cheek.

Sitting on the couch, I set my beer on my knee and relaxed. "Eh, I can cook, so it's not a deal-breaker for me. Bucs fan?"

"Fuck no, Browns fan born and bred." He stretched out, placing his free hand behind his head.

"No shit? You like an underdog or abuse?" I smiled before lifting the beer to my lips.

"I stay true to my roots, you?"

"Bears fan. No other way to be."

"They've had some fuckin' horrible seasons, but the Browns have the market cornered on losing."

"Give ya that," I said as I tipped my beer toward him. "Suzy said you three lived together."

"Yep, for a while. She was a lifesaver, and I owe her. Don't fucking break her heart—I'll beat the fuck out of you." He laughed. "Seriously, you'll have a few more holes to match the ones you currently have."

What? I could see the girls had talked about me in detail. "Not my plan," I said. "Suzy isn't like other girls."

Suzy leaned against the counter and watched Sophia as they chatted. They looked over at us and started laughing.

"No, she's not. She's kind, pure, and too trusting. I feel like she's my little sister, and I'll protect her like she's my family."

"Gotcha. Loud and clear."

"You boys done with your pissing match?" Sophia said as she walked in the room with a plate of burgers. "These won't cook themselves."

"Let me handle the meat," Kayden said, handing Jett back to Suzy.

"That's what she said." Sophia chuckled. Kayden grabbed the plate from her and kissed her on the lips. She looked at him with a dopy grin as he backed away.

"If you're a good girl, I'll let you handle my meat later."

"Not in front of our guests," Sophia said as she smacked him on the shoulder.

"They're kind of nauseating aren't they?" Suzy stood next to me and rocked Jett in her arms. His eyes were almost closed as he sucked his fingers.

"A bit." I felt content with the three of them. I could almost feel the bond that they had, the love for each other.

"They've endured more than most people have in a lifetime, and they came out on the other side with an unbreakable bond. Someday I'll tell you their story. If fate is real, they're the perfect example. They were made for each other." She smiled as she watched them on the patio.

They touched each other and kissed, never moving apart. His actions portrayed adoration for his woman. "Are they married?"

"Not yet. Someday, I hope. They've both been married before, and they use that as an excuse not to rush into things." She curled her lips up and rolled her eyes. "I remind them that they have a baby. I guess I'm old-fashioned." She shrugged.

I made sure not to fuck that up. I never fucked without a condom or took that kind of risk. "I was brought up that way too, but you can't deny what they have. I'm sure they'll do it in time."

The evening was relaxing, and I liked talking with Kayden. He didn't bullshit, and Sophia was something else. She was a spitfire, and loved to tease Suzy mercilessly. "Did I pass the test with your friends?" I asked as we climbed on my bike.

"You did well. You got the thumbs-up from Sophia."

"She's not the one I'm worried about."

"Kayden? Oh, please. He likes to talk all his macho crap, but he's the sappy one. He just wants me happy, City."

"He said he'd kick my ass if I broke your heart, sugar."

She wrapped her arms around me as I walked the bike away from the building, trying not to be too noisy. "Kayden's been known to take matters into his own hands, but I'll set him straight about us," she said in my ear, chuckling.

"Whatcha mean?" I said as I started the engine.

"Oh, nothing." She rested her head against my shoulder and toyed with my nipple piercing. It was the first time I didn't feel her tense against my body when riding on the back of the bike.

Maybe she was finally letting go and enjoying herself without over analyzing the situation.

Chapter 12

S [uzy]

I had become used to being the third wheel around Sophia and Kayden, but tonight everything just felt right. Kayden and City had laughed and talked about sports for hours as Sophia and I talked about work and Jett.

I didn't want to be alone anymore, and I couldn't waste time with City. My heart ached around Kayden and Sophia, and I envied them, wanted what they had—that great love, the one that you can feel and almost touch, and I wouldn't settle for anything less. I had to walk away from City and move forward in my life.

Tears formed in my eyes while I thought about having to give him up as we pulled in and I climbed off the bike. I put my helmet on the bike and started to walk away from City. I didn't want him to see the glistening in my eyes.

"Where you hurrying off to?" Reaching out, he grabbed my wrist, pulling me into his arms.

"Nowhere, I was just going to unlock the door." I shrugged, keeping my arms down and not melting into his touch.

"You okay, sugar?" he asked, looking at my eyes with a question on his face.

"Yeah. The wind made my eyes water." I smiled at him.

"Glasses will block the wind. We'll have to get you a pair."

Thank God he bought that crock of shit. He wrapped his arms around me, smashing my face in his t-shirt. I inhaled, enjoying the musky scent in the material. I closed my eyes and luxuriated in the smell of him.

"Maybe." I felt shitty and my heart ached. Why bother buying me glasses? I didn't plan to spend the rest of my life riding on the back of his bike. Although Sophia and Kayden were opposites, they worked, but City and I didn't have a future.

"What's wrong?" he asked, squeezing me tighter.

"Nothing. I'm just tired." I squeezed him back and relished in the feel of his tight muscles. Don't say it; don't look like a girl whose head is filled with fairytales.

"Sugar, that's bullshit. You've never walked away from me or been snippy. Your sparkle's gone. Spill."

Don't do it. He isn't your knight in shining armor riding in on a white horse.

Shifting my weight, I stared at the ground, trying to avoid his gaze. "Nothing, City. I just need sleep. I swear." That lie felt easier than I'd thought.

"Look me in the eyes and say that." He pulled my chin up, forcing me to look into the clear azure eyes that showed sadness. I swallowed hard and steadied my breathing. I knew he could read me like an open book, everyone could, and I had to pull this off. Don't cry or blink, girl—breathe.

"I'm just tired, really." I stood on my tiptoes and placed my lips against his. This would be the last time I'd kiss him. I couldn't spend more time with him without risking my heart. I could fall in love with him easily, but I wouldn't risk the heartbreak that would follow. "Call me tomorrow?" I said as I backed away.

"You don't want me to come in, beautiful?" he asked, drawing his brows together and studying my face.

"Not tonight, City. I want to crawl in bed and drift off. If you come in, I know what will happen." I grinned at him as a sly smile spread across his face. He ran his finger down my cheek, and I wanted to lean in to it—I wanted more. "No, no. Don't even think about it." I giggled as he tried pulling me into a kiss. "Down, tiger."

"Tomorrow then," he said as he kissed me on the lips.

I instantly felt the loss of his heat as he let go of my body, and I looked at him. He really was beautiful. He looked like every girl's fantasy with his bike behind him, hard muscles, dreamy eyes, and kindness. I couldn't let myself fall any deeper for him. Every time my phone rang, my text alert chirped, or I stood in his presence, my heart raced. My heart and body responded to him, but my mind kept saying run. He wasn't the type that settled down and had a family, and I couldn't blame him. He was a playboy that led a different life than I did. He was on a different path.

I stood at a fork in the road—travel down the path of heartbreak and further immerse myself in his world, or make a clean break and continue on my journey to my ultimate destination of happiness and the love I couldn't live without.

"Tomorrow, big boy," I said with a meek smile, and waved to him before disappearing inside the house without watching him drive away. I threw my keys on the table, walking through the darkened house to my bedroom. My eyes felt heavy, and they burned from the tears that wanted to break free.

The roar of his engine made the walls in my bedroom rattle. I'd never hear that sound again without thinking of him and feeling butterflies in my stomach. He'd altered my thoughts and invaded my mind.

I undressed and put on my favorite comfy pajamas, catching a glimpse of my reflection in the mirror. I wanted to turn back the clock to a time when life felt simpler. When I didn't know the pure animal magnetism and sexual chemistry like I felt with him, but I couldn't. He ruined me and stole that from me.

My phone vibrated as I turned it in my hand and caught a glimpse of his message.

City: It's tomorrow—one minute after midnight.

Setting the phone on my nightstand, I stared at the empty bed and thought of how different the night could've been.

Me: Night, City. Drive safely.

I crawled under the sheets, loving the crisp material against my skin. I stared at the ceiling and watched the fan whirl, causing a shadow to form against the white background. I couldn't fall asleep, and turned on the television, praying that the mindless entertainment would help calm my thoughts and help me forget him.

My phone danced across the wooden surface. Don't pick it up. I couldn't do it. I wanted to see if I could break free of him—quit cold turkey like a junkie. I had to try to put distance between us. I'd only known him a week, but he invaded my life.

Flipping through the channels, I stopped on a show about a group of bikers. I'd heard about the show but never found interest in it until now. I couldn't bring myself to turn it off. Every man on the screen reminded me of him. The roar of the engines made my heart flutter and my stomach hurt. Curling on my side, I hugged the pillow as tears poured out, plopping on the material. I wanted to feel the wind in my hair and my arms wrapped around his body, but it could never happen again. My eyes burned as I gave in and drifted off to the sound of roaring engines.

I woke to a couple of messages from City wishing me good morning and asking when I could see him again. Leaving my phone on my nightstand, I made a glass of tea and sat on my front step sipping the warm cinnamon liquid. The neighborhood was quiet as a few couples walked down the sidewalks and children played in the front yard down the street. I stared at the sun shimmering off the wet grass and thought about him. I couldn't sit here all day and think about him. I had to find something to do today to keep my mind off him and move toward my future.

I needed a shower, had to wash his scent off me and start my day. No more wallowing in self-pity and the whirlwind that I'd lived for the last week. I grabbed my phone off the nightstand, but there were no new messages from City. Maybe he got the hint after I didn't send him a good morning text.

The ringing of my phone made me jump as I waited for the water to warm. I walked to the phone slowly and peeked at the screen—relief flooded me as I saw that it was Derek and not City.

"Hey," I said, as I stood there naked, staring in the mirror, the fog blurring my reflection.

"Hi, Suzy. What are you doing later?" Derek had a deep voice, but it didn't have half the effect on me that City's voice did.

"Not much, just about to jump in the shower. What's up?"

His sharp intake of air made it evident that he had just pictured me naked. "I wanted to know if you wanted to go to dinner tonight and maybe play some mini-golf. Do you want to go with me?"

"Oh, well..." I gnawed on my thumbnail and debated a date with Derek. He worked on paper, and we ran in the same circles. Our worlds were similar and we could relate to each other. Maybe he was the path that I needed to follow—or at least he'd help keep my mind off City.

"Come on, Suzy. We'll have fun. What do you say?" His voice was hopeful. Couldn't blame a guy for being persistent—he'd never taken no for an answer.

"Okay, Derek." I ran my hands down the bare skin between my breasts, loving the feel of the softness. I instantly felt like crap for saying yes when all I wanted to do was run to City.

"It's a date. I'll pick you up at six."

"See you at six."

"Great. I can't wait to see you tonight. Bye for now, Suzy."

"Bye, Derek." I heard him celebrating his victory before the line went dead.

I stood in the shower and daydreamed about City before touching myself, relieving the ache between my legs. The orgasm wasn't as satisfying as I had hoped. It dulled the need I felt for City. I craved the earth-shattering orgasms I felt under his deft fingertips, but I couldn't let my sexual desire cloud my judgment.

City sent me two more text messages before Derek picked me up for dinner. I ignored the urge to reply and finished my make-up, smacking my red lipstick together before running the brush through my hair one last time. The tight black miniskirt and yellow tank top helped show off my fading tan. Soon the winter cold and weakened sun would cause my skin to return to its almost ghostly shade of white. Grabbing my strappy black stilettos out of the closet, I thought of that last time I'd worn them—the night City rode into my life. I put my favorite Reef sandals in my purse for later, when my feet ached and we played mini-golf.

The chime of the doorbell snapped me out of my memories of the first night in City's bed. Opening the door, I took in the sight of Derek in a pair of khaki dress pants and crisp white linen shirt, with his toes peeking out from the fabric around his feet. His smile beamed as his eyes roamed my body, taking in my outfit before stopping on my breasts. He licked his lips before he settled on my face with a goofy smile.

"Wow, you look sexy, Suzy." His nostrils flared as his gaze drifted down my body again.

The way he looked at me made my skin crawl. "Thanks, you look great too." He did look nice, but not heart-stopping or panty-dropping.

He held out his hand to me. "Ready?"

I placed my fingers against his smooth palm, "Yeah," I said, although I was anything but.

Derek opened the door to his beat-up Nissan Altima, waiting for me to climb in before he kissed my hand and slammed the door.

I sighed as I watched him walk around the car, a brilliant and victorious smile on his face. "God, this is a horrible idea," I mumbled to myself as he opened the door and climbed in.

"What did you say?" he asked as he climbed in, closed the door, and looked at me.

"Just saying how hungry I am. Where are we eating?"

He brushed the hair off my shoulder, gliding his fingertips across my skin, lingering longer than felt comfortable. My body involuntarily moved away from his touch. "Sorry," he said as he turned away and gripped the steering wheel, his knuckles whitening from his firm grasp. "We're going to Paesano's for some Italian, if that's okay with you?"

"Sounds great."

I stared out the window, watching the trees pass by as Derek chattered about work. I looked forward to my weekends and escaping the stress and my job, but that was all Derek wanted to talk about. I listened to his words and answered when asked a question, but he already bored me. Thankful that the drive to the restaurant wasn't long, I climbed out of the car as Derek jogged to me and grabbed my arm, hooking them together.

The conversation during dinner was stagnant. We didn't have much in common besides work. It became evident as he talked about video games. My idea of a great night did not involve playing a mindless game on the television. When the food finally arrived, I found myself thankful for the silence as he shoveled the food in his mouth without care. He ate like a pig, with sauce from his pasta dribbling on his chin and resting at the corners of his mouth. I moved the food around on my plate, trying not to stare.

"You want to go for some drinks after here or you want to go to mini-golf?" he asked with a full mouth, a small piece of pasta falling in his lap.

Why the hell did I think this was a good idea? "Drinks sound great." I prayed that a few drinks would make him interesting and have the evening end on a high note.

We skipped dessert and headed to Club Karma for drinks. The club had opened a couple months ago, but I hadn't set foot inside. It had a big-city feel, not like the typical small-town hangouts. The walls were blood red, decorated with black-and-white photos of couples in various sexual positions and states of undress. Colorful lights bounced off the shiny black tile floor as dancers moved their bodies against each other. There were small seating areas with couches filled with couples laughing and touching, and a large bar on the opposite side of the entrance.

"Drink first?" Derek asked. I nodded and looked around as he guided me through the overcrowded space. Derek rested his body against the bar, his arm touching my skin. "You want to dance?" he shouted in my ear above the music.

I shook my head and waited for the bartender to come in our direction. A large mirror hung above the liquor bottles on the wall behind the serving area. Watching people dance with such erotic and methodical moves made me think of City and our dance last weekend. I never felt sexy on the dance floor, but with him I had been able to feel the music instead of thinking of my next move.

I ordered a martini, wanting the alcohol over a virgin daiquiri, needing to forget City and find a way to make Derek more palatable. His arm brushed against my back as he rested his hand on the bar, effectively trapping me. I ignored him, staring into the mirror as the bartender placed my drink on the bar.

I took a sip, testing the sweetness of the raspberry martini. This whole night had been a bad idea. I knew it from the moment I accepted his invitation to dinner. I wouldn't have said yes to him if I weren't trying to forget the tall, muscular Italian man.

"Suzy," Derek whispered in my ear, further invading my personal space.

"What?" I said into the glass still pressed against my lips.

"Drink up, babe, because I can't wait to get you out there." Derek bobbed his head like a character in a skit from Saturday Night Live. I could see his reflection in the mirror, and my cheeks felt heated at the thought of someone seeing me with him.

"Uh huh." I didn't turn to look at him but kept my eyes on the scene in the mirror, like I was watching a television show. I'd find a way to stall. I couldn't go on to the dance floor with him. No way in hell would that happen. He didn't have the ability to make me dance like City had, and his awkward movements would only draw more awareness to us, when all I wanted to do was blend in.

His fingers touched the skin of my arms and hand as I fought every urge to kick him in the balls. He rambled on about his clubbing days in college and how he mastered the dance floor and people would stop to watch him "bust a move." Almost spitting my drink out, I broke out into laughter, tears forming in my eyes. I could imagine the scene. Derek thought people stopped to admire his ability, when in actuality they were stunned or entertained beyond belief.

"What's so funny?" His lips were turned into a frown as he moved his head away from mine and stared at me.

"Oh, nothing, Derek. Just something I remembered from college." God, I had always been a shitty liar, but I didn't want to hurt his feelings. The man had confidence, and who was I to kill it?

"Ah, okay. I thought you were laughing at me." He shrugged before sipping his beer and wiping his lips on his shoulder. "Come on, just one dance," he begged, and released me from my human cage.

I sloshed the pink liquid in my glass, now half drained, and lifted it to my lips. I owed him at least one dance for his efforts. I swallowed the last mouthful and placed it on the bar. "Just one."

His eyes lit up as he grabbed my hand and pulled me toward the writhing bodies in the middle of the room. The beat of the music made me unable to feel my pulse, even though I knew it had to be hammering. I wanted to throw up at the thought of anyone watching me make an ass out of myself. Just as we reached the spot that Derek wanted, dead center, the DJ switched songs. Fuck, why me? A sad, slow melody filled the air as Derek pulled me into an embrace. I'd rather make a complete asshole out of myself with a wicked beat that didn't require touching.

"Perfect," he said, wrapping his arms around me, his hands resting a little too close to my ass.

Placing my hands on his shoulders, I tried to keep some distance between us, but Derek didn't get the hint. His body felt nothing like City's; there was no hardness to it. Derek's hands roamed my back as he swayed our bodies side to side to the music, and I gave in, letting him control our movement. He didn't speak as he moved us back and forth to the beat. Time passed slowly, and I felt like I had been wrapped in his arms for hours with no escape.

When the song ended, Derek broke the embrace and backed up to look at me. He gave me a silly grin, "Thank you."

"For what?" I yelled as the music began to thump through the speakers.

"The dance, Suzy. I loved having you in my arms," he said, as he reached for my hand and kissed the top.

"You're a sweet guy, Derek." I blushed. He wasn't a bad guy—he just wasn't City.

"Another drink?"

"If I didn't know any better, Derek, I'd think you're trying to get me drunk."

He smiled, his face turning pink as he pushed on my back and led me off the dance floor. "Can't blame a guy for trying."

We passed a set of couches, and something drew my attention. There before me was a woman in a skintight, barely there dress with red stiletto heels and long brown hair. The woman didn't draw my attention, but the man whose lap she sat on was City. He didn't notice me as he talked to her, giving her his total attention. His hand rested on her ass as she nibbled on his lips. I wanted to throw up. He didn't seem to have a problem forgetting me.

Bile rose in my throat at the sight of the two of them together. I'd spent the entire day trying to forget him without success, but he had moved on to someone else. "I'll take you up on that offer, Derek." No longer able to watch City with another woman, I walked to the bar with Derek right behind me. Derek only had eyes for me tonight, and the smile on his face made it clear that I had made him happy with my response.

Even though I had been the one that ignored him, it still stung to see him enjoying the company of another woman. "What'll it be, sweetheart?" the bartender asked me as she leaned against the bar with a smile.

"Shot of anything sweet and another raspberry martini, please."

"I'll have another Miller," Derek said before she walked away. "A shot, huh?"

"It's Saturday night and I could use a little something stronger."

"I didn't know you were a drinker, Suzy." He grabbed our drinks, pushing mine in front of me before throwing down a twenty for the bartender.

"I'm not, but what the hell. Why not?" I shrugged before picking up the shot and smelling it. Raspberry something or other, but I wasn't quite sure. It would do the job and help dull the pang of jealousy I felt from seeing City with the girl in red. "To life and love," I said, raising my glass before swallowing the sweet concoction.

Derek tipped his beer in my direction and watched me as he raised it to his lips. "Why aren't you taken?" he asked from behind the brown bottle.

I shrugged. "Looking for the right one." The martini sloshed the glass as I brought it to my lips too quickly. One drink and a shot and I didn't give a fuck that some of it splashed on my breasts. Tears stung my eyes as I gulped the martini and hoped that it would put my brain in a temporary haze. The feel of a hand touching my breast caused me to jerk, sending the last bit of raspberry heaven to the floor. "What the fuck?" I said, looking down to see Derek's hand move away from my breast.

"Sorry." He grinned. "Just thought I'd help you with that little spill." He sucked on his fingers as he stared at my chest.

I snarled as I put my face close to his. "No matter how drunk I am, you don't touch me without asking. Am I clear?"

"Yes, ma'am," he said, raising his hand to salute me.

What a cocksucker. Poking him in the chest, I spoke very slowly. "I mean it, smartass. Do. Not. Touch. Me." Turning away, I looked in the mirror and saw the red dress still sitting on City's lap, and my fingernails dug into the wooden bar.

"Okay, Suzy. Let me make it up to you, since I made you spill your drink. Let me buy you another?"

I closed my eyes, rubbing the bridge of my nose, before turning my attention back to Derek. "I don't think so, Derek. Will you just take me home?"

"One more, Suzy. I swear I'll keep my hands to myself. I don't want the night to end like this. Please."

I studied his face, and he looked genuine, with a sad smile and pleading eyes. I held up my index finger to him. "One more and then I want to go."

"Excellent." He raised his hand in the air and snapped his fingers, grabbing the attention of the bartender.

As I leaned against the bar, my eyes kept wandering back to the mirror. The third martini was easier to drink; my legs felt weak and the bar became necessary to keep me from tipping over. Derek chattered in my ear and kept his distance as we polished off our third drinks.

"Ready?" he asked as he set the empty bottle on the counter.

"Are you okay to drive?" I asked. I may be drunk, but I knew enough to ask.

"Yeah, I can handle more than three beers, babe."

Hearing the word "babe" come out his mouth when he spoke made me want to throw up on his shoes. Everything about him made me crazy, and I knew that I'd never go on another date with Derek. On paper he seemed right, but in person he was a creepy mess that revolted me and did nothing for my libido.

"Okay, let's go." I grabbed my purse and walked on unsteady legs toward the door, leaving Derek to walk behind me.

"You want to hold my hand?"

"Why?" I stopped and turned to face him, almost falling over. I'd had too much to drink and didn't realize it until now.

"Because you're walking funny. Just hold on to my arm until we get to the car." He held out his hand and waited for me to take it.

He didn't grin or smile, and I believed he was sincere in his offer. Clearly the alcohol had made my brain fuzzy. I didn't hold his hand, but snaked my arm through his and leaned on his body as I swayed through the parking lot, thankful when we made it to his car.

Leaning against the car, I waited for him to open the door. I closed my eyes and soaked in the feel of the cool air against my warm, clammy skin. The air inside the club had felt stagnant. My anger and hurt over City made my body feel flushed and caused me to sweat. I had done this. I pushed City away. I had been an idiot, and I knew it when I saw him with her in his arms.

Derek's lips were on mine before I could react. I pushed at him, hitting his chest as he trapped me between him and the car. My arms felt like jelly, and I couldn't gauge how hard I was hitting him as the beat of my heart filled my ears. "Stop," I mumbled between breaks in the kiss, but he didn't stop crushing his body against mine harder. His lips moved over my cheek to my neck as he grabbed my breast and squeezed. "Derek, stop, damn it!" I yelled, hitting him in the ribs.

"You know you want it, Suzy," he said against my neck.

"I don't! Stop!" I pushed against him again, but his weight was too much. I swung and connected with his face with a loud smack. My hand stung from the contact.

His face moved away from my neck, and he looked me in the eyes. He glared at me with his mouth set in a firm line. "You hit me. What the fuck? I'm just giving you what you want, baby."

Clearly I had sent the wrong signals, or he was just a dumbass. "Get the fuck off me."

"You're such a prick tease in this outfit tonight. You can deny it all you want, but I know you want me."

"I do—"

His lips were on me again before I could stop him. I struggled against him, bending my knee up to make contact with his balls, but hit nothing as his body flew backward.

City held Derek by the throat, bringing him to eye level. "Why don't you pick on someone your own size, motherfucker?" City said with a look of pure hatred.

"This has nothing to do with you, man," Derek spat. "This is between the lady and me." Derek clawed at City's hands, trying to escape his grip.

City turned toward me. "He your boyfriend?" His eyes moved over my body, taking in my outfit. I shook my head, my hands gripping the car, not moving. "You want him to touch you?" He looked at Derek and back to me.

Derek's face had turned a deep shade of red, on the verge of purple, as City's grip increased. "No! I told him to stop!" I said. "But I work with the scumbag. Don't hurt him."

City growled; his chest heaved with rough breaths while deciding his next action. "Fuck," he muttered before dropping Derek to the ground.

Derek gasped for air as he tried to stand, but collapsed on his hands and knees. Air filled my lungs, and I realized I had held my breath, waiting for City to beat the hell out of Derek before my eyes. Did he deserve it? Hell yes, but I didn't want to witness it or deal with the aftermath.

City stood in front of me, his hands clenched at his side as he stared at me. The hard features of his face looked more pronounced by his anger. His cheeks flexed, his nostrils flaring as he studied me. "What the fuck, Suzy? I called you and you don't fucking answer and then you're here with this fucking prick and almost let him maul you in a parking lot." Running his fingers through his hair, he turned and looked at Derek before returning his attention back to me.

"I'm sorr-ry." I didn't know what else to say. I didn't have an excuse. "I didn't know I had to answer to you. You seemed to have your hands full inside, anyway." I snarled as I spoke.

"What the fuck are you talking about?"

"Brunette, red dress, almost dry-humping you on the couch. Ring any bells?" Who the fuck was he to question my actions?

"Fuck." His arms flexed as he clenched his hands into a hard fist at his sides. "Kaylee means nothing to me."

"Neither do I, I suppose."

"Woman, you have no idea what the fuck you're talking about." He stepped closer, and my body instantly registered his nearness, moisture pooling between my legs.

I swallowed, the dryness in my mouth making it hard to move anything down my throat. "I saw your hands on her ass as she kissed you. How the hell do you explain that? It seems women have no value to you."

"Shut your mouth, Suzy. I followed you out here because I saw you stumbling out of here with someone I didn't know. I came here to check on you. Kaylee is no one, hear me now, no one. I didn't come here with her or ask her to sit on my lap. I was trying to be nice to her."

"Well, if nice means you feel her up, I'd say you were very kind to her."

"Suzy, listen to me. I called you and asked you back out. You blew me off. What was I supposed to do? Sit home and wait for you to call?"

Breath escaped me as he closed the small space between us.

Tears began to stream down my cheeks as I took in the enormity of the situation. If City hadn't stopped Derek, would I have been able to get away from him? He just saved me, and I was being a total bitch. The sob tore through my chest as I broke down. City wrapped his arms around me and kissed my forehead. He felt so right against my body. I felt safe and comfortable with him, no matter how much we didn't seem to fit on paper. He said nothing, but made sounds to calm me as I buried my face into the soft material of his t-shirt. My fingers found the piercing on his nipple as I toyed with it and tried to catch my breath.

"Can I take you home, sugar?" he asked with his face buried in my hair.

"Yes," I whimpered, clinging to him like a lifeline.

Without speaking, he drew me into his arms, carrying me across the parking lot. I melted into him, resting my head against his shoulder. The thought of Kaylee still stung, but I couldn't be mad at him anymore. He saved me from a totally fucked-up night, and for that he'd earned my forgiveness. The jostling movement as he placed my bottom on the cool seat of his bike made my stomach churn. I said nothing as he put the helmet on my head and fastened the harness against my chin. He had the right mix of pissed-off male and swoon-worthy alpha to make any girl's heart go pitter-patter.

"Can you hold on?" he asked as he held my chin between his fingertips.

"Yes." My tone was breathy and betrayed me with the sound of need.

He climbed on the bike, scooting his ass between my legs and gripping the handlebars. I molded my torso against his and interlaced my fingers. The usual jitters I felt anticipating the ride ahead didn't register.

"Hold on, sugar." He throttled the engine and took off for the short drive to my house. The cool air whipped my hair around as I nuzzled against his warm back. My mind grew blank with the movement of the bike and the roar of the engine. I allowed myself to get lost in the moment and the sensation of the vibrations from the bike—and the feel of City between my legs.

Lost in the City coma, I didn't notice as we pulled into my development and weaved through the winding streets to my house. Maybe I'd drifted off, but I wanted to stay like this forever—wrapped around his body, in a stress-free haze of contentment. I mumbled against his shirt as he turned off the bike, placing his feet on the ground, securing it and tapping my hands. "Sugar, we're here."

"Mm hmm," I said into his back before raising my head and looking through blurry eyes at my house. I sat up, letting go of his chest before wiping the drool off my lips. "Thanks, City. I don't know what would've happen tonight if it weren't for you." I started to climb off the bike but didn't have the energy, and plopped back against the seat with an "oomph."

City laughed as he climbed off, pulling me off the bike, cradling me in his arms. "Can I come in?" he asked, brushing his nose against my cheek.

"Depends. You mad at me?" I asked, praying he said no.

"I'm not mad. We gotta talk, Suzy." His eyes begged me to let him in as his brow furrowed.

"Okay." I rested my head against his hard chest and rubbed my palm against his pec.

I handed him the keys as we approached the door. Anger was no longer visible, but the tilted grin I'd grown accustomed to had vanished. He kicked off his boots before he walked across my white carpet, placing me on the couch. The couch dipped from his weight, but I couldn't look him in the eye. I fiddled with my fingers as the silence became deafening. The alcohol-induced haze had started to wear off, and I felt a small buzz.

"Why the hell didn't you call me today? I thought we made plans. What the fuck did I do wrong?" His words made me cringe; sadness was evident in his voice.

"I wanted to put distance between us. You didn't do anything wrong." I shook my head, meeting his eyes.

"Distance? What for?" His eyebrows drew together as the skin wrinkled in between.

"I just don't think we'll work out." I shrugged.

"Woman, you think too damn much, and it's fucked up. Blew my ass off for that douchebag tonight, and how'd that shit turn out for you?" He paused before continuing. "What makes you think we don't have a shot?"

I looked away from him, unable to look him in the eyes. "We're just so different, City. I don't see a future between us, and at my age, I'm looking forward. I don't live life by the seat of my pants like you. We have nothing in common and we run in different worlds." Water clouded my vision as I stared at the wall across the room. I blinked, trying to clear the tears from my eyes.

Sighing, he reached for my face, touching my cheek and pulling my face to look in his directions. "Look at me, sugar." His eyes moved around my face. "I don't know how you think I live, and you sure as hell don't know who I am. We're getting to know each other, but you shut me out without a reason. You said it yourself, Sophia and Kayden are opposites but they work. Why couldn't we?"

I drew in a shaky breath, his words making my heart ache. "I know I said that, but I don't know, City."

"What don't you know? Talk to me." His hand closed over my fist in my lap as he stroked his thumb across my sensitive skin.

"I like you a lot. So much that it scares me, and I don't know if I could deal with the heartbreak when you walk out of my life." A tear slid down my cheek as I spoke.

"You never gave us a chance to see if we could work." His finger slid across my skin, wiping the tear away.

"You're not a one-woman man. I could tell that about you, and I don't work that way. I don't want to share you."

"Suzy, I'm not a whore. Since I met you last week I haven't been with anyone else. I don't want anyone else, just you."

"I'd like to believe that, but you looked a little too cozy with Karen tonight."

"Kaylee, not Karen. I'll be totally honest with you about her. I had sex with her twice in my life. Not my proudest moment, but she offered and I accepted. She wants to be my girlfriend, and I've told her no. I'm very clear with her that she and I are nothing and never will be. Should I have pushed her ass on the floor when she sat on my lap?"

"No, I guess not." I didn't want to think about the visual I had of another woman sitting on him and fawning.

"I wanted to be with you tonight. You blew me off. We had such a nice time last night, and as soon as I brought you home, you shut down."

"I don't know, City," I said.

"Joey."

"Joey, I watched Kayden and Sophia all night. They reminded me of what I want someday. I want someone that's going to love me and be mine alone. I want to be important to someone," I said, staring into his eyes without blinking, worried another tear would slip down my cheek.

"It's what everyone wants—"

"Let me finish." I shook my head. "I like you, Joey. No one has ever made me feel the way you do, but I can't risk falling for you. I can't have my heart broken." I bit my lip, trying to focus on pain instead of sadness. I didn't want tears to flow freely. "I think it's best if we stop now. The time we've spent together has been amazing, but I can't do it anymore. I can't lie to myself."

"May I speak now?" He smiled at me, but it was a sad smile.

"Yes."

"Do you think I'm incapable of love?" He stared at me, waiting for an answer, his mouth set in a firm line.

"No, I just don't think it's who you are now, and I can't wait around for that part of you. It wouldn't be fair to either of us."

"Suzette." Formal names always meant something serious. "I never allowed myself to think of a future with anyone, but last night I saw a world of possibilities. I realized what I was missing out on—I want what Kayden and Sophia have." He squeezed my fingers, and I watched his thumb rub the back of my hand. "Look at me. I've never allowed myself to get close to anyone in years, but your innocence and sweetness have pierced my heart."

"Oh," I said, my eyes growing wide with surprise.

"I didn't want to rush into anything with you. I don't want to ruin anything, but you need to understand where I'm coming from. You need to know my past." His Adam's apple bobbed in his throat as he swallowed before continuing. "I have been in love before. I had a fiancée and I thought my entire life was made. Plans don't always work out exactly as we think."

"I'm sorry," I said, breaking a hand free from his grip, touching his cheek, running my thumb across the rough stubble.

"It was a long time ago. We were in college and her name was Joni. We were high school sweethearts." He closed his eyes, and I could see the pain on his beautiful features. "I loved her more than anything in the world, and she was ripped from my life."

My heart skipped with the thought that anyone could break his heart.

"A fucking drunk driver hit her on her way home from work and she was killed instantly." He hung his head, hiding his face from my view. I could only imagine the pain that he'd felt losing his love that day in such a brutal manner. "I've never allowed myself to get that close to anyone after she died. It fuckin' wrecked me, and I didn't know if I'd ever fully heal."

"I'm sorry, Joey." I kissed his cheek, allowing him the time to gather his thoughts and hide a small part of himself.

His eyes rose to meet mine. "You remind me a lot of Joni...your kindness and playful nature. It's infectious. You two would've been good friends. She was my light, and I couldn't remember life without her until the day she died. I thought the heartbreak would kill me, Suzy. I've been so scared to open myself to anyone again, but you made me want to try. Don't shut me out. I can't promise forever, yet, but I want you to be mine, Suzy."

My breath caught. "What do you mean?"

"Woman, I swear sometimes I have to spell shit out to you. For a smart girl, sometimes you amaze me." He chuckled. "I want you to be my girlfriend. Mine and only mine. I'd planned to ask you tonight before you blew me off."

Yes, yes, yes! "What about you?" I asked. Would he see other girls? My heart couldn't take that.

"Just you, Suzy. I want a full commitment, and it's a two-way street. Your body is mine...no one else's. I haven't wanted to be with only one person in a long time."

"Okay," I whispered, a smile creeping across my lips. My body vibrated with excitement as his words sank in. City wanted me to be his girlfriend. Wow.

"So, you'll be my girlfriend?" he asked.

"Yes," I said as I crawled into his lap. "I've never wanted anything more," I said against his lips.

"Mine," he growled as he crushed his mouth to my lips. The kiss felt different than the others. There was a hunger behind it—a claiming.

City lifted my body as he stood. Wrapping my arms around his neck, I kissed him back with more passion than I had before. I wanted him more than I ever did. I wanted to make love to him and convey all the passion I felt for him—I wanted to heal him. He may have been broken, but I'd help his heart heal and show him all the love I had to offer.

Chapter 13

Suzy

Sharing the loss of Joni was easier than I'd thought. I rarely spoke about her, and only my family knew about my past. I felt Suzy needed to know to understand. I owed it to her. I'd let it go beyond a casual relationship by meeting her friends and seeing her more than once. Fuck, I'd seen her more than any woman that I'd allowed in my bed since Joni.

Placing her feet on the bedroom floor, she slid down my body before standing, leaning against me. Her soft eyes stared into mine as the corners of her mouth turned up into a smile. Cradling my face in her hands, she rose on her tiptoes and touched her lips to mine. She tasted sweet, and my body craved more. We kissed with our eyes open, and I watched as her pupils dilated and her blinking slowed. Her hands began to move, and I heard the fabric of her shirt rustle as her knuckles brushed against my abdomen. I grabbed her hands, stilling them. "I undress you," I said, and her hands went slack at her side.

She swallowed, smiling at me before lifting her arms. Pulling up her shirt, I exposed her soft belly before the white lace of her bra became visible, her hard nipples calling for my mouth. I dropped her shirt to the floor behind her and ran my hands down her still-raised arms, over her collarbone, over her breasts, stopping at her nipples. I palmed her breasts in my hands and felt the heaviness in them. Her breathing changed as I ran my thumbs over her hardened nipples and stared in her eyes. Her mouth opened, and she sucked in a quick breath as her head fell back.

I wanted to take her hard and fast, but after the talk we'd just had, I knew I had to show her the gentler side of sex. I couldn't be rough with her, not this time at least. I had to show her that I cared for her and didn't think of her as a fuck toy.

I forced my hands to leave her breasts and moved them over her soft stomach, hooking my fingers inside the cloth hugging her hips, as I pulled her skirt down her legs, to reveal matching white lace panties. I kissed the delicate material and placed my knees on the floor. She stood there and swayed, but didn't move.

"Feet, sugar." I tapped the tops of her feet as I waited for her to react. I could hear her giggle above me as she crawled out of her skirt, and the sound of it made my heart skip a beat. Innocence and bliss. I grabbed her hips and moved her body until the back of her knees hit the soft mattress. She sat down and looked at me with wide eyes.

"Lie back," I growled as I held her knees, spreading them wide. "I want to taste that sweet pussy of yours. I'm going to devour you until you're begging for my dick, sugar." I grinned at her. I could hold out an eternity feasting on her body—worshipping her center with my tongue.

She rested on her elbows and smirked at me as I sat between her knees. "All the way down, sugar." I squeezed her knees in warning.

"Damn, you're pretty between my legs. I just wanted to watch you," she said with a playful grin on her face.

"Keep your eyes on me." I reached for her lace panties and wrapped my fingertips inside the material.

"Wait," she said as I began to move the material away from her body.

I pulled quickly, and the material disintegrated in my hands.

"Well, crap, those were expensive." She blew out a breath.

"I'll buy you new ones, sugar. No more talking; my mouth has other things to do that are more important." My hands glided down her legs, pulling them apart as they reached her knees. I moved my mouth to the soft, sensitive skin of her thigh and licked, causing her body to shudder.

I could smell her arousal, and the sweet scent of her pussy made my dick ache. I kissed and licked to the V where her leg connected to her body, only inches from her pussy. Sucking her flesh in my mouth, I lapped at her juices as I twirled my tongue over the smooth skin and listened to her tiny moans. Continuing the slow, sensual assault on her body, I gripped her knees as I ran my tongue across her pussy, but didn't stop to pay her engorged clit any attention. I stopped at the same exact spot on her right leg, pulling the skin into my mouth to leave a mark. I hadn't given a hickey since high school, but I wanted to leave something to remind her of who owned her body.

"You're killing me," she said, all breathy. I smiled against her skin as I bit down on the flesh and she flinched. "Jesus," she yelped, and the bed dipped as her back dropped against the mattress.

My tongue soothed the red skin where my teeth had left a mark, leaving no doubt where I'd been and to whom she belonged. I couldn't wait any longer to taste her and feel her on my tongue as I moved toward her heat, inhaling her scent before my mouth descended on her body. I buried my nose in her blonde hair and smelled her sweetness. My flat tongue rested against her clit as I began to circle it with my tongue, but I denied her the contact she wanted. I sucked her lips into my mouth, like a starved man, tasting her wetness on my tongue. Her fingers laced in my hair and pushed my face into her core.

I dipped my tongue into her wetness and swallowed her arousal. I didn't think I could ever get enough of her taste. I wanted to hear her scream and couldn't wait any longer. I licked upward, capturing the last drops from her pussy as I sucked her clit hard.

She moaned, pulling my face harder against her body, writhing under my touch. I pushed two fingers inside her and her body stilled. Her pussy clenched against my fingers as I thrust them inside her. Her body arched and she gripped the sheets as she moaned. Moving my palm against her skin, I placed my fingertips on her nipple. Pinching it, my grip pulsated against her stiff peak, and it tipped her over the edge. She lifted her head, and her body grew rigid as her breathing became erratic and shaky.

I stared at her face, watching her fall into oblivion, overcome by the orgasm gripping her body. She dropped her head on the pillow as her eyes opened, sucking in a shuddering breath. Listening to her ragged breaths, I grabbed the condom from my back pocket before standing and removing my clothing.

The look on her face was one of a predator staring at their prey. I stroked my cock and stared at her body, waiting to be filled. Her mouth opened as she stared at my hand, and I stroked it with a firm grip, catching the piercing as I touched the tip.

"You want me inside you, sugar?" I asked in a slow, deep tone as I stood at the foot of the bed stroking myself.

"Well," she said, caressing her skin and licking her lips. "I mean, your fingers are magic and your mouth is divine..."

I held up my free hand. "Shhh, sugar. No more talking. The only sound I want to hear is you screaming my name as you come on my dick."

"Oh," she said, her eyes still glued to my shaft like she'd never seen it before. She was so easy to fluster. I tore the condom wrapper open with my teeth and rolled it over my aching member. I couldn't wait any longer to be inside her luscious cunt and seek my release.

I moved up her body and nestled between her legs. "For the first time, I'm taking you as mine." I laid my palm against her pussy, cupping it as I gripped it in its entirety. "No one else gets to touch you understand, Suzette?" I asked with my lips against hers.

"Yes, Joseph. It's yours and only yours," she said, staring in my eyes.

I kissed her and claimed her body as mine, fucking her with passion. I took her slow and gentle, showing her body the attention it deserved, and worshipped her in a way she'd never experienced before collapsing on the mattress.

I stretched out in bed and stared at the ceiling as she went to get ready for bed. She walked out of the bathroom in a t-shirt, but I wanted to feel her skin against mine as we slept. "No clothes."

"What do you mean?" she asked as she touched the edge of the mattress.

"When you sleep in bed with me, I don't want you wearing clothes. They're a barrier I don't want to deal with—I want all of you whenever I want you, even in the middle of the night." I patted the mattress.

"Underwear?" She smiled and lifted the shirt.

"No underwear either. Strip and get your fine ass in this bed." She didn't move, looking at me with a silly smile. "Do it," I said, eyeing her.

"But—"

"No, buts, sugar. I've seen every inch of your body, even that beautiful little asshole of yours. That'll be mine someday too."

Her smile faded, but her eyes twinkled as she stepped out of her panties and threw her nightshirt on the floor. She curled against my body and rested her head on my shoulder.

"Hand, sugar."

She placed her hand on my chest, not forgetting where I'd put it the first night we spent together. My heartbeat thudded below her palm as I rested my hand on top of hers. I placed my lips against her forehead. "Sweet dreams, beautiful."

"Night, Joey," she said as she yawned. Her breathing changed quickly as she drifted to sleep.

I listened to her tiny breaths as she slept beside me, wrapped in my arms, and curled into my body. I held her hand against my chest and felt her fingertips rub my skin. I felt my eyes grow heavy as I rubbed her hand and tangled my fingers in her hair.

I felt someone staring at me as I opened my eyes in the darkness. "You awake?" she whispered.

"I am now," I said, moving my fingers in her hair. "What's wrong, sugar?"

"I couldn't sleep. I didn't want to wake you, but I..."

"What's bothering that pretty little head of yours?" I moved my fingers out of her hair and rubbed the soft skin of her arms, thrumming my fingers back and forth rhythmically.

"I'm just scared," she whispered.

"Of me?" I moved my head away to see her face barely lit by moonlight cascading through the blinds.

"Not really." She rubbed my chest. "I've had boyfriends, but only a couple. I've never felt about them the way I feel about you, Joey. It scares the piss out of me."

"How did you feel about them?" I asked, more curious about how she felt about me than the previous men in my shoes.

"They were nice, but I didn't get butterflies every time I saw them. We'd go days without talking, and I was fine with that, but with you I'm always checking my phone for a message. I'm feeling needy with you, Joey, and I don't like it."

"Sugar." I reached for her chin, drawing her shadowed eyes toward my face. "That's not needy. Needy and clingy is if you're up my ass all day and want to know my every move. Needy is when you show up at my house all hours of the night and at the shop during the day." I shook my head and smirked at her. "You're not needy. Wipe that shit from your mind."

"If you say so. It's just a new feeling for me. If I overstep or act like a crazy person, please tell me." The worry in her eyes began to ease.

"Deal." I kissed her forehead, lingering over the soft flesh with my lips.

"What was your longest relationship?" I asked. I hadn't been the pillar of normal relationship behavior since I lost Joni, but I had an inkling that she had been just as unlucky in love as I had been.

"Four months," she whispered.

"Did you love him?"

"I think I loved him, but a week after I said those words to him, he left me. He's the only man I've ever said that to—he broke my heart."

I rubbed my hand up her arms to soothe her while she spoke.

"I've never really allowed myself to get that close to anyone after that. It was during my freshman year in college, and after that breakup, I just spent my time studying and avoiding anything that felt like it could lead to a relationship." She yawned and burrowed her body a little closer to mine.

"I understand heartbreak and wanting to guard your heart from the pain. I've lived it for more years than I'd like to admit." I pulled her closer, leaving no space between us. "Let's just take this slow. It's best for both of us."

"Slow," she said, as she reached up and rubbed my face. I pulled her hand back to my chest and held it against my heart.

I could hear her breathing change as sleep took her. I closed my eyes, content and happy for the first time since Joni had last slept in my arms. I looked forward to what tomorrow held.

Chapter 14

Suzy

"How'd it go with Mr. Piercings?" Sophia chuckled in the phone as I chewed my bagel.

"He gave me a little going-away present this morning before he headed home to change." I chomped down, letting the cream cheese slide across my tongue.

"Oooh, someone had a sleepover. I like him, Suz. He looks badass, but I can see a kind heart underneath. Reminds me a bit of Kayden, but I hope without the other bullshit."

I swallowed down the dry leftover bagel. "I almost messed everything up with him, Sophia." I grabbed the glass of milk off the counter, taking a sip, while I waited for her to scream at me.

"Are you fucking crazy? Why in the hell would you do that? What happened?" she yelled, her shrill voice causing my ear to throb.

"I just didn't see us going anywhere, and I didn't want to get too attached to him. I ignored him yesterday and ended up going on a date with Derek instead."

"Derek? What the fuck, Suzy? You know that guy gives me the creeps."

I sighed as I leaned against the counter, wanting to smash my head into the gray Formica for being so stupid. "I know. I just wanted to forget City—epic disaster that I'll tell you about someday. Anyway, City came to my rescue and took me home."

"Well, thank Christ for small miracles."

"He asked me to be his girlfriend, Sophia. Can you believe that?"

"I do. You're an amazing girl, little mama. Any man would be lucky to have you as his woman. City was smart enough to realize it. Kayden was the same way with me, but his hard exterior melted. Sometimes you just have to roll with it to get to the good stuff. Nothing in life is risk free, Suzy."

"I know, Sophia. My entire body vibrates when I'm around him, and my stomach fills with butterflies. I've never felt that way with anyone, and it scares the crap out of me. I tried to push him away, but he didn't let me."

"You must have some fine shit."

I choked on my milk, and it started to come out my nose as I wiped my face. "What in the heck are you talking about, woman?"

"Well, you tried to get rid of him, and I know you usually hold true to your plan, so I know you didn't relent first and he came to you. Most guys would just say fuck that and walk away without looking back, but you must have something special that made him come back for more. Huh, who knew?" She giggled.

"Shut it, whore. We had a long talk about relationships and love when he brought me home. He's been hurt before and hasn't had a real girlfriend in years."

"We've all been hurt before. It's part of love. If you never hurt, then you've never truly been in love before, Suzy. What happened to him?"

"His fiancée died," I said, putting my cup in the dishwasher. I leaned against the counter and rested the phone against my shoulder.

"Wow, that's horrible. I couldn't image losing Kayden. I'd be a complete and total mess. I don't know if I'd love anyone the way I love him. I couldn't allow myself to love anyone that way again if he was ripped from my life."

"Yeah, I just wonder if he'll be able to make room in his heart for me. I'll always be competing with her for his love, I'm afraid."

"It's not a competition, sweetheart. There's room for both of you. He's taking a risk with you—just give him time to deal with his feelings. Don't rush into the L-word."

"You did with Kayden," I said, smiling even though she couldn't see me.

"I know." She sighed. "I couldn't imagine anyone else in my life. Kayden was it for me, babe. He ruined me and I could never be without him—I knew that after our first weekend together. It felt like all the planets aligned. I was finally with the man I was meant to be with my entire life."

"I'm just going to enjoy his glorious body filled with extra holes and pretty pictures. Jesus, girl, you should see his fine ass naked."

"Did you say ass?" she asked, sounding shocked.

"I am an adult, Sophia. I do swear."

"I think City's dick stirred your brain and altered your thought pattern. My Suzy sunshine never uses profanity," she bellowed.

"Suck it."

"What am I sucking?" she asked.

"Kayden's dong." I started laughing at how immature that sounded.

"Listen, whore, no matter what you do—do not fucking say 'I want to suck your dong' to City. His hard-on would vanish, as he would fall on the floor in a fit of laughter. It's not sexy, not at all. Funny as fuck? Yes, but not come here and fuck me talk. Got it?"

"I know. Just wanted to see what you'd say."

"Silly, girl. Oh, and don't call it a penis. Use the dirtiest, crudest words you can think of when you speak to him. Men love it dirty and raw. If you can find it in the health teacher's textbook, avoid it like the plague."

"Got it. All right, I'm going to go get ready."

"Where you going so early? Your ass usually isn't out of bed before noon, and it's only eleven."

"I have grocery shopping to do today, and I feel like browsing at a couple of stores. I plan to look at all the things I'll never be able to buy. A girl can dream, right?"

"Grocery shop today and window browse tomorrow. I'm so glad we have a long weekend, and I want to go shopping and have a girl's day out. We need to practice your dirty talk."

"Don't you want to stay home with him and Jett?" I asked, walking in my bedroom, searching my closet for something to wear.

"Nah, let them have some male bonding time. What time you want to pick me up tomorrow?" she asked.

"Noon, okay?"

"I'll be waiting for you, my pretty." She cackled as she hung up the phone, and I shook my head. Sophia was going to make it a very long day.

"Come on, you big pussy, let's go inside," Sophia said, yanking my arm as we sat in the parking lot of Inked. Once Sophia had something in her mind, she was like an Italian woman I knew—totally unbendable.

"Sophia, please. It's not nice to surprise him at work. What happen with the 'no cling' stuff?" I shook my head and put all my weight on the seat.

"It's not clingy. I want a damn tattoo. I want to surprise Kayden, and I never get a chance. I either have the baby or him with me. I'd rather him do it than some stranger. Please get out of the car before I pull you out by your hair."

Her hands were on her hips and she was giving me the pushy teacher look that always cracked me up. Sophia was just as much of a softy as I was, but her look was nastier and usually made people do as they were told.

"Fine, but when it all implodes I'm blaming your bossy butt." I closed the doors and hit my remote twice, making sure that no one could steal my collection of vintage hip-hop cassettes.

Sophia whistled as we approached the door. "This is a nice shop, not like most of the shit-ass tattoo places around here." She grabbed the door handle, and my palms began to sweat as my heart pounded in my chest, causing my breathing to grow ragged.

"Can I help you ladies?" a man asked. He looked like a younger version of City. His muscles bulged from under his shirt; his arms, covered in tattoos, flexed as he rose from his chair.

"I'd like to get a tattoo today. Any possibility of that?" Sophia asked.

Looking around the shop as Sophia spoke with the one of the Gallo boys, I took in all the vibrant colors on the walls—reds and oranges with yellow on the ceilings. No white space invaded this realm of his life.

I walked over to the beautiful artwork on the walls to get a closer look. The pieces on the wall were body parts that had been decorated with some of the most stunning work I'd ever seen. I turned my head and my stomach dropped. City was sitting next to a beautiful brunette with his hand on her breast and his face only inches away. They were laughing and talking, but he didn't see me. They looked comfortable together, like there was something between them, or maybe there had been at some point. My heart thumped against my chest and I felt flushed looking at them.

I walked back by the desk quickly and grabbed Sophia's arm. "Can we go, please?" I asked quietly.

She turned around and gave me a confused look. "What's wrong?"

"He's touching some girl's boob and I just can't look at it. It hurts to see it."

She touched my shoulder. "Babe, it's a boob. He's an artist and some girls like tattoos on their breasts. It's like a gynie looking at a snatch; it's just another body part. Don't get caught up in what you think you see." She smiled.

"You're crude. It was more how they were looking at each other." I shrugged.

"Was he looking at her or what he was doing?" She eyed me.

"He was looking at her breast, for Christ's sake."

"He was looking at his lines. Calm the fuck down before you have a coronary. Lemme see." She pushed me back and peered through the doorway to the tattoo area. "Look," she said, yanking my arm and pulling my body to see what she saw. "He's concentrating on his artwork." She held my body so I couldn't move, and forced me to view City touching someone else.

"Call me a prude, but I don't want to see it." I pulled away from her grip. "I'll go wait in the car—you get your tattoo or whatever. I can't be in here, Sophia."

"God, you're so dramatic. Get over your shit. He's not fucking the bitch in the chair, he's creating a masterpiece." She looked pissed at me. "Suit yourself, go wait in the car and I'll be out in a bit."

I pushed the door open as I heard Sophia say, "Hey, City."

Damn it. I wanted her to leave with me. I knew she was going to spill her guts, or should I say mine, and tell him everything that happened. I sat in my car and waited for over an hour. I tilted the seat back and closed my eyes, enjoying the warmth of the sun. I cracked the window an inch so I could feel the cold rush of wind on my face every so often.

"What are you doing, sugar?"

I jumped, his voice waking me from a nightmare. His face was buried in someone else's legs, kissing them with his mouth like he had done to me the night before.

"You scared the crap out of me. Jesus." I placed my hand over my eyes to block out the sun as I looked out the window to see his beautiful body.

"Why aren't you inside with Sophia? What the fuck are you doing out here alone? You didn't want to see me?" He looked hurt, but I couldn't get the visual of him with the woman's boob out of my mind.

"I thought it was best if I waited out here."

"Are you going to open your door so we can talk face to face? Or am I going to talk to you through glass like it's a prison visit?"

"You looked like you had your hands full," I said, and looked out the front windshield, avoiding his glare. "I'm sure you have more boobs to fondle." What the hell was wrong with me? The pang of jealousy hit me hard, and it felt foreign. I had never been a jealous person. No one had evoked this kind of emotion before him.

"Open the damn door, Suzy." He pulled on the handle, bending down to peer through the window. "So that's what it is. You're jealous?" He laughed.

I wanted to smack that shit-eating grin off his face. He looked so smug. "I'm not jealous." When had I reverted to acting like a childish crazy person? Get a grip. I knew it was only part of his job, but it was foreign to me, and I couldn't wrap my mind around the image and reality.

"Sugar, come on. I wasn't looking at her breast. I was working, for shit's sake. It's a piece of canvas to me. Don't be jealous—although I kinda like that emotion in you. Shows me that you care."

"I need time to process it all. Did you start Sophia's tattoo?" I asked, wondering how long I'd have to sit here.

"She needed a break. I won't go back in and finish until you get that fine ass out of that car and we talk about this."

The man knew how to hold me hostage. I closed my eyes and took a deep breath before unlocking the door.

City pulled on the handle, opening the door before crouching down next to me. "Sugar, look at me." The grin on his face made me want to smack him. "Only you. She's a married woman with children, and I've known her for years. I wasn't staring at her nipples—I watch my lines. If I make a mistake, it can't be fixed. Outta the car, Suzy." He backed away and waited for me to climb out.

Closing the door behind me, I leaned against it before he placed his arms on either side of my body, pinning me against the car.

Rubbing his crotch against my stomach, he said, "You're the only one that does this to me."

I wanted to stake my claim and ward off any woman that thought he could be theirs. His hand snaked around my neck, gripping me roughly as he crushed his lips against mine. My lips parted, granting him access as he pushed his stiff shaft against me.

He broke the kiss and searched my eyes. "Are we good?"

"I just didn't like seeing it, City, especially so soon after seeing you with Kaylee. It's going to take some getting used to for me." I could get lost in his crystal blue eyes. "I'm sorry I was so childish," I said as I leaned my forehead against his cheek.

"Childish and jealous," he stated. "I'll be patient with you, but I'm going to make you pay later for your little temper tantrum." He laughed.

"What do you have in mind?" I asked with a cocked eyebrow and a grin.

"It's on a need-to-know basis, sugar, and you don't need to know...yet." He licked my bottom lip and grabbed my hand, pulling me to the shop door.

"That's not fair, City."

"Sometimes life isn't fair, sugar. I can guarantee that you'll be screaming through it, and it won't be out of pain, unless you're into that sort of thing." He waggled his eyebrows and chuckled.

Oh, hell. I knew trouble when I saw it, and it was standing right in front of me. City would be the death of me, but hell, at least I could say it was fun while it lasted. I did the thing I never, ever did—I took the plunge and jumped in feet first without holding my nose.

Chapter 15

·

C ity

I had plans for my little darling. She needed to pay for her temper tantrum, but I wanted to give her plenty of time to think about her actions and worry about what was ahead of her.

Suzy stared at the ground as we walked through the door of Inked. Mikey sat at the desk and was engrossed in his work until I cleared my throat. He looked up, a smile breaking out across his face.

"Suzy, this is my brother Mikey."

"Michael," he said, holding out his hand.

Suzy smiled at him and placed her hand in his. "Nice to meet you, Michael."

"Pleasure is all mine." He brought her hand up to his mouth and kissed it.

"Hey, dickhead, break this shit up. Suzy's mine." I smacked his shoulder and gave him a glare.

"I'm just giving her a proper welcome, bro. Chill the fuck out," Mikey said, looking at me with a smarmy grin. Asshole.

"Do you want to come in the back or stay out here with Mikey?" I emphasized "Mikey" just to get under his skin. He'd always been Mikey, but he didn't like the nickname when women were nearby.

"I'll keep you company," he piped in, and I turned to give him the look of death.

"Um, I don't know. I don't really like blood. Is it bloody?" she asked.

"Not too bad, sugar. Tattoos are done with needles, so there's some." I pulled her close and buried my face in her hair, inhaling her sweet, flowery scent.

"I think I better wait out here," she said into my chest.

"I'll keep her company—no worries, Joey." The fucker winked at me, and I wanted to punch him in the face. I knew he was just fucking with me, because one thing my brother sure as fuck wasn't was a woman stealer. He wouldn't try and fuck Suzy or take her from me, but it still grated on my fucking nerves.

I'd never felt so territorial over someone, and especially not as quickly as I had with Suzy. Maybe it was her similarities to Joni or her kind heart, but I didn't want anything bad to happen to her, and I sure as hell didn't want to lose the opportunity to get to know everything about her.

"I'll be done soon with Sophia. I just have to finish the color." I kissed her, making sure to leave her breathless and her mind only filled with thoughts of me before I left her in the capable hands of my wanker little brother. "Don't let Mikey fool you. He's not as innocent as he looks."

"I figured that. I'm not completely naïve." I chuckled, because she was that naïve. Mikey had the look of a kindhearted person, with his charming, boyish good looks, but I'd seen him beat the piss out of men almost twice his size.

"Okay, sugar. Just don't believe a goddamn thing that comes out of that mouth of his, got me?" I smiled at her, and all I wanted to do is take her home and fuck her brains out, but I had to finish Sophia's tattoo and leave these two to talk.

"Gotcha, big guy. Go finish that tattoo so I can get her home to Kayden before he starts blowing up her phone. I'll be okay."

"I still have plans for you, sugar. I haven't forgotten. Catch ya in a few." I slapped her ass hard enough for it to sting. She yelped and jumped from the quick swat.

"Dang, City," she said as she rubbed her ass, and I laughed as I walked to the back of the shop.

Sophia was typing on her phone, and looked up as I approached.

"Get the pussy out of the car?" she asked as I pulled on my gloves.

"Yeah, we had a little talk." I laughed. I sat down and grabbed my machine and dipped the needle in the yellow ink.

"You have to understand her, City. She's not like most girls. She's in a class all her own," Sophia said as she looked up from her phone.

"Whatcha mean, darlin'?" I asked, rubbing the salve over the design before placing the needle against her skin.

"She hasn't really had a boyfriend or been in love. Shit, I'd never been truly in love with someone until I met Kayden. She's not used to any of this. God, I'm so fucking this up, but you're fucking killing me with that needle, City." She giggled.

"Just a little bit longer. Tell me more about her, Sophia. You guys were with each other, like, twenty-four-seven there for a while. What don't I know about her? What won't she tell me about herself?" I looked down and shaded in the beautiful hibiscus on her hip with shades of pinks and yellows.

"Well, where should I start? I'm sure you've figured out she doesn't swear, but trust me, that girl has one dirty-ass mind." She laid her head back in the chair and her body grew less tense. Talking seemed to help people get their mind off the needle scraping against their skin.

"Really? This I gotta hear."

"I don't want to give away all her secrets, but she needs a guy like you."

"What's that mean?" I had an idea, but I wanted to hear her best friend say it.

"Suzy is a control freak. She needs someone that won't give in to her, but—and this is a big but—she also needs someone that's going to care about what she wants. She's been with men that don't really live up to the promises in the sack, or make her feel like a freak."

Now she fucking intrigued me. "What would make her feel like a freak?"

"She has this fantasy about being kidnapped and sold into slavery."

She whispered the last words, and I looked up at her. I almost fucking choked. "Suzy?"

"Don't be so shocked, Joey. She just wants to be owned, if you know what I mean. She may be a control freak, but in the sack she wants to be used and controlled. Think you're up to the challenge?" She moved her eyebrows up and down, with the biggest smile plastered on her face.

"I think I'm just what the doctor ordered. Tell me more—this shit is good."

"She has fantasies, but will probably never share them with you."

"Why not?"

"No one has ever asked her, so don't expect her to just cough up that shit. You have to pull it out of her."

"Got it."

"Just don't break her heart, City, or I'll crush your balls. Got me?"

"Loud and clear, and I think you'd do it too, Sophia." Sophia didn't seem like the type to not follow through on her words. She reminded me of those strict teachers that you didn't want to fuck around in class and get that pissed-off-teacher look from, but I knew she was sweet too, 'cause Suzy wouldn't be friends with someone who wasn't.

"Oh, I have no issues inflicting bodily harm when necessary."

"Kayden must be one hell of a guy to handle you, Sophia."

"He's complicated."

"Suzy mentioned something along those lines about Kayden." I dipped the gun into the black to finish the shading as I hit the home stretch on the design on her leg.

"I normally wouldn't take as much shit as I did from him, but when you love someone and you know you're meant to be with them, you stick it through. I couldn't abandon him in his time of need. Someday I'll tell you the whole story, 'cause it's a long fucking tale."

"Almost done, just a few more lines. Was it worth it?" I knew the answer, but I wanted to hear her say it was worth the struggle that I feel she had to endure to find the love of her life.

"I wouldn't trade a moment of our fucked-up journey. We were meant to be together. I don't regret a second of my time with him."

I liked hearing about Kayden and Sophia. All my friends and siblings were single and had been put through the ringer. I wanted to hear that it was possible to find love in today's jaded world.

I put the machine on the table and began to wipe the tattoo to clean her skin so she could get a good look at it. "There ya go, darling. Hop up and look in the mirror." I leaned back in my chair and stretched my back.

Sophia jumped up and walked up to the mirror, holding the side of her pants down. It was beautiful and permanent.

"Whatcha think?"

"Oh my God, City. It's amazing. I fucking love it." She turned to the side and stood closer to the mirror. "The color's amazing."

"Will Kayden like it?" I asked. I was sure he'd love it; what man wouldn't love their woman to have their name on their skin? She was marked and his forever.

"He's going to freak out. The guy has a thing for tats, and he has my name on him. I can't wait to show him." She just stood there and stared in the mirror with a giant smile across her face.

"He does?"

"Yep, huge down his leg. There's no way to cover that shit up, either. He's mine forever and I'm his," she said as she walked back over to the chair.

"I never advise anyone to tattoo a boyfriend or girlfriend's name on their body. It's asking for disaster. You're brave."

"Brave? I'm never leaving that man, City. No one will ever love me like he does."

"I've seen the chemistry you two have. I did my part in warning you, but I can't deny you the design you want." I rubbed the salve on her skin and covered it to keep it clean. "You know how this works and about after-care?"

"Yep, it's my fifth tattoo. I got this shit."

"Well then, darling, you're all done."

"I have to use the ladies' room. Where is it?" she asked.

"Down the hall to the right. I'm going to go check on Suzy." I wanted to see her and make sure Mikey kept his paws off her.

I pulled my gloves off with a snap and threw them on the table. I cracked my neck and rounded the corner to see Mikey and Suzy sitting in the chair talking and sitting a little closer than I'd normally feel comfortable with—but this was Mikey.

They began to laugh. "Oh stop, Michael, you're killing me." She covered her mouth and slapped her knee.

"I shit you not," Mikey said, then looked up at me and cleared his throat. "Oh, big brother. How'd things go?"

"What the fuck are you two talking about?" I knew Mikey wanted to find any way to embarrass me; my family was fantastic for that shit.

"Nothing at all."

Suzy's face turned red, and she could barely look me in the eyes without breaking out into a fit of laughter. "Don't you worry, we're just sharing family memories."

Cocksucker. Someday I'd make him pay for this shit. I wouldn't normally give a fuck, but I didn't want Suzy to think of me in the way Mikey had probably described me. Thank the motherfucking gods that the rest of the group wasn't here today. Izzy would be all over Suzy, grilling her and filling her head with stories that should stay in the past. "That's what I'm afraid of."

"No worries. Michael was just reminiscing," she said between her fingers, trying to hide her laughter.

I wanted to choke the motherfucker. I knew he had a knack for making shit up just for his amusement and my embarrassment. I rubbed the back of my neck, trying to stop myself from punching him in the face.

"Where's Sophia?" Suzy asked, getting up from her seat.

"She's using the ladies' room. Go back and see the work I did on her." I kissed her, patting her ass as she walked away. "What the fuck did you tell her?" I said to Mikey.

He started to laugh as he stood. "Oh, nothing."

"Bullshit. What lies did you fill her head with, asswad?"

"I told her you slept with a teddy bear and sucked your thumb until you were ten." He doubled over in laughter, and I saw red.

"You're a dickhead, Mikey. Why do you always do this shit to me?" I closed my eyes and calmed my breathing.

"You never got all worked up before. You must really like this one." He plopped his ass in the chair and pulled himself up to the desk.

"Fuck you."

"Oh, testy. Definitely a boner for that blonde bombshell. Hey, you told my last girlfriend that I pissed my bed until high school. All's fair in love and war, rat bastard."

I burst into laughter. That was the last time that woman came around the family. She broke up with Mikey shortly after our Sunday dinner. "You didn't even like her. You were just fucking her." I heard the door creak, and Suzy and Sophia emerged with smiles on their faces. "Guess you're right, I deserved it, but for fuck's sake—I really like this girl. Don't fuck it up for me. Got me?" I said, leaning over the desk so only he could hear.

"Righto. Don't get your panties in a wad, man." Mikey stood quickly, and smiled as the ladies walked up to the desk. "Everything okay, ladies?"

Sophia's smile couldn't be any bigger. "Fabulous. You did such an amazing job, City. I fuckin' love it, and Kayden's going to be shocked as hell."

"Kayden?" Mikey said, his voice filled with curiosity.

"Yes, Kayden, my boyfriend and father of my baby."

"Fuck, all the good ones are taken," Mikey muttered as he walked away.

"I'm glad you're happy. Let me know what Kayden thinks about it."

Sophia wrapped her arms around me and said, "Thank you."

"Anytime, babe. I'm your man if you ever need any more work. Give that some time to heal. You're going to be sore for a couple of weeks. The hip is tender. Watch what type of clothing you wear, too."

Suzy stood off to the side and smiled at us both. I couldn't wait to get her alone later, but I still had work to do. "Come here, sugar." I held my hand out to her, and she placed her tiny fingers in my palm.

I wrapped her in my arms and pulled her body against mine. "I haven't forgotten that I owe you for your little display earlier." Her eyes went wide as she stared at me. "I never break a promise, either, sugar." I kissed her and rubbed my dick against her stomach. I couldn't wait to bury myself in her pretty little cunt. "I'll be over around eight. Be ready." I smiled and said goodbye as the two girls walked out of the shop in a fit of giggles.

Chapter 16

S uzy

I collapsed on the bed, exhausted, sweaty, and out of breath. City stretched out next to me, hands behind his head, a smug-ass grin stretching his lips. "What's that look?" I asked.

"I fuckin' rocked your world."

"Cocky much?" He fucking did, too. I'd never come so hard or as much as I had with him. He knew all the right things to do and all the perfect places to touch. "If that was your punishment, it didn't work."

"Oh, I don't know about that. I heard you yelp a few times when I smacked your ass." He laughed.

I stared at the ceiling and thought about his words, remembering the stinging feeling of his hand landing on my ass. It set my skin on fire and made everything more intense.

"More out of shock than hurt. You surprised the heck out of me."

City turned on his side, rested his head on his hand, and gazed at me. He ran his fingertips across my stomach, and my flesh broke out in goose bumps. "I hope it's not the last surprise I ever give you."

I closed my eyes and wanted to stay in this moment forever.

"Whatcha thinking about, sugar?"

I opened my eyes and looked into his beautiful blue eyes. "You, Joe. You're just so, so...I don't know how to describe you." I sighed.

"Unlike anyone you've ever been with?" He arched his eyebrow.

"Yeah, and I don't know if that's a good thing, either." I didn't want to say that he also made me half neurotic. The jealously I'd felt in the tattoo shop was something foreign to me, and I didn't like it—not one bit. I barely knew him, and it gutted me to think of him with someone else. I was starting to question my sanity.

"Oh...it's good. The way you screamed my name couldn't be anything but good, sugar."

My face flushed, and warmth crawled down my skin. I had never been a yeller or made much noise at all, but then again, I'd never had a reason to before.

"Don't be embarrassed." He pulled me against his body and kissed my temple as he fisted my hair.

I couldn't escape him—his smell, skin, and warmth. Everything about him made me want more, and I couldn't block it from my mind or wish it away.

"Want me to go?" he whispered in my ear.

"No!" I opened my eyes quickly, turning toward him. My lips brushed against his. I didn't close my eyes and neither did he—we stared in each other's eyes for a moment as I melted into his body.

"Stop overthinking shit, Suzette. You want to be with me?"

"You scare the hell out of me, honestly."

"Why?" He brushed the hair from my face, and my skin tingled from the innocent touch.

"Like you said—you're unlike anyone I've ever known. You're like one giant damn mystery to me."

"I'm an open book. I don't hide my feelings and I don't pussyfoot around shit. I do what I have to and I say what's on my mind."

"I guess I'm just not used to someone being so...so..."

"Cocky, sexy, manly?" He chuckled and started to grab my side, causing me to break out into laughter.

"Stop!" I couldn't catch my breath.

"You think too damn much instead of saying what's on your mind."

"Okay, okay," I puffed out through my giggle, with tears running down my face. His hands stilled at my side and his tongue darted out and licked the tear from my cheek.

"Like that. No one has ever done that."

"Sugar, maybe I need to ask what they have done to you. I feel that list is shorter than what they did do. Have you come during sex before?"

I didn't want to answer that question. "Um."

"Yes or no?" I felt like his azure eyes were staring into my soul and trying to unwrap all of my secrets.

"Not really." I gave him a shy smile, not wanting to divulge that no one had ever gotten me off like he did. City was cocky enough without thinking he was my own personal sex god.

"Hmm. Did you come with me or were you faking that shit?"

Oh, here we go. "I did and I sure as hell wasn't faking—I never fake it."

"Besides me, ever? Without having to do it yourself?"

"No, no one has ever really cared if I did."

"Fucking assholes." He shook his head. "Why do women date assholes like that? I know no one's ever smacked your ass. What do you want that no one has ever done to you?"

Oh my God. I couldn't be any more embarrassed than I felt in this moment. "I don't know."

"That's bullshit, sugar. Everyone has fantasies." He nuzzled my hair, and I didn't feel so under the microscope, but I didn't want him to laugh at me.

"Tell me one of yours." I stroked his arms and traced the tattoos on his skin. The artwork really was beautiful. My parents always told me that tattoos were trashy, but on City they were works of art. They were a timeline of his life, and I wanted to peel back the layers and hear the story.

"I want to fuck you on my bike."

My breath caught in my throat. The thought of him taking me on his bike hadn't even crossed my mind, but now the image was burned into my brain.

"I want you spread eagle, my face planted between your legs, licking every ounce of wetness from your body before sinking my dick in you." The vibration of his words in my ear caused wetness to pool between my legs. Damn him. "Your turn." I knew he had a smile on his face without even seeing it. Bastard.

I sighed. "Where do I begin? God, this is so embarrassing."

"Sugar, if you can't share your fantasies with your boyfriend, who can you?"

One point, City—Suzy, Zero. "I swear I need to have my head examined." I covered my eyes with my hands. City would think I was nuts.

"Out with it. Sophia told me you two read a lot of those smut books. Fantasies can become reality, sugar."

"It's just so weird. You're going to think I'm completely insane."

He stroked my arm as I tried to cover my face. His body shifted as he moved my hand away from my eyes.

"I gotta know now. I can call Sophia and ask, or you can tell me. Give me the naughtiest thing you've always wanted."

I swallowed and shut my eyes. I didn't want to see his reaction when he heard this one. "Fine. I have this fantasy of being taken against my will."

He didn't gasp or scream, but very calmly said, "Rape or kidnapping?"

I opened my eyes and turned to look at him. He had a grin on his face, and the butterflies dancing in my stomach calmed. "Kidnap. I know it's weird," I mumbled.

"No, Suzette. It's not weird at all. We all have our kinks and fantasies. Okay, so kidnap and then what?" He looked so damn eager to hear the rest, like he was hanging on my every word. How could I not share the rest?

"Do you honestly want to know?"

"Yes."

"I've read so many amazing books that deal with kidnapping and being owned by someone. I don't really want some crazy person to kidnap me, but the books make it seem appealing and sexy as heck."

"I'll see what I can do to make that happen."

"Oh, God."

"I won't surprise you, you'll know when it's coming—when I'm coming for you."

He pulled my body against his, our skin touching, his hands pressed into my back; he made me feel normal about wanting something so taboo. He smelled so good. His masculine and musky scent mixed with the smell of sex. I didn't think I could ever get enough of him.

His hand glided up my back, on to the nape of my neck as he grabbed a fistful of hair. The feel of his calloused hands against my skin and the prick of pain on my scalp felt like electricity throughout my body. Holding my head still with his firm grip on my hair, he looked into my eyes. The brilliant blue of his almost glowed in the light and burned with passion. "As for being owned, I plan to own every inch of your body. You are mine, sugar, don't forget that shit. I'm going to fucking ruin you."

Why the hell did that sound so amazing? Damn trashy books altered my sense of right and wrong. I wanted him to own me—ruin me.

I was lost in thought until his lips crashed against mine. His kiss wasn't gentle or kind, but demanding and all-consuming. My body molded around him as I wrapped my leg around his waist.

"I'm going to be rough, Suzette," he said against my lips.

I searched his eyes and could see the lust and need within. "I'm yours," I whispered.

He grabbed my torso and flipped me on my stomach. He moved faster than I thought possible, and he was behind me in a moment. He grabbed my hips and pulled my ass in the air. "Stomach down, sugar." He pushed on the small of my back. "Head too, only your ass in the air." I buried my face in the sheets and could smell him on the fabric.

I started to hyperventilate. I'd had sex doggie style, but this was something different—new. His fingers raked through my wetness, stroking my clit and squeezing it lightly. A jolt coursed through my body, and I cried out.

Smack. "Don't move," he said, rubbing my ass with one hand and pinching my clit with the other. "Unless you want another swat on the ass."

I wanted to squirm or rub against him like a cat in heat, but the sting of his last swat kept me rooted in place. His hand left my ass, and I turned to look at him. His tall, muscular body stood on the bed, and he stroked his cock. The metal piercing at the tip would disappear in his hand. His beautiful black hair was a mess and lay across his forehead, and the light reflected off his eyes. I could stare at him for hours—he was everything my mother told me to steer clear of in life. Just looking at the man made my panties wet. I'm so screwed.

I was so exposed in this position. My ass and pussy were on display for him. He pumped his hardness in his fist as he positioned himself behind me. I could feel the head rub through my wetness. His cock was hard as it poked at my entrance. I closed my eyes and held my breath as I waited for him to fill me. I instantly felt the loss of his body, and opened one eye to see what he was doing.

"What's wrong?" I asked, staring at him just standing there, stroking the shaft as he looked at me.

"Relax, sugar. I'll make it fanfuckingtastic." He rubbed my ass, and I knew his words were true.

I relaxed my muscles and closed my eyes as I felt his hand on me again. The head of his dick touched my opening, and I wanted him inside me. I gripped the sheets and braced myself for the impaling I was about to endure. He rested his hand on the top of my ass as he pushed himself inside. I felt stuffed, and I knew he wasn't fully seated inside. I squeezed the sheets tighter as the sensation of him became overwhelming, and more intense than I'd felt before.

His body slammed into mine as he pumped in and out. His body worked like a well-oiled machine, and his shaft was the piston battering my insides. The tip hit parts of my body that had never been touched before, and I wanted to crawl away—the fight-or-flight instinct started to kick in. My ass stung as the sound of his hand striking my ass filled my ears.

"Ass up, Suzette," he growled, grabbing my hips and molding my body exactly how he wanted it without going out of rhythm.

I bit my lip. I wanted to cry out. I wanted to crawl away. I didn't know if I could take one more minute as I reached back and grabbed his ankles. I dug my nails into his skin and grounded myself. I had to fight every urge in my body to flee.

I could feel every inch of him as it moved inside my body. His breathing was harsh and quick, and I buried my face in the sheets to stop from crying out. My muscles tightened as I felt an orgasm building inside me, but how? He hadn't even touched my clit in this position, and I hadn't touched myself.

His speed increased and his hips slammed against the sore spot left by his hand. He grabbed my hips and pulled me closer, allowing himself to be buried to the hilt.

"Fuck, your cunt is so tight." His fingers dug in my hip as I was held captive by his hands. "I can feel it squeezing my cock. Fuck, sugar," he said as he pulled my body against him to meet his thrust.

I squeezed my eyes shut as a moan escaped my mouth that I could no longer hold. I needed to yell as the orgasm crashed over me, my body becoming rigid. My core gripped his shaft as the aftershocks tore through me, and his rhythm became more intense, and eventually more erratic. He moaned and my body became limp, but I kept my ass in the air because of his rock-hard grip.

His body twitched against me before he pulled out and collapsed on the bed. "Fuck," he muttered.

My body ached. Rolling over, I stretched out across the mattress and rested my arm across his body. Our labored breathing filled the air. My hand rose and fell with his chest as I gulped for air and tried to swallow the cotton taste from my mouth.

Neither of us spoke as we lay there. City had been more than I could ever imagine. I liked being with him. He was easy to be around. He made me feel beautiful and wanted. I needed to turn my brain off and stop thinking of the reasons I should run away from him and enjoy our time together.

I felt like I was in a dream world, half awake as City rolled over and placed his arms around me. He kissed my face and whispered, "Night, beautiful," in my ear.

Chapter 17

C ity

We spent a few nights together during the week—work took up our days and kept us apart, but the evenings were filled with fucking her raw and leaving no doubt in her mind of my feelings toward her. Saturday she had a wedding to attend that she'd already RSVPed to and couldn't change.

As I locked up the shop, my phone chimed.

Bear: Get your pussy ass over to the Cowboy. Where the fuck you been, man?

Suzy would be gone until around midnight, and a drink with the guys was in order.

Me: Headed that way, asshole. Save me a seat and you better have a fucking cold beer waiting for me.

Shoving the phone in my pocket, I climbed on the bike and headed toward the Neon Cowboy. Steam rose from the dampened streets as the tires parted the mist. The moonlight flashed through the trees lighting my path. The cool breeze felt good against my flesh as I barreled down the road to hang with my guys.

Walking in the bar, I took in the familiar smell of smoke, the sound of the country guitar, and the murmur of the crowd, and I realized how much I'd missed this place.

"Yo," Bear yelled, grabbing my attention. "I almost sent a search party looking for your ass," he said as I approached the table. Tank and the others laughed.

"I've been busy, fucker." A frosty glass sat waiting for me, as I'd hoped it would be.

"Busy nestled between that sweet blonde ass, I assume," Tank said as he twirled the beer bottle between his fingers.

"You're just jealous because you gotta pay for your pussy, shithead."

He shrugged, bringing the bottle to his lips. "Less complicated that way. I just wanna bust a nut without the cuddling and whining."

"You're an asshole." Frisco laughed, slapping Tank on the shoulder, causing the bottle to move from his lips.

"Fucker, you made me spill my beer."

Frisco covered his mouth with his hand as his eyes turned into small slits. We called him Frisco because he hailed from sunny California and grew up in the San Francisco area. His features were unique—his Chinese mother and American father were both evident in his features. His eyes were almond-shaped and dark, his hair pin straight, cropped at the top, and coal black. He was taller than me, and thin with a slight, muscular build.

"So, City, tell us about the li'l woman? How are things going?" Bear asked.

I leaned back in my chair and rested the beer against my knee. "Fucking perfect."

"You're serious about this one?" He raised an eyebrow and studied me.

Everyone at the table stopped, turning their attention to me. "Serious as a motherfuckin' heart attack." I sipped my beer, looking at their faces. Frisco smiled, Bear's mouth hung open, and Tank scowled. "What?" I said, moving the bottle from my lips.

"Didn't think I'd see the fucking day, dude," Bear said with a sappy grin.

"She's too pretty to be with your loser ass," Tank piped in before I could speak.

"Fuck off, Tank."

"I'm happy for you, man. This calls for another round." Tank raised his fingers to his lips and whistled. He was so crass, but the girl always ran when she heard him call. "Another round, sweet cheeks," he said as he patted her on the bottom.

"Hey, City. Nice to finally have a gentleman back in here." She winked at me before turning her attention back to Tank. "Anything for you, handsome?" she said, running her fingers down the side of Tank's face. He blushed as he placed his order.

"You know your ass would give up this shithole for a piece of that every night," I said to Tank as he watched her ass swaying in her Daisy Dukes as she walked toward the bar.

"Won't deny that shit." He laughed before slapping the table roughly, causing all the bottles to jump.

We talked for hours about motorcycles, tattoos, women, and, of course, the bar. The guys filled me in on the events of the last week. It was always the same old bullshit—bar fights, hook-ups, and booze. The town was so small that everyone knew each other's business, and word spread like wildfire.

"Fuck," Bear hissed. "Speaking of bitches, Kaylee was in here looking for your ass."

"What the fuck? When?" I gripped the bottle in my hand, trying to control my anger.

"Last night. Mumbling some bullshit about how she was yours. Spreading that shit around here like it was the gospel. I told her to fuck off," Bear said, leaning back like he was about to beat on his chest.

"She's a fucking train wreck. Stuck my dick in her twice and she won't let me fucking forget it. I'll set her ass straight, unless one of you boys wants to take her off my hands?" I looked around the table and waited for someone to accept.

"Fuck no, that bitch makes my skin crawl. Hate clingy women," Frisco said, shaking his head.

"My dick, my problem," I said, feeling the phone vibrate in my pocket. Pulling it out, I glanced at the screen under the table.

Suzy: Drunk and tired. Sophia's taking me home, but you're welcome to join me.

"Ball and chain wrangling your ass in?" Tank asked.

"Such a ball buster. It's late and I worked all day. I'm heading home. Thanks for the drink, Bear." I shook his hand and turned to Frisco. "Good to see you again, buddy. Tank, it's been real."

"Whipped," Tank mumbled as I stood to leave.

I left the guys to end the evening how they always did. Bitching about life and women. Thankful that my night wouldn't end like it had for countless years, I sent Suzy a text.

Me: Leave the door unlocked. I'll meet you in bed.

When I arrived, Suzy was half dressed and passed out across the bed. Her mouth hung open, hair was half covering her face, and her dress was halfway off, exposing her breasts. It took everything in me not to snap a picture of her and remind her of it later, but I didn't want to be a dick.

"Wake up, sugar." I grabbed her leg, pulling her body down the bed. She mumbled but didn't wake. I pulled the hem of her dress, removing the clingy material. I rarely had the ability to just stare at her body without her trying to cover her skin. I stood and looked at her—white skin, perky breasts, and long, muscular legs. She was a vision.

Gathering her in my arms, I placed her head on the pillow before I removed my clothes and climbed in next to her.

"City," she muttered as she shimmied her ass into my dick.

"Fuck." I sighed. My cock throbbed from the warmth of her soft cheeks rubbing against it. "Go back to sleep, sugar." I pulled her tighter, burying my face in her hair before drifting off to sleep to her soft snores.

"How's the shop doing?" my father asked as we sat around the dining room table. Today was gnocchi, and it always sat in my gut like a ton of fucking bricks.

"We're doing good, Pop. We're turning a profit and we're constantly booked when I can get everyone to show up for work," Mike said before shoveling in a heaping forkful of gnocchi.

"Mike, you aren't always there either, so don't be a martyr and skip the bullshit." Anthony pointed his fork at Mikey before stabbing the gnocchi on his plate.

"We all have other shit to do. The shop is for fun and to have something of our own, so get off our damn backs, Mike. You aren't the boss,'" Izzy said emphasizing the word to sound like a great big "fuck you." "You just aren't an artist like the rest of us." She picked up the wine glass and brought it to her lips to hide her smile. Izzy always had been a spitfire.

My mother and father sat at the opposite ends of the table and exchanged looks as my siblings had a war of words. As children, we battled with our fists and usually one of us ended up bloodied, but now we used our mouths. Sometimes words leave a greater mark than any punch ever could.

"I'm every bit an artist as you are, baby sister. I just prefer to use my hands for other things. I may not draw pretty pictures, but I can pierce anything and knock a bastard on their ass in a single punch."

My father cleared his throat. "Is the shop too much?" he asked.

I needed to speak up. The shop was doing great and we all got along. Sundays often made us crabby because we wanted to do anything but be trapped in this house. A one-weekend reprieve would be fucking mind-blowing—and a totally bullshit improbability. "Pop, the shop's great. We're packed. Everyone shows up on the days they have appointments. I'm there more than anyone and I know the business the best. Mike may organize shit, but I know what happens inside the walls of Inked." I soaked my garlic bread in my mother's homemade sauce, which had spread out around my plate. "We need to keep ourselves busy during the day, and the shop has more than done that."

"Good, son. I'm proud of all of you. You could be sitting on your asses at home, but you're business owners and successful—not to mention your other hobbies." Oh fuck. Everyone hated to have their true passions and dream careers referred to as a "hobby."

I heard forks drop to the table and clatter off the dishes. Such drama queens in this goddamn room.

"Sorry about that. It's not what I meant." My father looked down at his plate, concentrating on his food, but I could see the smile on his face. He loved a good punch to the gut and ego whenever possible.

"I have a big fight coming up after the first of the year," Mikey piped in, to show my dad how far he'd risen.

"Around here?"

"New York. I got the call yesterday. I've been training for months for this opportunity."

"That's fantastic, son. Wish your mother and I could see it."

My mother looked green at the thought of her son being in a closed ring beating the piss out of someone—or getting the shit beat out of him. I'd put my money on Mikey in any fight, but I know my mother still thought of him as her baby. Fuck, we were all her babies.

"Michael, why can't you be like your brother? Go into music or something without violence and bloodshed?" She dabbed her lips with her napkin and then placed it on the table.

"Ma, I'm great at it and I love it. It's my dream to be a well-known ass kicker."

Pop reached over and slapped him on the back. I was surprised he didn't start beating on his chest at how proud he was of his ass-kicking son.

"I just don't like the whole idea. Become a musician or something else."

"Tone deaf," Mikey mumbled as he placed more food in his mouth.

My mother sighed and fidgeted with her fork on the table. "I was fine with it when I thought it was just a hobby or a passing phase, but now, I'm scared for you, Michael."

"No worries, Ma. I got this shit. You'll see." He grinned at her and flexed his muscles. "It's going to be on pay-per-view, so you'll be able to watch, Pop. I'm not the headliner, but they show all the opening fights before the main event."

"I'll have to have the guys over to watch my son kick some ass."

I rolled my eyes and hoped someone would change the conversation.

"Anyone talk to Thomas this week?" Mom asked.

Not the topic I would've liked, but anything to not hear about Mr. Badass and his upcoming match.

"I did, Ma, he texted me. It's hard for him to call with work," Anthony said.

She sighed and closed her eyes, pinching the bridge of her nose. "I worry most about him. He's in such danger every day, and I don't like him being so far away. I need all my children around this table every week."

I could see the pain on her face. She worried about my brother. He'd been an undercover cop for the last year. He was trying to infiltrate a motorcycle group notorious in Florida for drug trafficking and gun smuggling. He rarely called or texted in order to keep his cover, otherwise his life would end.

Why the fuck my brother risked his life was beyond me. It's one thing to work the streets every day walking a beat, but to go undercover and be discovered was something cops rarely fucking came back from. If something happened to him, my mother would never recover. Tommy had always been an adrenaline junkie, but this was extreme. Jump off a fucking bridge or skydive like normal people; don't risk being shot in the fucking head when they realize you're there to help bring them down.

"He said he's fine, Ma. He said not to worry and he's well and living the life. You know, Tommy would have made a great actor. He can bullshit the best of them." Izzy always tried to console my mother about Tommy's work, but it was always there—the worry. We all felt it like a ton of bricks, waiting for the phone call that he was missing, but thankfully it hadn't happened.

"I know, baby girl." My mom smiled at Izzy. "He could always charm the ladies."

"Speaking of charmer, Ma, Joey's girl was at the shop yesterday and I missed it." Izzy pouted and winked at me. She knew she'd just thrown me under the goddamn bus, and my mom would have a shitload of questions...again.

"Still seeing her, Joseph?" Her face lit up. I knew she was already picking out the baby names, but fucking hell, I wasn't ready for that shit.

"Yes, Ma." I hated talking about this shit with anyone, especially my mother.

"Is she your girlfriend?"

I sighed, wanting to reach over and choke that shit-eatin' grin off Izzy's face. "Yes."

"Don't chase her away because she isn't Joni. You hear me?"

"Yes, Ma."

"I met her, Ma." Fucking Mikey.

"What's she like, Michael?" My mom knew she wasn't going to get much more out of me than she had last week in the kitchen. She knew to ask the blabbermouth of the group.

"She's beautiful and deserves so much better than that punk." His head moved in my direction, and I wanted to bitch-slap him.

"Better as in you, Mikey?" I eyed him.

"Calm down, bro. She's a nice girl, Ma. Reminds me a bit of Joni. Innocent, and her laughter is infectious. You'll like her." He grinned at me.

What a fucking asshole.

"You'll have to bring her for Sunday dinner soon, Joseph." Exactly what I didn't want to do. I didn't want her to be around my crazy-ass siblings, especially Izzy. Iz was dying for another girl, since the testosterone to estrogen level was off balance.

"Maybe soon. I don't want to get ahead of myself."

"The holidays are coming up. Christmas, maybe. Is she a Catholic girl?"

Already planning the wedding ceremony. Religion weighed heavily in an Italian family—christenings, baptisms, weddings… everything seemed to revolve around the church.

"Ma, you haven't been to church in years," I said flatly.

"I know, but it's still important. It makes life easier. Is she Italian?"

"I never asked." I grabbed my plate and headed for the kitchen. I could hear the giggles from the table as my mother and sister always liked to rag on me most of all. No one was in a relationship in the group, but for some reason I was always the target.

I didn't know where Suzy and I stood and what the future held for us. She was always so wrapped up in her fucking thoughts and second-guessing our relationship. She couldn't get beyond the tattooed façade and the beat-up shack I called home. I needed to know that I was enough for her. I wanted to be liked for me—the good, bad, and the ugly.

Chapter 18

S uzy

I could hardly contain my excitement all week. City and I talked every night on the phone and texted during the day. I couldn't stay away from him and couldn't get him out of my mind. I tried to keep myself busy and find reasons not to be with him, but it didn't work. I was falling for the man, and falling hard.

Growing up, my mother had drilled in my head that I needed to find a man with a stable job. I needed to settle down, have a family, and live the American dream. I tried for years to find that man, the perfect mold, but all of them were just...boring as hell.

I'd never been willing to settle for anything less than perfect. A picket fence and a beautiful home are worthless if you dread going home to the one you're supposed to spend your life with. I prefer being single to the doldrums in which some of my friends currently dwelled. Sophia and Kayden were the happiest couple I knew, and they were complete opposites—they were the yin to the other's yang.

The students cleared the building as soon as the last bell blared at two in the afternoon on Friday. I had another thirty minutes left and couldn't seem to function. All I could think of was tonight and what could be—what would be. I couldn't stare at the clock and watch another minute tick away. I knew Sophia would be tidying up the library, and I needed to talk to her. She'd questioned me all week about City and when I'd see him again, but I hadn't told her the plan we had. I needed her opinion.

The lights in the library were dimmed, but I could see her wandering around, returning books to their rightful spots. I took a deep breath and walked through the door to the torrent of questions I knew I'd face.

"Sophia," I called out. I didn't want to scare the hell out of her. I knew most of the staff had snuck out early, but the two of us never took the chance at losing our jobs for a few minutes of our time.

She turned the corner with a stack of books in her hand and a smile on her face. "Hey, Suzy Q, what are you doing up here? Don't you have any big plans for tonight?" She winked at me. I couldn't hide the smile on my face. I felt like the electricity and joy radiated off my body. "How many hours until you see him?"

"Maybe I'm not going to see him tonight." I was so full of shit, and I knew I couldn't fool Sophia, but sometimes I hated that she could read me like an open book.

"Whatever, whore. It's written all over your face. You're going to get some cock tonight, and by the red creeping across your cheeks, I'd say it's fucking amazing."

"Do you hear how you talk in a school?"

"Prude ass. Every child has run away from this place screaming at two. There isn't a soul within earshot except for us. What time are you meeting him tonight?"

"We're meeting at seven." I plopped down on one of the comfy couches as Sophia placed the books on the table and sat down next to me.

"My feet are freaking killing me in these damn heels." She kicked off her shoes and rubbed her feet. "What's the plan tonight?"

"I don't even know if I can repeat it." I shrugged. My stomach was a jumbled mess from just thinking about the possibilities.

"You can and you will. This is me, girl. I know all your darkest secrets. Shit, you used to lie in bed with Kayden and me and grill us on our sex life. We have no secrets. I know you're a kinky bitch underneath that polished veneer."

"It's your fault. I was happy with my bland sex life and you had to go and ruin me with all those trashy novels."

"Stop changing the subject. What's the plan with the sexy-as-sin City?" She grinned and waggled her eyebrows up and down.

I'd always wanted sex that was worthy of girl talk, and for years, I'd lived off the stories that Sophia and my other friends had shared with me. City had made sex worth talking about; I'd finally have some wild stories to share.

"I kind of shared one of my fantasies with him and he's going to make it happen tonight." I covered my eyes with my hand, avoiding her stare. I was scared to tell her any more, but she knew every fantasy I had and always reassured me that I was normal, that my sanity hadn't been replaced by impure thoughts.

"Oh my God. Tell me, tell me." She practically bounced on the couch cushion. "Don't hold back now, bitch." She slapped my arm.

"I told him the darkest one."

"You didn't?"

I grinned, and my cheeks almost hurt from the smile that had been plastered on my face all day. "I did, and he said I'd have it."

"Kidnapping?" She looked shocked, but I saw the twinkle in her eye.

"I can't believe I told him, but yes. Oh my God, it's happening tonight, Sophia."

"I'm so proud of you." She wrapped her arms around me. "My baby's all grown up." She squeezed me and ran her palm down the back of my head. "Tell me more. I want to hear about him. Now."

"We're going to meet at the Neon Cowboy, that biker bar out in the country. We're going to have some dinner and drinks before I leave alone and he makes it become a reality."

"You're going to chicken out. Oh God, he's giving you time to change your mind." She stood up and started pacing the room.

"Calm down, Sophia. I'm not going to chicken out. I've wanted someone like him, and tonight I'm getting more than I could ever dream of—my fantasy becoming a reality."

"You've never done this shit. You're like I used to be—Ms. Missionary Style. I expect details tomorrow, and I mean a full report."

"Yes, ma'am. I'll give you a full briefing."

"I want every last fucking detail too, got me?"

"I got ya, Sophia. I better go get my stuff and head home. I want to rest a bit before I see him."

"Good luck with resting." She snickered.

"I know. I could barely sleep last night." I sighed.

"I used to get that way when I would see Kayden after time apart. There's no feeling like it." She smiled and hugged me. "Now go. I have to finish up and get home to my fantasy man."

"You still feel that way about Kayden after all this time?"

"I still get butterflies when I see him, Suzy. That's the difference, you know—that feeling has never gone away. I'm still get excited like the first time we met."

"I envy you, Sophia."

"You'll find your Kayden, babe. I think you may already have, if you don't let your stupid OCD checklist get in the way." She tapped me on the forehead.

"I got to go. We'll debate my sanity and compulsions another day." I waved to her as I walked out the door. "Later, Soph."

"Don't forget to call me, Suzy, or I'll hunt your ass down," she yelled to me as the door closed behind me.

"Hey, sugar." His voice filled my car via speakerphone, but he didn't sound as excited as I felt.

"Hey, City. I'm almost to the bar."

"I'm going to be fifteen minutes late. Fuck, I'm sorry. The tattoo I was working on took longer than I thought. Can you wait for me in the parking lot?"

Damn. That bar gave me the heebie-jeebies, and I didn't fit in, not even in the parking lot. "Yeah, City. I wouldn't dream of walking in there alone." I felt sick. "This isn't part of your plan, is it?"

"Hell no! We're still having some drinks first. I need you to not overthink everything tonight. I want you a little tipsy for what I have planned." He laughed.

The excitement took over, and all second thoughts vanished. "Okay, City. I'll be waiting for you."

"Do not go inside alone. Understand me?"

"I won't. I promise."

"See you soon, sugar."

After tossing my phone on the passenger seat, I rolled down the window, welcoming the cool air against my clammy skin. The events of the night played through my mind. City would be my kidnapper. My lungs burned as I screamed along with the song on the radio, "Dark Horse" by Katy Perry, the bass causing my windows to rattle with each beat.

Pulling into a spot hidden in the shadows, I turned off the lights and waited for City to arrive. In the rearview mirror I saw my face glistening from the humidity in the air, and I wanted to look flawless. City had seen me at my worst, but I wanted to look beautiful for him in front of his friends.

The lighted mirror behind my visor was more forgiving as I blotted my face with an old napkin I found in the glove box. My lips lacked color as I smacked them together, making kissy lips. After slathering on some Buxom lip gloss from my purse, I rubbed my lips together with a pop. They tingled as the peppermint oil started to plump my lips, soaking into my skin.

A loud knock on the window made me jump, and I hit my head on the visor. "Shit," I said. I turned to get a glimpse at my knight in shining armor, but it wasn't City outside my car. It was a guy that looked vaguely familiar. He stood there staring at me, and alarm bells went off in my head.

I cracked my window an inch, thankful I had rolled them up when I arrived. "Can I help you?"

"Why's such a pretty lady sitting out here alone? Come inside, beautiful."

Hell, he creeped me out. "I'm waiting for someone." I didn't want to hold a conversation with him. His hair was a mess, gray hair lined his face, and dirt was smeared across his tattered t-shirt. A sour smell caused me to wrinkle my nose—he was the asshole that wouldn't leave me alone the first time I came here, until City and Bear stepped in. Shit, where was City?

"You can wait inside, let me buy you a drink." His face came closer to the window, and I could smell the alcohol on his breath, mixing with the body odor that I couldn't escape. My heart raced and my palms started to sweat. Just stay in the car.

"Thanks, but I'm going to wait here." I couldn't stand looking at him anymore. Why won't he just go away? I heard a motorcycle pull in the parking lot and come to a screeching halt next to my car. Peering through the passenger window, I saw City climbing off his bike quickly and coming at the scumbag outside my window.

"Get the fuck away from her," City roared as he stood toe to toe with the asshole.

"I just asked her to come inside for a drink." He looked City in the eye and didn't move. He must have had a death wish.

"She doesn't want to be bothered. Go the fuck home, you drunk bastard. Stop bothering all the ladies here, or at least mine. Do I need to beat that message in your stupid-ass head?" City grabbed his shirt, crumpling it in his first.

The man threw his hands up in surrender and tried to back away, but City had a firm grip on his shirt.

"Come on, man. I didn't know she's yours. You need to keep better track of her. Pretty things disappear all the time around here." He grinned, and my skin began to crawl.

"Beat it, jackass. Next time I won't speak. I'll just bash your fucking head in so the only thing you can do with that mouth is drink through a goddamn straw." City released him and shoved him backward. The man stumbled before falling on his ass.

City opened my car door and held out his hand, but I couldn't take my eyes off the guy on the ground. The look he gave me was pure hatred.

"Come on, sugar. I'm here, he won't bother you."

Placing my hand in his, I didn't say a word as I closed my door. I stayed close as we approached the bar. My nerves were shot, and I needed that drink more than ever.

He stopped, grabbing my arm and turning me to face him. "Are you okay, Suzy?"

"Yeah, Joey. He didn't hurt me, but he's creepy as hell."

He wrapped his arms around me, cocooning me. Melting into him, I buried my face in his shirt. Unlike the man from the parking lot, City smelled amazing—the mix of musky cologne with his natural scent. My hand drifted across his chest until I found the piercing I'd become fond of touching.

"Sugar, keep doing that and we won't make it through the first drink before I take you in the bathroom and fuck you raw."

I leaned back with a smirk on my face. "I can't help myself. It's nice to finally touch you after such a long week." I buried my face in his shirt again, not letting go of the little metal object attached to his body.

"I have another piercing that could use some attention," he said through clenched teeth as he ground his cock against me.

"Nah, I'm good. Drink first, then you can do anything you want to me."

Did I just say that? I needed to learn to filter my promises—he was not a bland and boring lover, he liked his sex hard and fast, and he had mentioned my ass. Don't even think about it.

"Anything?" he whispered.

"Within reason." I smiled against his chest—thank God my face was hidden.

"That's my girl. Always thinking." He laughed and wrapped me under his arm before walking through the doors of the Neon Cowboy and into the firing squad of males that had egos to protect and manhood to show off. Lord, help me.

The guys I'd met the first night insisted that we sit with them. I reassured City that it was fine as long as he never left my side. The asshole in the parking lot had already put me on edge, and a tableful of strangers didn't help put my mind at ease.

Bear and Tank talked me into lemon drop shots and beer. I couldn't exactly order my virgin daiquiri sitting at table full of bikers. I tried to fit in, calm my nerves, and get in the right frame of mind for my "kidnapping." I listened to them talk about bikes and tats—a world foreign to me, but still entertaining. They looked scary, but they were good guys that just wanted to hang out, drink beer, and bullshit.

Bear looked just like his nickname—wild, curly, overgrown hair; a beard; big and burly. When he stood, I could picture him like a grizzly bear on its hind legs ready to attack. When he spoke about his kids and old lady, he reminded me more of a teddy bear. I quickly learned my first impression of him had been wrong, and I needed to be more open-minded. Wilder shit had happened.

"What are you two kids doing tonight?" Bear asked as he washed down the last sip of beer.

I felt the heat crawling up my face, and I couldn't answer his question. I sat there and stared at City. I'd let him field that question.

"Nothing much, Bear. Just going to kidnap this beautiful creature and use her how I see fit." He winked at me and looked at Bear with a cocky smile.

I glanced around the table, and everyone was staring at me. I was sure the picture in their mind was accurate, minus the actual kidnapping part.

Bear slapped City on the back. "That's my boy," he said with a laugh.

City leaned over and nuzzled his face in my hair. "Why don't you head out and I'll find you, sugar," he whispered in my ear. I shivered at his words. I wanted him to play this game.

I turned my face and kissed him on the lips. "Yes, sir. Catch me if you can." The guys at the table started to hoot and holler as I stood from the table, almost knocking over my chair as City caught it. "Sorry about that," I said as I stood on shaky legs.

"Get going, sugar." City swatted me on the ass, and I yelped. I shouldn't have done that last shot.

I kept my eyes on the floor, making sure not to trip on my way out the door. My eyesight felt fuzzy, and my head was cloudy from the vodka. I turned to look back at City before walking out the door. Every man at that table stared at me. City looked excited as he winked at me with a tilted grin that made my panties wet, but the rest of them looked in shock. Maybe City had clued them in on our little role-playing adventure that lay ahead.

I smiled and waved; the cool air touched my skin as I walked outside to wait for my captor to find me. My heart thundered and my stomach gurgled as I made my way toward my car. I was ready for him.

Chapter 19

"Were you being fucking serious?" Tank leaned forward.

"About what? Using her?"

"Fuck, all of it," he said with an eyebrow raised and one side of his mouth curved in a smile.

"All of it. I got to go, boys. Time to go find my victim for the night." I stood from the table and threw a fifty down. "You gentleman have a good night with that image rolling around in your head right now."

They couldn't even begin to process what we were really going to do. They thought "kidnap" was just a nice way of saying I was going to take her away from the bar and have sex with her, but I was going to literally kidnap her.

"Can one of you take my bike home tonight and I'll grab it in the morning?" I asked before walking away.

"I'll take it," Bear said. "I'll tow it to Tank's shop."

"Thanks, man—my dick thanks you too." I laughed as I tossed him the keys.

"At least someone's prick will be happy tonight," Bear mumbled as he placed the keys in his jacket pocket.

I didn't say anything, but couldn't stop laughing. Poor bastards.

I rolled my neck as I headed for the door, cracking it almost like I was prepping for a game. I'd give Suzy everything she wanted and more.

"City!" a voice rang through the crowd. Fuck. "City!" A hand waved above the crowd, and I knew the voice but pretended not to hear her.

I didn't turn around, but walked faster until a hand wrapped around my arm.

"Oh, Kaylee, I didn't see you."

"I was screaming your name," she huffed, trying to catch her breath.

"Didn't hear you, either. I'm in a hurry and got to go."

"I've missed you, City." She tried to wrap her arms around me, but I grabbed them and forced them away.

"Stop, Kaylee. I really don't have time for this shit."

"You've always had time for me before." She pouted and tried to play the guilt card.

"I don't now. I have to go meet my girlfriend," I said, hoping she'd get the fucking hint.

"Girlfriend? Since when?" She looked in shock as she held my arm, digging her nails into my flesh.

"Bye, Kaylee. I don't have time for a goddamn chitchat. My girl's waiting for me, and I don't mean you."

I left her there with her mouth open and gulping for air like a fish. I needed to get to Suzy. I'd already left her entirely too long outside by herself. Damn it. She had to be in knots by now, but then again, it probably helped build her excitement.

Rubbing my face as I walked outside, I couldn't believe fucking Kaylee. I was supposed to be only moments behind Suzy; she'd fumbled with her keys trying to unlock her car when I grabbed her from behind. She could've changed her mind and gone home with the amount of time that had elapsed.

Her car was parked in the same spot, but her door was open and she wasn't inside. I looked around—where the fuck was she? I studied every inch of the parking lot, but couldn't see her. My heart thundered in my chest. I felt sick. I heard a muffled cry, but couldn't tell where it came from over the street noise. "Suzy," I screamed, panic taking hold.

Her purse lay on the ground near her car; I just had to find her. I couldn't stand there and wait any longer. I had to move. I ran into the woods behind her car and surveyed the area. I listened for any sound; a man's voice caught my attention—faint but enough to pull my gaze to behind the bar.

I ran in the direction of the noise and saw a man on top of a woman, Suzy, raising his fist before striking her. "You bitch," he seethed. It was the motherfucker that had bothered her earlier when I arrived.

I grabbed him by the throat before he could land another blow and slammed his body to the ground. The force of his head connecting with the concrete made a horrific sound from his skull cracking. Straddling him, I pummeled him with my fists, feeding off the sound of his jawbone crunching underneath my knuckles. He moaned, but I didn't give a fuck. He hit a woman, my woman. I punched him again then grabbed his head, and I wanted to bash it into the cement to watch all of his blood ooze out, but a pair of hands began to pull me off him, stopping me.

"City, you're going to fuckin' kill him," Bear said as he tried to pull me back.

"Fuckin' bastard deserves to die." I moved my hand to punch him again, but Bear grabbed my wrist.

"Goddamn, man. He's out cold. Get the fuck away from him and take care of your girl."

Suzy. I had been so busy beating the fuck out him, lost in my anger, I forgot to check on her. She lay on the cement with her eyes closed, not moving. She was limp in my arms as I cradled her against my chest. Blood dripped from her lip and nose, and I brushed the hair from her eyes to look for more damage. She had a red mark that would turn into a bruise near her temple.

"Suzy," I whispered, brushing my fingers across her face. "Suzy, wake up, sugar." I gathered her legs off the cold ground and placed her in my lap.

I looked at Bear as he stood over me with wide eyes. "Call an ambulance, Bear."

"On it, buddy." He stood over the asshole lying on the ground unconscious, and I saw Bear kick him. "The attacker is knocked out on the ground. I'll keep him restrained," Bear said to the person on the phone.

"Suzy, come on, sweetie. Wake up, beautiful." I kissed her warm lips. This was my fucking fault. "I'm so sorry, Suzy." Fuck. Her clothes were in place, nothing was torn, but they had dirt on them from being on the ground.

Her eyes started to open, and I felt like I could breathe again. I smiled at her, touching her cheek. "City," she said with a shaky voice. Her arms started to move, reaching for me.

"Don't move, sugar. Wait for the ambulance." I didn't want her to injure herself worse than that fucker may have already done.

"What happened?" She stared at me with her big, beautiful blue eyes. I could see the confusion and hurt in them.

"I'm sorry, Suzy. I got held up inside and I showed up too late. This wouldn't have happened if I didn't force you live out one of your fantasies."

She smiled sweetly at me. "Ouch." Her tongue slid across her lip and stopped on the blood.

"You're bleeding, sugar. Just lie still until the paramedics can check you out."

"What about?" She didn't have to finish the sentence—I knew what she wanted to know.

"He won't hurt you anymore."

She closed her eyes and a tear slid down her cheek. "What did you do, City?"

"I gave the fucker a taste of his own medicine. He's out cold." I wiped the tear away from her cheek with my thumb.

"Is he"—her lip began to tremble—"dead?"

"He's alive. I wanted to kill the prick, but Bear pulled me off him." Sobs tore through her as her body began to shake. "Shh, I got you. No one's going to hurt you ever again, Suzy."

I held her until the paramedics arrived, and a second ambulance pulled in a moment later. Two men pulled her from my grasp, assessing her injuries before placing her on a stretcher and completing their evaluation. I watched as they checked the fucker's body on the ground. Fuck him. I hoped the bastard fucking died.

"We need to take her to the hospital. She's sustained some head injuries and we want to make sure it's not serious," the EMT said. "Would you like to meet us there?"

"I'll follow you." I looked over his shoulder and saw them loading Suzy into the ambulance. "Can I speak to her first?"

"Yes, quickly, so we can leave."

I climbed in the ambulance and crouched down next to the stretcher. Her body was strapped in and machines were attached to her arms. Suzy looked worse with the lights shining on her face. "Sugar, you want me to go with you or follow them?"

"Take my car, City. I don't want it here, please."

I leaned over and kissed her. My heart felt like it was going to explode in my chest. "I got it. I'll be right behind you. Don't worry," I said, not wanting to leave her, but wanting to obey her wishes.

She gave me a weak smile before I climbed out and headed for her car, moving as fast I could to be by her side. I had to beg for her forgiveness, and I prayed her injuries weren't serious. I could never live with myself. I found Suzy's phone lying by her purse, and I knew what I had to do. I dialed Kayden and Sophia and knew there would be hell to pay.

Chapter 20

S uzy

Time seemed to pass in slow motion as a flurry of doctors and nurses poked and prodded me. I repeated the story of what happened so many times I could've recited it in my sleep.

"One more time, ma'am. What happened to you tonight?" the doctor asked as he placed a small light in my eyes.

I sighed and wanted to tell him to fuck off as he moved the light back and forth, momentarily blinding me. "Do I have to say it again? I've told you the story already." My patience was wearing thin.

"I need to make sure you have no memory issues from the blow to your head. Last time, I swear."

"You said that last time we did this." I rolled my eyes.

The doctor snickered. "I guess there's no short-term memory problems."

"My boyfriend and I were at a bar tonight, and I walked out before he did. I thought he was right behind me, and when I unlocked my car someone grabbed me from behind. By the time I realized what was happening, I was already on the ground and tried to fight back, but it was no use. I don't remember much else."

A police officer stood in the corner and scribbled on a little notepad as I spoke.

"I remember waking up in Joey's arms and then the ambulance arriving."

I couldn't give the truth. My boyfriend was supposed to kidnap me as we played out my fantasy for him to abduct me and make me his sex slave. Who did shit like that?

"We're just going to keep you here overnight for observation. You have a couple of bruised ribs, the laceration on your lip, and a concussion, but nothing that will cause long-term damage," the doctor said, staring at his clipboard. "We'll get you into a regular room as soon as possible so you can rest. We will release you in the morning."

"Is anyone here to see me?" I couldn't believe that City hadn't shown up, or anyone for that matter.

"Yes, but he's been instructed to wait outside until we complete your assessment."

"Can he come in now, please?"

My body ached, my face throbbed, and my head pounded from the aftereffects of the attack. I wanted to rest my eyes and turn off the light, but I needed to talk to City. I had to find out what happened, and why he wasn't the one to find me alone in the parking lot.

"Yes, I'll have the nurses talk with him and send him in. I'll see you tomorrow, Ms. McCarthy."

"Thanks," I said with a fake smile. I had nothing to be thankful for. All I wanted to do was crawl in my own bed and sleep against City's body. Crunchy hospital sheets, plastic mattresses, and thin blankets were not my idea of comfortable.

I threw my head back onto the thin pillow, squeezing my eyes shut. I wanted to cry, but I didn't have any tears left.

"Ma'am," the officer said, and cleared his throat. "I've taken down your statement, but I may need more details. We have your attacker in custody and the statement of Joseph Gallo and another gentleman, but we may still need your side to fill in the gaps. Here's my card. Call me when you can talk. It can wait until you're home and more comfortable." He smiled at me, and I could see he was genuine.

"I'll call you, sir. I just don't feel like talking about it anymore tonight." I rubbed my eyes. The lights were making my headache worse, and I wanted to sleep.

"No problem, ma'am."

Drawing back the curtain to leave, I caught a glimpse of City. A frown was visible as he looked at me. I could see the pain on his face. His hands appeared swollen, and red dotted his knuckles—blood from the pounding he must have given to the asshole.

"Hey," he said as he approached my bed.

"Hey yourself."

"Are you okay, sugar?" He sat down on the bed and held my hand.

"I'm okay, City. They're just keeping me for observation." I shrugged.

Touching my cheek with the rough pads of his fingers, he studied my face. His eyes roamed over every inch, stopping on my lips and cheekbone. "God, I'm so sorry, Suzy. It's all my fault." Deep lines appeared on his forehead.

"It wasn't your fault. You meant well. I give you an A for effort, but a D in completion, big boy." I smirked. I couldn't really be mad at him.

"Don't make jokes, sugar." He tried to keep a straight face, but I saw a small smile tug at the corner of his lips. "I could've lost you tonight." He squeezed my hand.

"What happened to you? You were supposed to be only a minute behind me, Joey." Closing my eyes, I remembered the fear I felt when I realized it wasn't City grabbing me from behind.

"I was on my way out of the bar after joking with the guys, but I got held up. I tried to get away as quickly as possible. I didn't want you to be outside alone. I should've never taken you to that bar. Fuck." He rubbed his face, "What happened before I got there, sugar?"

Tears began to fill my eyes as I spoke. I couldn't hold them back. "I pretended to drop my keys when I heard someone behind me. I thought it was you. As I bent down to pick them up, he grabbed me by the hair and knocked me off balance." I paused, trying to steady my voice. "He pulled me by my hair behind the building, and I tried to get free of him. I kicked and screamed, but no one heard me. He hit me in the face and called me names. I could taste the blood in my mouth. I don't remember anything else until I woke up in your arms." I cuddled into City, needing the feeling of safety.

"Shh, sugar. I'll never let anything bad happen to you again." He crawled in the bed and wrapped his arms around me. I cried in his chest until there were no more tears left. He stroked my hair, kissing my head, rocking me until I calmed.

"Where is she?" Sophia's voice woke me from my peaceful slumber. "I don't give a shit, I want to see her now."

Jesus.

"Ma'am, you can't go in there."

The curtain opened in one quick motion, and a scared Sophia appeared. "Oh my God, Suzy. I've been worried sick about you." She rushed to my bedside.

I saw movement out of the corner of my eye—Kayden. He looked pissed. More pissed than I'd ever seen him, and I'd seen him pretty crazy at times over the years.

"I'm okay, Sophia. Just some scrapes and bruises. I'll heal."

"You could've been killed, for shit's sake. And you." She glared at City, pointing at him. "You were supposed to protect her from shit like this. How could you let her go outside alone?"

"It's not his fault," I said, but she held up her hand.

"Well?" she asked.

"City, may I speak to you for a moment?" Kayden asked in a calm voice.

I didn't like pissed-off-looking and calm-sounding Kayden. "You both need to back off," I said.

"Suzy, this is between City and me. I won't keep him long," Kayden said.

I looked at City, silently pleading with him not to go. He squeezed my hand as he slid off the bed. "I'll be right back, don't worry." He gave me a wink and a smile before leaving with Kayden.

"Let the boys talk. What the fuck happened, Suzy?" Sophia sat down next to me, tilting her head before she grabbed my hand. "God, I was out of my mind when City called. This is all my fault."

"It's no one's fault, Sophia. I walked out and everything was going perfectly. I guess City got held up for a second, and that's all it took." I wiped the remaining tears off my cheek. "The same creep had bothered me before and must've been waiting for me. It was stupid to think we could live out that fantasy. It's not as sexy as it sounds anymore."

"Fuck, it's my fault." She hung her head.

"Sophia, why would it be your fault?"

"I kinda told him about your fantasy." She didn't look me in the eyes.

"You did what?"

She stood up and moved out of reach. "When he was doing my tattoo, I told him that you don't like to share your fantasies, and told him about your kidnapping thing you've been dying to live out."

Jesus Christ. "Sophia, I know we're best friends and all, but that was between you, me, and Kayden." I took a deep breath and tried not to be angry. Sophia loved me, and so did Kayden. We always talked about sex, and they were the two people in the world that never judged me. Kayden was the only male that let me pick his brain on the subject, and he answered honestly without making me feel like an idiot. "I'm a little embarrassed here. I thank you for trying to give me what I want, but that was my secret to tell."

"If it would've worked out, he would've knocked your socks off, babe. City is exactly the type of guy you need to be with. Don't let this experience put doubt in that pretty little head of yours. He was a wreck, Suzy. I feel a little shitty now that I got bitchy with him. He really cares for you, my little OCD friend."

I laughed. I always made Sophia insane with all my little quirks and lists. The woman lived life by the seat of her pants, and I wanted everything planned. I had lists for my lists, and I would even include her on my lists when we lived together. "I know he cares, Sophia. I saw the pain in his eyes tonight. I don't think I've ever seen anyone so afraid for me before."

I could hear the murmured voices of Kayden and City but couldn't make out the words. "What is he saying to City?"

"You know Kayden is very protective of you. He's just having a man-to-man."

"I'm not a child, Sophia. Kayden better be nice." I crossed my arms over my chest.

"Kayden's always nice. They're just chatting." She smiled, but I could see the worry on her face.

Life had become so complicated, and my plans seemed to unravel before my eyes. I felt like Sophia on the rollercoaster she experienced when falling in love with Kayden. She put her hands up and screamed through the ride, while I wanted to jump off and keep my feet on the ground.

Chapter 21

City

"How in the fuck could you let her walk outside alone?" Kayden stood toe to toe with me. I didn't blame him—he cared for Suzy.

"Kayden, I know, man. I was supposed to be right behind her. Everything got fucked up." I kept eye contact with him. I wouldn't show weakness, even though I knew the entire thing happened because of Kaylee and my past. My fucking cock always caused trouble.

"Yeah, I'd say. If anything happens to her, City, I'll kick your ass. I may look small compared to you, but I'll crush you. Hear that shit."

I clenched my hands, stopping myself from beating his ass right here in the hospital. I knew he wouldn't hit me. Throwing down with Kayden would only drive a wedge between Suzy and me. I'd let him say his piece. "Got it loud and clear, Kayden. I'll protect her with my life."

"I know you didn't mean for any of it to happen, City, but I expect more." He stepped back. "She's like a sister to me. Just protect her and we won't have an issue. I don't want to be a dick, but I had to tell you that you fucked up."

"I know, and I will, Kayden. I'm happy that you love her and you'll look out for her if I'm not around. I know I fucked up and I'll do everything in my power to make it up to her."

"Are you planning on breaking her heart, man?" He crossed his arms over his chest and stared. "If this shit is just a game to you, then you need to end it now."

"Fuck no, but I don't know where her head is right now." I rubbed my eyes, exhausted from the events of tonight.

"Don't give her a choice, City. She's quick to overthink everything. She needs a little push sometimes."

"I'm happy to show her the way. Are we good, man?" I asked. "I need to get back to her."

"Yeah, we're good." He held out his hand to me.

"Thanks, man." I shook his hand.

I walked through the curtain to the girls whispering on the bed. "Hey, ladies," Kayden said behind me. "Suzy, how are you, love?" He walked in front of me and stood next to her bed.

I stood at the foot of the bed and watched them as they interacted. They were a family, anyone could see that. There was a love and a shared past that brought them together. They chatted as I stood there, transfixed. Suzy looked battered, with bruises and a split lip. It would take forever for the effects to fade from her beautiful face.

"We have a room ready for you," a nurse said as she entered the small space.

"Oh, great," Sophia said. "We better head home, Suzy. Sleep well, and we'll stop by tomorrow to see you." She kissed Suzy on the cheek, and Kayden did the same.

"Night, Suzy." Kayden turned to me. "City, make sure she's okay tonight. Don't leave her alone." He wrapped his arm around Sophia.

"I wouldn't be anywhere else, Kayden."

"I love you guys. City will take good care of me. Go home—Jett will be up soon."

"Bye, love," Sophia said before they walked out.

I sat down next to her as the nurse started to unhook the machines. "Hey, sugar. How are you really feeling?"

"Sore." She winced as she moved her limbs. "Can you find a mirror? I want to see my face."

Oh God. Her face was swollen, with a small amount of dried blood in the corner of her mouth. I didn't want her to see herself all bruised. "I'll find one soon. Wait until you're moved."

"You can follow, sir. We're taking her to the second floor for the night." The nurse removed the brake on the bed as I stood and moved out of the way.

"I'm not leaving her side, ma'am," I said as Suzy laid her head on the pillow and smiled at me. I wouldn't leave her tonight.

The trip to her room was quick, and the nurse left us alone and didn't ask any questions. I sat down in the chair next to her as she yawned. My eyes felt heavy and my mind cloudy.

"Will you sleep up here with me? I mean, there isn't much room, but I want you to hold me tonight. I need you."

How could I say no to anything she asked? I'd stand on my head all night if it made her fucking happy. "Anything you want, sugar." I kicked off my shoes, climbing in the small twin bed before lying on my side, pulling her face to my chest. "Try to sleep. I'm not going anywhere."

The tiny bed was perfect as I cradled her in my arms. She gripped my shirt, resting her face against my shoulder. I enveloped her in my arms, I wanted her to feel safe, and I needed to know that she was okay.

Listening to her breath as she slept, I smelled her hair, but it had the scent of the cigarette smoke from the bar, and dirt. Her body twitched as she whimpered in her sleep. I wanted to crawl inside her dream and rescue her.

I flexed my hands; the stiffness from the bruises and small cuts made me wince. It wasn't anything I hadn't felt before, but I couldn't work for a couple of days until they healed. After pulling my phone from my pocket, I adjusted her body without waking her then sent Anthony a message. My other siblings would be in a panic and the entire crew would be here, but Anthony I could count on to keep the information low key—at least for tonight.

Me: Won't be in tomorrow. Tell Mikey to reschedule my appointments. Thanks, bro.

Anthony had a gig in Clearwater, and he was a sure bet to get the information.

Anthony: I told him, he's with me.

Fuck. Might as well have put it on the evening news or taken out a fucking billboard. Mikey would have a million questions and would want details.

Anthony: What the fuck happened? Not like you to not work.

I didn't want to give them the details, but I had to give enough to get them off my back. I didn't have a fucking choice in the matter. I'd have to cancel dinner with the family. My mother would want to know why—no one got out of dinner without a legitimate excuse. I wanted to stay with Suzy for the weekend and make sure she was okay before I let her be alone.

Me: Situation at the bar tonight. I need to stay with Suzy. Tell Mom I can't make it and clear my schedule for a couple days at least.

Anthony: WTF happened? You okay?

Suzy didn't move as I typed with one hand, trying not to break the embrace.

Me: Beat the shit out of some fucker that attacked her. She's in the hospital for the night and I want to stay with her after she's released. Don't tell anyone. I don't want them to flip out.

Anthony: Gotcha, but Mom is going to want details. Which hospital?

Me: County Hospital, but we're okay. My hands are just swollen. I'll be fine.

Anthony: Gotcha. Mum's the word.

Nothing stayed a secret in my family. It was like the mafia party line. I knew Mikey had probably read over Anthony's shoulder, and soon the entire brigade would be on high alert. I set the phone above my pillow and closed my eyes, wrapping Suzy in my arms.

I tried to think about happy things, Suzy's laugh or how she kissed me, but all I could think of was her limp body and bloodied face in my arms. I kept opening my eyes to remind myself that she was okay. I waited for exhaustion to take me and wipe that vision from my mind.

The sound of plastic squeaking against the tile floor woke me early in the morning. "Sorry, I didn't mean to wake you," a nurse said as she moved to the IV stand.

I grunted and waited for her to leave before closing my eyes again. Hospitals aren't the place for rest. The movement outside the room is constant, alarms and announcements echo through the halls, and people talk loud enough to wake the dead. I felt like a Mack truck had hit me. My back was stiff, my eyes burned, and my hands throbbed. I wanted to get the fuck out of here and crawl in a real bed with her.

A quiet knock caused Suzy to stir, and my mother stood in the doorway. Fucking brothers—always mama's boys.

"Hey," she said, smiling.

I held put my finger to my lips, hoping not to wake Suzy as my ma entered the room. "It's early, Ma. What are you doing here?" I whispered.

"Your brother told me something happened and that you were here with Suzy. You know I can't sleep good when I worry about my children." She stood next to the bed, looking at Suzy's face against my chest.

"I'm fine, Ma. I couldn't leave her and I want to stay with her when she gets out for a couple days. I didn't think Mikey would put out an all-points bulletin."

"Always so quick to blame Michael, aren't you, Joseph? It was Anthony that texted me. I just wanted to stop and see if you two were okay." She shook her head at me.

When did my mother learn how to text?

"We will be as soon as we get out of this shithole."

"What happened, son?" My mom pulled up a chair and waited for my answer.

"Someone assaulted her. When I found her, I kicked his ass." I didn't want to meet my mother's eyes. She was the only person in the world I never wanted to disappoint. I wasn't a mama's boy, but in an Italian family a mother is the queen bee, top dog, and wore the pants. Even my father bowed down to her and cherished the ground she walked on. He wasn't a pussy, and could kick ass in his youth, but Mrs. Gallo wasn't a person any of us wanted to piss off. "Trust me, Ma, he looks worse than me."

She wrinkled her nose; she never liked to think of any of her children fighting, even Mikey. "Where were you?"

"Neon Cowboy, and we were on our way out after having a couple drinks." I definitely didn't want to share that I'd planned to kidnap my girlfriend. Sex wasn't something I talked to my mother about, and usually not even my father.

"I told you I hate that damn bar. There's nothing but trouble in those types of places. Haven't you learned anything from Thomas?" She wasn't mad, but I could see the fear in her eyes.

"Yes, Ma. I have friends there, clients even, and I like it there. I'm not going to stop hanging out there because of the what-ifs."

"Is she okay, son?" She peeked over my shoulder, her eyes growing wide as she took in the sight of Suzy's face.

"Yeah, she'll heal. Just waiting for the doctor to come and release her. I won't be there Sunday, but I promise to be there next week."

"Sure, baby. Can I drop off food, at least? That way you can spend time taking care of her without having to cook."

How could I say no to my mother? When she offered food it was the highest honor. She lived to cook and take care of her family. If I said no, it would be an enormous insult and there would be hell to pay.

"Sure, Ma. I'd love if you'd stop by with some food." I didn't entirely mean that statement, but I knew it would make her happy.

"I'm going to go and let you two rest. I don't want to wake her. I'll call you later, Joseph." She stood up and kissed my forehead. She was the only person in the world that I'd let treat me like a child. No matter how many times I told her I wasn't, she just made it all the more unbearable, smothering me with her love.

"Okay, Ma. Thanks."

"I love you, Joseph. Take care of that one."

"Love you too, Ma."

She walked out of the room and I ran my fingers over the bruises on Suzy's face. They were brighter in color and more visible than they had been the night before. She began to stir at my touch, and her eyes opened. The side crinkled from the smile on her face.

"You stayed?"

"Where else would I go, sugar?"

She closed her eyes and made a sound like "I don't know" as she smashed her face in my chest and inhaled. "Can we get out of here?"

"I'll go see if I can get the doctor to discharge you. Let me get up."

She winced as I helped her move out of my arms and climbed off the bed. "You're going to spend all day in bed when I get you out of here."

"Oooh, that sounds so sexy." She laughed and held her side.

"Bad girl, you're injured—rest only." I was happy to see that her spirit hadn't vanished with the attack. "Be right back or I'll break you out of this joint."

I found a nurse sitting at a desk and pleaded with her to process the paperwork quicker than normal. "You can help her get dressed to speed up the process if you'd like, sir," the nurse said as she typed.

"Sure, we'll be waiting, ma'am." I returned to the room to find Suzy trying to climb out of bed. "What the hell are you doing?" I said, rushing to her side.

"I needed to pee." She looked up at me with a shy, embarrassed smile.

"I'll help you, sugar. Then we got to get you dressed."

"Fine. I hate having to need help to walk, City. This is a little ridiculous."

"It's what I'm here for. You're mine and I'm going to take care of you this weekend. No arguments. Got it?" I waited for her reply before taking her hand.

"Yes, sir. I'm yours for the weekend. I thought it would be a bit different, but..." She shrugged.

"Makes two of us. Come on, sweetheart." I helped her to the bathroom and then grabbed her clothes. I hit them a couple times to get the dirt off before she dressed.

"I need a shower," she said as she hobbled out of the bathroom.

"I'll help you as soon as we get you home."

"You're the boss."

I liked the sound of those words coming out of her mouth. I wouldn't take any lip from her this weekend. She was mine.

Chapter 22

Suzy

I settled in my bed, thankful to be home, and watched City as he undressed. I'd never been with a man that I couldn't stop staring at. I wanted the image etched in my brain. His muscular build flexed as he took off his pants. The tattoos on his torso and arms moved, and I was mesmerized as if watching a movie. I ached to tug on the bar that hung from his nipple, salivated to taste his flesh, and shivered at the thought of him inside me.

He kicked his pants in the air and caught them. "Don't look at me like that, sugar." His shaft bobbed, catching my attention; my mouth suddenly felt dry.

I blinked and looked at his face. "Like what? I was just thinking about how skilled you are at catching your pants." I giggled.

"You just looked at my dick in a way that makes me want to jam it down your throat." He grinned at me, and even though my face hurt, I wanted nothing more than for him to do that to me. "Not today, sugar."

"Tomorrow?" I raised my eyebrows, hoping that I could entice him, or at least get a promise of something before the weekend ended.

"We'll see. I decide when and how. What can I get you?"

"Your cock." I knew when I said dirty words that he couldn't resist me. If he continued to deny me, I sure as hell wouldn't make it easy on him.

He rubbed his face and muttered something I couldn't quite make out. "Want something to drink or eat?"

He stood there, buck-naked and mouth-wateringly delicious, and waited for my answer. How could I think of water when his beautiful body was on full display? I shook my head and patted the mattress with a crooked smile.

"Tomorrow, sugar."

A pout hung on my lips, but inside I was happy to at least get a concession. "Good enough. I don't have anything in the fridge, City. I didn't think I'd be here much this weekend." Admitting to an Italian man that you lacked even the staples in your pantry wasn't easy.

"My mother wants to drop off food later. Are you okay with that?"

"Really?" My mother had never brought me food, even when I had the flu. I always fended for myself, even if it meant crawling to the kitchen to grab a glass of water. His mother, a woman I'd never met, would bring me food, and I had a twinge of jealousy. What would it have been like to grow up in a house like his?

"I can call her anytime and she'll drop something off. You just say the word."

"Word, word, word! Does your mom use Ragu like mine?" My mother never cooked from scratch. As a child I thought Chef Boyardee was the bee's knees, until I grew up and realized it was closer to vomit in a can.

City laughed, and his smile made my chest ache. "Don't even mention the word Ragu to her. She'll have a mental breakdown."

"Good to know," I said. "Remind me to never cook for her, okay?"

City grabbed his phone as he crawled in bed. "Hey, Ma. Suzy's going to rest for a bit, but we'd love for you to drop by with some food." I could hear her talking on the phone, and it reminded me of Charlie Brown's teacher. I couldn't make out the words, but I heard a garbled voice as I put my head on his chest. I played with the piercing, which earned me a stern look. "I'll text you her address. Thanks, Ma."

He put the phone down and stared at me, but I just smiled. "What?" I asked innocently.

"You must've hit your head harder than I thought."

"Maybe." I kissed his nipple, tugging on the hoop with my lips. He inhaled sharply as I bit down.

"Sugar, not now. I'm trying to be real good here, and you're not in any shape right now to do the things to you I want. Later, when you've rested and had something to eat, I'll give you more than you can handle...if I feel you're up to it."

"Party killer," I said, as I laid my head back down in the crook of his arm.

"Be a good girl and sleep." His fingertips trailed down my back, leaving a wake of warmth against my skin. I closed my eyes and enjoyed the feel of his hands on me, even if it wasn't the way I wanted.

I didn't know how long I slept, but when I woke up, I was alone in the bed. His side was still warm. My muscles rebelled and ached as I stretched. "Damn," I whispered, wanting to move without pain.

The doorbell rang and my heart started to pound—his mother. I didn't look presentable, and my face had to be a mess. I'd stared at it in horror this morning at the hospital. This wasn't the way I wanted to meet his mom.

I could hear them talking in the kitchen. The door cracked open and I turned my head, praying it was City. "Hey, sugar, ma's here. Do you want to meet her?"

"I look like crap, City. I can't have her see me like this."

He sat down next to me. "Sugar, she was at the hospital this morning. She's seen your face. She's not going to stare at you."

I sighed. "You didn't tell me."

"Sorry. Come on, just a quick hello. She made you lasagna." He brushed the hair away from my face, following the curve of my cheek.

I'd do anything this man asked me to. A smile, touch, or kiss and I was totally and utterly his. "Let me get dressed and I'll come out."

Meeting parents always scared me to death, and it meant a step deeper into a relationship. His mother obviously loved her son enough to bring us food, and I wanted to at least thank her for her kindness.

I looked into the mirror, touched the stitching on my lip with my tongue, noticing the coppery taste of blood. There was no need to bother with makeup. I couldn't look any worse than I did, and if she liked me now then I'd knock her socks off when she saw me at my best. Dressed in my favorite hoodie and sweats, I walked out to meet Mrs. Gallo.

"There she is," City said, standing from the couch with a smile plastered on his face.

Mrs. Gallo stood up and turned around. Her face was lit up and she looked like the mom I always wanted. She had long, wavy brown hair, big brown eyes, and a kind smile. "Suzy, it's so nice to finally meet you," she said as she wrapped her arms around me. "I'm sorry for how we're meeting, sweetheart. How are you feeling?"

"Thank you, Mrs. Gallo, I'm feeling much better." I moved to sit next to City, and grabbed his hand. "Thank you for making me lasagna. It's one of my favorites."

"My pleasure. Food always helps make everything better," she said.

"Italian motto," City muttered, and I laughed.

"I'm going to get going now and leave you two kids to enjoy your food. I just wanted to say hello. Is there anything else I can do before I leave?"

"No, ma'am, you've done more than I can ask for."

"Mrs. G or Maria, please. You need anything, just have Joseph call me."

"Joseph." I laughed. It sounded so serious, and fit him well.

"Watch it," he said in a playful tone, and squeezed my hand.

We all stood and hugged his mother goodbye. We walked to the door and watched her leave. I pictured her climbing into a minivan, even though she didn't have small children. I never pegged her for a woman that drove a Mercedes. I dreamed of a new Honda and knew it would be a budget killer...maybe someday.

"Your mom is great," I said as I wrapped my arm around his waist.

"She can be, but she's a pit bull when you cross her—just ask my father," he said. "Want some lasagna?"

"What's for dessert?" I asked as he closed the door.

"Anything you want, sugar."

"You know what I want," I said.

"Are you up to it?"

"Question is, big boy, are you up to it?" I wanted him, and I figured that if I challenged his manhood, he'd finally cave. All men are the same in that regard.

He laughed. "Don't ask questions if you can't handle hearing the answer. Eat your food and I'll show you how up to it I am, sugar."

He placed a giant piece of lasagna with cheese oozing out in front of me. My stomach growled at the smell, and the feeling of hunger finally registered. I cut into the slice and watched all the insides squish onto my plate. The hot lasagna spread across my tongue, and I wanted to moan from the taste.

"That good, huh?" City asked as he scooped a chunk in his mouth.

"What? Did I?"

"Yep, you moaned, sugar."

My face became heated. "Well, I'm used to Stouffer's lasagna. This is amazing, City. You don't know how lucky you were to grow up on this type of home cooking." I slid the fork across my tongue and slowly chewed, letting all the flavors dance on my tongue.

"I never thought about it." His fork stopped near his mouth as he looked at me with piercing eyes. "Suzy, you keep making noises like that and I won't let you finish the next bite." He set the fork on his plate and leaned back.

"I need my fuel to get better." I placed another sliver in my mouth, closed my eyes, and made a small sound in the back of my throat.

"You have thirty seconds to finish what's in front of you before I take your ass in the bedroom and give you something to really moan about." He crossed his arms over his chest and looked at his watch.

I shoveled the food in my mouth. I felt torn in this moment, but the lasagna could always be reheated.

"Fifteen." He smiled at me, and I felt everything in my body convulse and scream to be touched. I chewed like a maniac.

"Five."

"Wait!" I held up my hand. "I need something to drink," I said as I hopped off the high-top café chair.

"I got something for you to wash that down with, sugar. Time's up."

"Slower, Suzette," City said in my ear as he rocked in and out of me. "It's not a marathon. I want to savor being inside you."

"I've just missed you. Missed this."

"We have the rest of the weekend. I don't want to hurt you. Slow." He grabbed my hips and held me still as he slowed his pace. I wanted to scream and claw him, but I knew it wouldn't help to fight him.

He rested his forehead against mine as he encased my body and assaulted my senses. This was more than just sex. He expressed his feelings, and I felt them seep into my body. I stared in his eyes as he stared into mine before he kissed my lips. The pain of the kiss didn't stop me from returning it with fervor.

My fingers dug into his shoulders and I felt them flex under my touch. Each thrust brought me closer to the release I craved. His breathing grew harsh as he curled his arms under my body, tilting my hips.

My hands rested on his hips, unable to reach his ass, as I felt them relax and constrict with each thrust. I wished I had a mirror to watch his ass and back as he moved with my body. I squeezed the soft skin and hard muscle as the orgasm tore through my body. It was stronger than anything I had felt before. My toes curled and my muscles clenched around him as his pace quickened, before he slammed into me one last time, reaching his own bliss.

He nuzzled my neck and kissed the soft skin, making a trail to my lips. "I don't know what I would've done if something happened to you, sugar."

I ran my fingers through his hair and pulled his face to mine, forcing his eyes to see me. "I'm fine, Joey. You saved me." I kissed him and didn't give him a chance to respond. He flipped us over, and I straddled his body before breaking the kiss.

"No more fantasies that don't involve me by your side, but I still want to make them come true."

"I'm looking forward to it." I smiled against his chest as I kissed the skin over his heart. I listened to his heart thud in his chest. I had never felt so content with any person, let alone a man.

City spent the rest of the weekend helping me. Even though it started rocky, it ended with me feeling more loved and adored than I ever had. I couldn't deny my feelings for him any longer. My checklist no longer mattered. He showed me that he would take care of me and treat me in the way I'd always wanted. My doubts about if he was the "one" had vanished, and were replaced by a fate that had been sealed.

Chapter 23

C ity

"Yes, sir, how can I help you?" the older lady at the reception desk asked. She leaned forward and rested her head on her hands.

I gave her my devilish grin and a wink. "I'm here to see Ms. McCarthy, ma'am."

"Oh, please, call me Kathy." She batted her eyelashes. "You're here to see Suzy?" She looked surprised, and her voice ended on a screechy high note. Her eyes no longer looked at my face, but traveled down my arms.

"Yes, I'm here to see Suzy, Kathy." I arched my eyebrow as she soaked me in, undressing me with her eyes. She looked like a nice enough lady, but I didn't like how she said Suzy's name, and I certainly didn't particularly enjoy the fantasy she must be having in her head. I cleared my throat, needing to pull her out of her lust-induced haze.

She blushed as she started fumbling with papers at her desk. She asked me for my identification and to sign the visitor's log. The school day had ended, but a few students milled around the receptionist area. I could feel their eyes on me. I wanted to laugh, but didn't want to be a total asshole.

Kathy gave me directions to Suzy's classroom in the next build-ing. I needed to make sure she was okay on her first day back to work since the attack. I was sure she'd had to explain the injuries to her face over and over again. People could be fucking merciless.

I checked the sign on the door, and it read "101 — Ms. McCarthy's Class." The large classroom had tables set up in neat rows, with cabinets lining the opposite wall. There was no chalkboard in the room like there had been when I was a kid, but a dry-erase board hung on the wall. Math problems that made my fucking head spin were written on the shiny white surface.

I didn't see anyone, but could hear voices talking from an at-tached room.

"I'm fine. Stop it," Suzy said. I picked up my pace to find out what the fuck was going on.

Entering the small office space, I saw Suzy pinned against the wall with Derek cutting off her escape. She looked like she wanted to become one with the wall and couldn't move farther away from his body. Her eyes grew wide as I reached for the prick and grabbed him by the shirt collar.

"What the fu—" he said, his eyes traveling to my face.

"The lady said stop. I think we've already had this conversation once before, dumbfuck." We were nose to nose, and I'd knock the motherfucker out.

"Suzy didn't mean it," he snarled.

He sure had a pair of brass balls, but my fists were made of platinum. I fisted his pansy-ass dress shirt, pulling his body to mine. "She's mine, you fucker, and when the lady says stop it she means stop and back the fuck up."

"I should've had your ass arrested the first time you hit me. Hit me again and I'll call school security."

"Need someone else to fight your battles, sissy boy? You pick on girls, but can't handle a man all on your own?"

Suzy had tears in her eyes as I looked at her over his head.

"Listen here, buddy, I don't know who you fuck think you are, but Suzy and I have a thing. She's not yours. Right, Suzy?"

She began to shake her head as her eyes grew wide. He turned his head to look at her, and I couldn't hold back my fist any longer. I punched him right in the jaw and watched the spit and blood fly out of his mouth. Served the bastard right. I held him upright with my grip as he wobbled on shaky knees and his eyes watered.

If we weren't in her office at a school, I'd beat the piss out of the motherfucker. He deserved to be taught a harsher lesson than one simple fist to the face, but I had to tamper down my anger for Suzy's sake.

I let go of him with a shove and watched him stumble before catching himself on her desk. "I'll have you arrested for this." He wiped the blood from his lip with the back of his hand and glared at me.

"I'll share the little tidbit with security. I'll tell them how I walked in on you sexually harassing Ms. McCarthy in her office. I heard her to telling you stop. Who do you think she's gonna back, asshole? You've touched her for the last time. Do it again and I'll bury you."

Suzy walked to my side and put her arm around me. "Derek, you mention a word and I'll make sure they fire your ass. I'll have no problem telling them about this and the other times." Smiling at me, she squeezed my waist. "I have Joseph and Sophia to back me up. Sophia knows all about you and your bullshit." Did she use two swear words in that speech? That's my girl, I thought as I beamed with pride.

"You wouldn't?" he asked, smoothing out his shirt, wiping the last bit of blood tricking down his chin.

"Try me, Derek," she snarled, showing the slightest hint of teeth.

"I'd put my money on the blonde." I smirked at the jackass as he stormed out of the room. "You okay, Suzy?" I asked, wrapping her in my arms.

She squeezed my waist and buried her face in my shirt. "Mm, you smell good."

"Answer me, sugar. Are you okay?" I kissed the top of her head.

"Yeah, I'm fine. Derek's an asshole. I don't think he'll be bothering me again." She laughed into my chest.

"I don't want you working with that dick anymore."

"I think he almost peed his pants."

"Promise me, Suzette? You need to go to the administration about him. He shouldn't work here or be near you."

She patted my stomach. "I love when you get all tough guy and use my full name." She laughed, and I squeezed her ass hard enough to make her jump. "I promise, Joseph."

"You seem to like it when I'm buried balls deep inside you, sugar, I don't hear you laughing then," I whispered in her ear. She shivered in my arms as the vibrations of my words touched her ears. "Why don't we put your desk to good use?"

She smacked me in the chest, but I could see the twinkle in her eye. She thought about it for a second before she answered. "No way, mister. I'm not getting fired."

"I thought maybe you went all bad girl on me, using all those curse words on Derek." I ran my finger over her bruise, but she didn't flinch.

"Two? I swore twice?" Her mouth hung open.

"You did, sugar. I'm proud of you."

"You must be rubbing off on me." She pulled away from my arms and smiled.

"Speaking of rubbin'." I looked down, wiggled my eyebrows, and moved my hips.

"Absolutely not." She looked away and started to move the papers on her desk.

I wrapped my arms around her and placed my face in her hair. "Whatcha gonna do, baby, give me a detention?" I asked. I couldn't help but laugh. God, if she was my teacher in high school I would've been all over her. My wet dreams would've been filled with visions of Ms. McCarthy leaning over my desk to help me with my math problems. I'd pray that her blouse would just happen to fall open and give me a glimpse of her beautiful tits.

She smacked my hands. "You're a naughty boy."

"You have no idea, Ms. McCarthy." I kissed down her neck, making my way to her shoulder before sinking my teeth into her delicate flesh. "You've smacked me twice, and I think I need to teach you a little lesson tonight." Her breath caught, and I heard a small moan escape as I ground my dick into her ass.

"Whatcha got in mind, Mr. Gallo?"

"I'm going to make sure you know you're mine." I cupped her breasts, squeezing them, and ran my palms across her hard nipples. "I'm going to fuck you so damn hard my cock will be the only one you'll ever think about. I'm leaving no inch untouched, no pore not kissed, and no hole unfilled."

"Um." She swallowed loud enough for me to hear. Perfect.

"Lost for words?"

"Not here," she whispered as she closed her eyes.

"My place, sugar. I don't want anyone to hear you scream when you think you can't come again, but I'll make you."

"Your punishment sounds so much better than detention."

"It's more like a retention program for at-risk little girls," I said as she turned around with a smile on her face.

"You know how to win a girl's heart." She stood on her tiptoes and kissed me.

I smacked her ass and she bit down on my lip, but not hard enough to break the skin.

"Oh, sorry, baby," she said.

"I'll get ya back, sugar. Let's get the fuck out of here or I'm tearing your clothes off right here." I pinched her nipple and felt her sharp intake of breath against my lips.

I needed to get the hell out of the school and take her to my bed. I kissed her goodbye after walking her to her car. I walked to my bike on the opposite side of the parking lot after she drove away. It would be hard as fuck to ride with the raging hard-on in my pants—I needed the walk to cool the fuck off.

Chapter 24

Suzy

Ruined. It was the only word that came to mind when I thought of Joseph Gallo, a.k.a. City McPierced Cock. He'd ruined me for any other man that could've had a place in my future. How could I go back to a boring anybody with a party pickle penis when I had Joey Sex God Gallo?

Joey made me scream in ecstasy; he'd been the first man I didn't have to fake it with. His voice alone made my skin break out in goose bumps, his kiss made the world vanish, and his cock—well, it was just damn unique and felt fucking amazing.

The idea of punishment didn't sound terrible coming out of his mouth. Anyone else and I would've run for the hills, but not City—he made my body feel like it was on fire. I wanted him to claim every inch of my body. What girl wouldn't want all the pleasure that would involve? I'd be an idiot not to want it.

I studied his body as he drove ahead of me on his sexy-ass Harley. I could see him watching me at the stoplights, and I never wanted the man to have eyes for another woman. He was everything I wanted, but never thought to include in my life plan. His muscles moved underneath his shirt as he hugged the road and gripped the bike. My mind kept replacing my body with the bike as we made our way to his house.

He became an addiction. He didn't ruin just my body, but he found a way to make himself a part of my life in a very short time. He invaded my dreams, and every thought I had involved him.

Watching him reminded me of the first time I saw him. I thought he would murder me on that country road. He looked mean and dangerous, but the only casualty would be my heart. Did I love him? It was a strong word to use in such a short amount of time. Could I go without him? Hell. No. Did I want him in my life? Damn straight. Love was a word I reserved for very few people in my life, and I wouldn't mess this up, no matter how fantastic his cock moved and how hard he made me scream. Love would come someday if he didn't fuck me to death first. Death by dick. Didn't sound half bad.

By the time we pulled into his driveway, my body buzzed with anticipation. It had been less than twenty-four hours since City had been inside me, but this felt...different. Turning the car off, I stared at him as he climbed off the bike and removed his helmet. He approached my car—his movement was like a lion stalking its prey—and I felt my cheeks flush with excitement. He looked handsome. Uniquely perfect.

His beauty wasn't only external. He had that nailed at first glance, but internally he was Prince Charming. Nobody had ever treated me like he did. He had just the right amount of caveman and Casanova to be destructive to a girl's mind—particularly mine.

"Come on, sugar. If I have to wait any longer, I'll fuck you right here in the driveway."

Although his words held promise, I'd never had sex outdoors; I wasn't ready to check that off my bucket list. Grabbing his hand, I followed him inside the small white farmhouse. I kicked off my shoes, and he grabbed me and pushed me against the wall.

His soft, wet lips crushed against mine as I gasped, and his tongue took that as an open invitation. "I can't decide which part of your body to assault first." His tongue slowly glided across my bottom lip. My heart pounded in my chest and he had to feel the rapid pace of the thump. "Do I start with this pretty little mouth?" He nipped my lip, causing a small moan to escape with the thought of my tongue wrapped around his cock. "Do I use this in your tight little cunt or your beautiful, tight ass?" He squeezed my ass, and I could feel his hardness against my stomach. I thought about all the ways he could and would take me, and a tingle ran down my spine.

"Perfect choice. Your mouth it is…to start." His eyes crinkled from the smile on his face. Fuck, I didn't make a choice.

"What? Wait."

"Not your decision. Watching you suck that lip in your mouth makes my cock ache to feel your tongue tugging at my piercing. On your knees, sunshine." The use of the nickname from our first meeting, when my world changed forever, made my insides warm.

Placing his hand on my shoulder, he pushed me on my knees, and I came face to face with his giant bulge. This time I knew what I would see, but it didn't dull the excitement I felt. Reaching up to unzip his pants, I peered at his face. The grin playing on his lips and the twinkle in his eye made my core pulse. His shaft bobbed and brought my attention back to the task at hand: sucking his beautiful cock and bringing him to his knees.

I unzipped his pants and began the task of unleashing his hardness. I rarely felt in control when City had me naked, but I felt empowered kneeling before him. Springing free, the tip glistened with a drop of moisture. My mouth watered as I palmed his cock, squeezing it, feeling the heaviness and hardness of his silky-smooth erection in my hands. I licked the tip, capturing the wetness on my tongue before taking him fully in my mouth. I loved the feel of the piercing, and every time I brought the tip back to my lips, I'd run my tongue over the metal, giving it a light tug. His body quaked with each thrust and pull. His fingers tangled in my hair. He gripped it roughly, trying to control my movement and depth.

I ignored his grip, welcoming the pain as I controlled the depth and speed. "Fuck, sugar, your mouth feels amazing." I squeezed his ass and felt a shudder take over his body. Pulsing my grip, I sucked harder and quickened my pace, and I squeezed my legs together, trying to relieve the ache. He moaned and twitched, and I could almost taste how close he was to losing it. I focused my effort on the tip of his cock, running my tongue along the underside, flicking the sensitive flesh and capturing the ring between my lips as I worked his length. "Fuck," he moaned, and he increased the grip on my hair. "Stop, sugar."

Screw that. I wouldn't stop until his body shook, he screamed my name, and I milked him dry. I grazed his shaft with my teeth and he hissed. "Fuck." I didn't stop in my relentless pursuit of his release. I watch his face as I sucked and licked like a starved woman on a mission—his eyes were closed, head tipped back, and mouth open. I gripped his ass with both hands, digging my fingernails in his skin, taking him fully in my mouth, hitting the back of my throat. I swallowed and tried not to gag. I clamped down on his cock as a moan escaped his lips, driving me forward, seeking the moment he'd say my name.

The feel of his rock-hard ass beneath my fingers, flexing and twitching, made me crazy. I wanted him, wanted to feel him inside me, but I wouldn't stop what I started. I felt in charge for once.

"Suzette," he hissed as my mouth filled with his release.

When his body stopped shaking and his cock stopped pulsating, I released him. I grinned at him, with his wide eyes looking at me with adoration. Swallowing, I licked my lips and captured a small drop seeping from the tip. His eyes had a twinkle in them as he watched me.

"You don't fight fair, sugar," he said with a shaky voice as he kicked off his jeans.

"I didn't see you stopping me," I said, pushing off the floor. He reached out, grabbed my neck, and pulled me to him, as he crushed his lips to mine.

He felt soft and warm. I wrapped my arms around his neck and soaked in the feel of his hands gripping my waist. He pulled my legs around his waist and I wrapped my arms around his neck, wanting the connection. We moved as one toward the bedroom where we'd begun weeks ago—my life hadn't been the same.

He leaned over the bed, but my body stayed attached to him like Velcro. "It's your turn to scream my name, sugar." He unlatched my hands from his neck, placing them at my side. "Don't move." He smirked as he moved down my body, running his finger across the exposed skin of my stomach from the bunching of my shirt.

His touch felt like electricity, a tingling sensation spreading throughout my body as he traced around my belly button. "Elastic?"

The word pulled me back into reality after I'd been lost in my dreamlike state.

"What?" I could barely think, let alone form a coherent sentence.

"You're wearing pants with an elastic waistband." He eyed them with curiosity. "Never met a girl that wore dress pants like these." His fingers grabbed the waistband and released it, snapping it against my skin.

Oh, shit. I had my granny panties on too. I didn't think I'd see him today. I just wanted to be comfortable, since I walked into a barrage of questions about the bruises and busted lip. I covered my eyes. "They're comfortable," I said as I swatted his hand.

He raised an eyebrow at me as he looked the material. "I'm sure. I think that's why my mom wears them too." His chest rumbled with a hearty laugh.

"Fuck off, City." I chuckled, kicking him with my foot.

"Watch the goods, princess." He grabbed my foot as I made another. "I have a fighter on my hands." He gripped the bottom of my pants and gave them a hard yank, exposing my underwear. Fuck. "You're full of surprises today, sugar," he said.

"Hello... didn't think I'd be seeing you today."

"Guess not, based on your attire." Smug bastard.

"This is who I am, City. I'm not a floozy and I don't like a string up my ass all day while I teach."

"Oh no, it's sexy. The best part about you is that you're not a floozy. Makes me feel special that you break out the sexy shit just for me."

"Well, since it's sexy, then I can stop with all the lingerie when I see you." I giggled. I'd never do it, but if he wanted to pretend it was a turn-on...

"I don't give a fuck what you wear, sugar, as long as you end up naked."

I didn't want to be the granny-panty-wearing girlfriend to the hot biker. I wouldn't change what worked. I'd wear my sexy lacy shit when I saw him, but maybe, just maybe, I'd throw him for a loop with innocent little pink flowers every once in a while. "You going to shut up and fuck me or sit here yapping about clothing all night?" I snapped.

"Oooh, I got a feisty one on my hands tonight." He moved his body as he covered mine before settling between my legs.

"You got a horny one that just sucked you off. She deserves a reward, and I can think of a million other things you can do with your lips than talk," I said, running my tongue across his bottom lip.

Lust filled his eyes as he tugged at my lips with his teeth. He pulled his shirt over his head as he balanced on one arm. I'd never get tired of seeing his body.

His fingers wrapped around the side of my underwear before he ripped them from my body with one quick jerk. "Hey," I yelled.

"I won't be buying you new ones, so don't ask." He laughed before nestling between my legs and licking his lips. The need I felt for him never waned like I'd experienced with other men—it only intensified.

I closed my eyes as his mouth closed around me and his tongue flicked my clit. The heat of his mouth made me melt into the mattress. I gripped the sheets, needing something to hold on to keep my body firmly planted. He didn't rush as he caressed and sucked every fold and inch of my core. I looked down, wanting to catch a glimpse of his beautiful face between my legs, and I was met with his blue eyes staring at me. His eyes didn't leave mine as he brought my body to the point of release. My body glistened as every muscle tensed.

"Please," I moaned. I was wound so tight; I sat at the tipping point and needed just a little bit more to tip me over the edge. I released the sheets and pinched my nipple between my fingers, rolling it back and forth. His eyes grew wide as he watched my fingers move against my skin.

The orgasm ripped through me, stopping my breath; I was paralyzed through the explosion of sensations. He moaned and lapped at my body as I screamed something that wasn't audible to my ears. My heart thundered in my chest as I tried to catch my breath. I opened my eyes to a very happy looking man.

"Sexy as fuck, sugar. Watching you touch yourself, coming on my tongue, and babbling all kinds of incoherent shit—priceless. You made me hard again. I want to feel you come on my cock."

City ripped open the condom wrapper before settling between my legs. The piercing nudged my insides, causing my body to tighten. I felt the pressure building inside my core as he pumped inside of me. He cradled my ass with his hand, and my world exploded around him—and he followed me over the edge.

Multiple orgasms had always been a myth, something I read about in books, but with him they were a reality. What had started as a journey of lust and carnal exploits had now turned into something more. I saw the man behind the muscles, tattoos, and piercings, and I didn't want to let him go. I didn't want to be Suzy Q, the goody two-shoes anymore. I wanted to be a woman that could let her hair down and be who I wanted instead of what everyone expected.

I wanted to do something that I'd enjoy, or at least I hoped I would. City would freak out if I told him what I had planned. I kept it a secret. I contacted Mikey to see if he'd help me pull it off.

Chapter 25

City

There was a chill in the air as I walked toward the doors of Inked. Fall rolled into winter in Florida, and that meant cold nights and days that felt like the Chicago of my childhood. It was a nice change, but I craved the warmth of summer on my bike instead of the coolness that stung my skin.

I pushed the door open to see an empty shop desk as the bell above the door chimed. Mikey wasn't at his usual post to greet me, like he had been for more fucking mornings than I could count. I could hear a female voice and Mikey whispering from the piercing room in the back of the shop.

I put my ear to the door to listen to their conversation, but the voices grew quiet. I knocked. "Hey, can I come in?"

"In a minute," Mikey yelled. "Kind of got my hands full." I heard laughing as I walked away.

I checked my schedule for the day and listened to the voicemail messages. My first appointment called to cancel due to the flu, so I had some extra time. I kicked back on the couch and sent Suzy a message. Last night I'd left her exhausted in bed before making my way home. We'd been spending almost evening together and usually never slept apart. The poor thing, I had been exhausting her with middle-of-the-night sex. She'd asked me if it was okay to sleep apart for a night and I agreed, although not happily. I understood, but I didn't fucking like it. The boner I woke up with this morning could've used some attention, but I did what needed to be done.

Me: Morning, beautiful. Sleep well?

I felt like a pussy-whipped fool, but for once I didn't mind feeling that way.

Suzy: Not really. I missed you in bed.

I smiled, knowing she felt the same. Never in a million fucking years would I have thought that I'd find love again in my life. Joni's sudden death had left me raw and reeling, not wanting to ever experience that hurt again. Suzy had changed that.

Me: Move in with me?

Did I really just type that shit? We'd been together only a couple of months, but I'd been with enough women in my life to know when it was right. I thought I'd get a quick response, but nothing. I was a fucking moron. I'd probably just scared her away.

The hinges on the door creaked as Mikey poked his head out. "Yo, bro. Wanna come see my handiwork?" He looked a little too happy for this time of morning.

"Who you working on off books?" There wasn't a name on his schedule before ten.

"Special request. Get your lazy ass up and come look, you prick." His head disappeared, and I could hear a hushed conversation.

"Mikey, I've seen every piercing out there." I climbed off the couch to make my brother happy, because he'd harp on me like a bitch in heat for the rest of the day. Plus, he could kick my ass if I didn't.

"What's so special about this one?" I asked as I walked in the room and stopped dead in my tracks.

What the fuck?

Sitting in the chair was Suzy, my Suzy, with her breast exposed and a small metal hoop through her nipple. I couldn't breathe as I stood there staring with my mouth hanging open. Mikey looked excited and proud of himself, but I wanted to rip his fucking throat out—fighter or not.

Suzy had a sly grin on her face. "You like?" she asked.

Should I be happy or pissed? I blinked, but I couldn't fucking respond. My brother had his hands all over my woman, even if it was for my benefit, and I wasn't there to supervise.

"Earth to City," Mikey said, and I swear to fucking Christ I wanted to knock his happy ass out of the chair.

"You don't like it, do you?" She frowned at me, and her eyes began to glisten.

"Oh no, sugar. It's beautiful. Sexy as fuck, actually." I grabbed her chin and kissed her. "I'll have fun tugging on it like you do mine. It feels amazing."

"You scared the crap out of me. Are you mad?" she asked as I rested my forehead against hers and stared in her eyes.

"I'm not mad. A little pissed my brother had his paws on your gorgeous tits and that you didn't let me be here for it." I turned my head and gave my brother a scathing look.

"Hey, seen one breast, you've seen them all. It's work, bro."

Dickhead.

"I wanted to surprise you, Joey."

"Well you fucking did that in spades, sugar." I kissed her forehead and inspected the piercing closely. "Next time you touch my woman, I get to be here, brother. Got me?"

"Got ya. I swear to God it was all for you. Get that stick out of your ass and look how well it turned out. She has the perfect nipples for piercings."

Did he just fucking say that to my face?

"Mikey, watch it."

"I look at it as another body part to be decorated. Chill the fuck out. I know she's yours."

"As long as we're clear on that fact."

"Crystal." He stood to leave.

"Mikey," I said, stopping him in his tracks. "I wouldn't trust her in anyone else's hands. You did well."

"Means a lot coming from you, Joe." He slapped me on the shoulder and gave us a moment alone.

"You're not feeling sick are you?" I asked. She looked flushed.

"Perfect. I thought it would hurt more than it did, though. I want to get the other one done eventually."

"It takes a while to heal. You're still riding the adrenaline high, but you'll be sore for a long time. Thank fuck you still have one nipple I can touch."

"Oh, just touch?" She smirked. I closed the door and locked it. I had time to kill, and Suzy sat before me with her breast exposed and a look of want in her eyes. "What are you doing?" Her eyes twinkled—she knew exactly what I had in mind.

"We're going to have a chat about my text you didn't respond to, and then I'm going to fuck you bent over that chair."

I loved her surprised face. "What text?"

"Look at your phone." I crossed my arms over my chest and waited for her to read it.

"You want to move in together?" Her eyes grew wide and her mouth hung open.

"Yes, sugar. We spend every night together, so why should you have to make a house payment when I have a place of my own?"

"Don't take offense, City, but your place isn't really my taste. The man cave, barren walls, and cottage feel. Can't do it. You can move in with me, though."

"Whatever makes you happy. As long as I have you in my bed and my bike in the garage, I'm a happy man."

"So that's it? We're doing it?"

"Oh, we're doing it. Undress, sugar. You're not leaving here until I've erased any scent my brother left behind and my cock is satisfied." I started to unzip my pants, and watched her carefully as she began to undress. Her nipple was red and slightly swollen from the piercing, and I'd have to remind myself not to touch it.

"Grip the headrest, ass out." I stroked my cock as she kept turning her head to see what I was doing. I liked to make her wait.

When she turned back around, I smacked her ass, causing her to jump and yelp. "What was that for?"

"Next time, ask before you change your body forever. I won't say no, but I'd just like to be clued the fuck in. I would've given that nipple a little extra attention before you took it off the market for a couple of months."

"Yes, sir." She smiled and rested her forehead against the leather.

Packing up my house didn't take long. We decided I would move my things during Thanksgiving break. I didn't put my house up for sale. It was paid off and I didn't see the need to get rid of it.

I loved the land that the small farmhouse sat on. I bought it for that reason, and thought that someday I'd build my dream house on the property.

I moved my clothes into her spare room. She bought a small drawing table for me to use in the evenings, and I decorated the space with my work and my Harley memorabilia. I didn't want to invade her space. Moving in together was a giant step, more of a leap of faith.

"Are you sure you don't want to put your clothes in my closet?" she asked, leaning against the doorframe in a tiny purple silk nightie.

"No, sugar. My things are just fine in here." I unpacked the last box of clothing, sliding them in the dresser drawer that she'd emptied for me. "You need your space, especially your walk-in closet."

She sighed as she pushed her body away from the door and walked toward me. "Be patient with me."

"Sugar, come here." Holding out my hand to her, I pulled her in my lap. "Don't do anything different because I'm here. I'm easy to live with. I don't require too much. Your body is the only thing I'm impatient about. It's mine."

Her eyes twinkled and her smile widened. "It's yours, City."

"Whenever I want?" I raised my eyebrow, giving her a sly smile.

"Yes." She giggled as I grabbed her by the waist, lifting her ass on the dresser. "What are you doing?"

"Taking what's mine." My hands drifted up her legs, spreading them, and raised the nightie to her abdomen.

The smile fell from her face and all giggles disappeared as I licked her clit. Her body relaxed, resting against the wall, as a small moan escaped her lips. My dick ached to be buried inside her, straining against my track pants. Her breath hitched as I dipped my tongue inside her. The sweetest nectar didn't compare to the taste of Suzy, and I always wanted more.

Her legs tightened around my head, as her breathing grew shallow. Her thighs began to tremble underneath my grip. I sucked harder, flicking her clit with my tongue to drive her over the edge. Her hands fisted my hair as she pushed my face deeper, and I growled, relishing in the prickling sensation of her tugging my scalp.

"Oh, fuck. City," she screamed as I sucked harder, drawing her entirely in my mouth. Her body twitched, and she shook under my tongue as she came on my face. I could never get enough of her. She gasped for air, swallowing with wide eyes as she looked down at me. The grip on my scalp lightened as she grew limp and her back collapsed against the wall. Her nightie had slipped off her shoulder, exposing her breast and the small silver hoop that I'd been dying to touch, but couldn't.

Adjusting my dick as I stood, I kissed her lips, sucking the last bit of air she had into my mouth. "I'll never get enough of you, sugar." Our tongues tangled, her juice mixing with her saliva. She drove me wild. The feel of her small hands on my shoulders, gripping toughly, her nails digging into my flesh, made me rock fucking hard.

"More," she whispered against my lips.

"Insatiable." I pulled her body forward as I opened the top drawer, pulling out a condom.

I fucked her hard and fast. The wooden dresser slammed against the wall, thumping with each thrust. I prayed it didn't collapse from the abuse. Her legs rested on my shoulders as I gripped her ankles, pumping inside her. Each thrust forced a moan from her lips. My balls tightened as her pussy clamped down on my shaft. Her eyes drifted closed as I tipped over the edge, spiraling into an orgasm so intense my legs almost gave out.

My chest heaved as I tried to catch my breath. Her eyes fluttered open, and her cheeks were redder from the second orgasm.

"That's how to start a day."

"Promise." She smiled at me, running her hands down my bare chest.

"I'd fuck you all day, but we wouldn't get much accomplished, sugar. Your pussy is fucking addictive."

"Ha, your cock isn't so bad either."

"You know what your dirty mouth does to me."

"No, we have too much to do, big boy." She pushed against my chest before hopping off the dresser.

I grabbed her around the waist, pulling her back to me. "I'm not done with you yet, sugar. I own your ass," I whispered in her ear.

"I love you," she said, as her eyes grew wide and she covered her mouth.

"What did you say?" I tried not to smile, but the corner of my mouth twitched; I was unable to hold back my happiness. As her hand fell from her lips, I gathered her face in my hands to look her in the eyes.

"I love you, Joey."

"Sugar, I love you more than I thought I could ever love another woman. I've wanted to say those words to you, but I didn't want you to freak the fuck out."

"I do, City. I love you for everything you are. You're everything I wanted and the only one I think about. You've invaded my heart, and I can't go another day without saying the words to you."

"Say it again," I said as I brushed my lips against her mouth.

"I love you." The whisper of her words on my lips warmed my body and sent a shock through my system.

Epilogue

Suzy

The transition of having someone live with me again had been easier than I thought. After Sophia and Kayden moved out, I didn't think I would ever allow someone else to live with me. Not because they were such a problem, but because I didn't think I'd find I could get along with. I know I'm not the easiest person in the world, and it's a fact that I'd always accepted. We talked about moving into a bigger place, but I didn't think we could afford it. My place was perfectly adequate.

It had only been a couple of weeks, but it had been wonderful. My house was small, but everything seemed to fit okay—with some adjustment on both our parts. I was thankful that it was Christmas break and that I'd get to spend the holidays with City and his family. My parents decided to go on a Caribbean cruise and leave me behind this year, and my sister had her fiancé's family to be with. If it weren't for City and the Gallo family, I'd be the third wheel at Sophia's apartment.

City had spent the morning making a special breakfast for us before heading to his parents' house. He told me that his mother always made panettone French toast every Christmas, and he wanted to treat me to his mother's recipe. It had been the best Christmas morning since my childhood.

I still hadn't mastered cooking, and stuck with the few dishes I could make edible. His mother had shown me some of her techniques and made notecards for me to follow, but it was useless. She would say, "No worries, love, you'll get the hang of it. It just takes practice." It was nice of her, but I knew that either you had it or you didn't—and I clearly didn't.

"Ready to go, sugar?" City asked from the bathroom doorway as I finished applying my lipstick. He looked handsome in a black pair of jeans and tight gray sweater. I wanted to unwrap him like a present.

"Just about, Joey. Do I look all right?" I turned to face him, and watched as his eyes traveled up the length of my body before he stared into my eyes.

"Always beautiful." He grabbed my face and kissed my lips, and the familiar want filled my body. I didn't know if I'd ever lose that feeling with him. I hoped I never did. "No time for what you're thinking, sugar. We can't be late today."

"I can wait. I'm not a total fiend." I laughed. "Did you load all the gifts?"

"Just waiting on you, sugar."

"Okay, I'm ready."

He held my hand and stroked it with his thumb as he drove. He looked happier than he did when we first met. He didn't look sad back then, but the happiness didn't radiate off him. It made me happy to know that I had put it there.

His parents' driveway was packed with cars as we parked on the curb. "Looks like a full house."

"Sugar, Italians do it big. My mom cooks for an army and invites all the neighbors to dinner."

"Oh, that's nice of her. I didn't get presents for everyone, though." A panicky feeling overcame me. I had met his family a couple of times and just started to feel comfortable, and now I'd have to sit in a room full of strangers.

"We do our gift opening later, after everyone leaves. Stop worrying—everyone loves you as much as I do."

City opened the door to a house of people; it looked to be bursting at the seams. His mom came toward the door with a smile on her face. She had on reindeer antlers and a cheery Christmas sweater. She looked like a mom, and one that any child would've been lucky to have.

"Suzy, love, merry Christmas." She enveloped me in a hug. City cleared his throat, and she chuckled in my ear and ignored him. "I'm so glad you came."

"Thanks, Mrs. G. I wouldn't want to be anywhere else. It smells amazing in here."

She held my shoulders and looked at me. "I made all the classic Italian Christmas dishes. Got to fatten you up, my dear." She rubbed my shoulder and stopped on the bone that sat below the skin.

"Not too much, Mrs. G, but I'll have some of everything."

"I knew I loved you, and yes, we do. Someday you'll be carrying my grandbabies." She smiled at me and made a face at Joey.

He choked and wrapped his arm around her to pull her off me. "Ma, let's not get ahead of ourselves."

"Just looking toward the future, Joseph. I want little ones running around. I'm too old not to have at least one. Try and make me happy for next Christmas, will you?"

"In time, Ma. Just give me a hug and we'll talk about it another day." He made eyes at me over her head, and I knew he was embarrassed, but I thought his mom was cute. Her words scared the piss out of me, but it was something nice to think about. I wanted him all to myself as long as possible.

"Come in and grab something to munch on before dinner's ready. Joseph, go introduce her to everyone."

"Yes, Ma." He wasn't always the most patient man, but that changed when he was around his mom. The reverence that was paid to a mom in an Italian family was something to watch. No one fucked with her or went against her word.

We walked around, and Joey introduced me to the family members that flew from Chicago for a warmer holiday, and the friends of the family. In my family, handshakes were the norm, but here hugs were expected. There was a warmth in the house and love could be felt in the chatter of the guests. I felt at home.

"Suzy," Izzy yelled above the crowd, and I could see her hand waving in the air.

"I'm going to go say hi to your sister. I'll be back," I said as I reached up and kissed his cheek.

He smiled at me with loving blue eyes. "I'll join you in a minute," he said before turning his attention back to the neighbor. They were discussing football and the possible Super Bowl teams. Boring didn't even begin to describe how I felt about the topic.

Izzy looked amazing, like always. Her long, flowing black hair framed her face perfectly. She had on a skintight dress that hugged her curves and showed off her beauty.

"Hey, Iz, it's good to see you."

"Merry Christmas, Suzy. I'm so happy you made it. How's my brother doing?"

"They're talking about football. Thank you for rescuing me." We both laughed and looked over at the two men waving their hands as they spoke.

"Boys and their sports. Did you guys exchange your gifts yet?" The look on her face told me that she knew what City had bought me, and she couldn't wait to get my take on the gift.

"Not yet. Do you know what it is?" I squinted at her. I never liked surprises, and maybe I could get it out of her.

"Oh, I know, and my lips are sealed, babe. City would be pissed if I spoiled his surprise."

A surprise. That means it was something big, and not a frilly dress or casual gift like we'd agreed on. I had purchased clothes and a cross pendant for him, along with new leather riding gloves. He was impossible to buy for, but I threw in some ultra-sexy lingerie that would have to wait until tonight.

"I hate surprises," I grumbled.

"This one you won't, trust me." She smiled and giggled, and my heart began to pound in my chest.

We hadn't discussed marriage, and I didn't know what I'd do if he bought me a ring and asked me in front of his family. Breathe—you can do it.

"Hey, big brother, merry Christmas." She wrapped her arms around Joey and they whispered in each other's ears.

The clinking of glass caused everyone to turn toward the kitchen. His mother stood, her antlers shaking with each stroke of her hand. A hush descended over the crowd as she began to speak. "I want to thank everyone for coming today. It wouldn't be Christmas without my family and friends. Dinner's served—feel free to help yourself."

"Your mother is really is adorable," I said to Joey as he wrapped his arm around my shoulder.

"Yeah, she loves the holidays. Anytime she can get people to eat, she's a happy woman. Hungry?"

"I just ate a ton of appetizers, but I don't want her upset so I'll figure a way to eat more."

"Better get used to it, sugar. Food's the name of the game in this house," he said as we moved toward the kitchen.

A line had already formed, and he stroked my back as we waited to grab a plate. Every granite countertop in the expansive kitchen had a dish of some sort filled with food. The woman should've opened a restaurant with her culinary skills. Every type of pasta dish, braciole, chicken Parmesan, and meatballs were waiting to be consumed.

We found an open space on the lanai and chatted with the table guests until we couldn't eat any more. I kept eyeing the bottles of wine on the table—Gallo Family Vineyard. Gallo was a common Italian name, and I was sure out of pride they chose this label above the rest. I could hardly move. If they celebrated every holiday with this much food, my waistline would be in serious jeopardy.

The ladies cleaned the kitchen, and I was told under no circumstances was I allowed to help. His mom wanted me enjoy myself, since I was a guest, while she and her sisters did the dirty work. I dozed off on Joey's shoulder during the chitchat and screaming at the football game on the television, but was woken up for the next round of eating—dessert.

The guests left a couple of hours later, after coffee was served and the football game ended. After the last person walked out, his mother yelled from the foyer, "Who's ready for gifts?"

"Anthony, get your ass in here," Izzy yelled from the floor.

His mother sat down next to the tree and waited for everyone to take a seat. "I love you all, but I miss Thomas. I wish he could've been here with us this year." The smile on her face faded as she wiped her eyes with the back of her hand. I knew little of Thomas, and he was the only sibling I hadn't met. "He called this morning and spoke to your father and I. He promises he'll be here next year." She cleared her throat. "I'm thankful that Suzy could join us."

She pulled a gift from under the tree and held it out to me. "For you," she said.

I placed it on my lap and looked around, noticing that all eyes were on me. "What?"

"We all take turns, sugar." City patted my leg.

"Oh, sorry. My family, it's more like a free-for-all. Not used to this, but I'll learn."

It took hours to open gifts. They ranged in all sizes and shapes. I watched the family in front of me with joy. I'd never experienced something as loving as the Gallo family Christmas.

"I love everything you got me, sugar. I'll use it all." He kissed my cheek.

I smiled at him and whispered in his ear. "Wait until you see your last gift, but it's at home—for your eyes only." I bit his earlobe and was rewarded with a deep kiss.

"Hey, I know I want grandbabies, but not right here on the couch, please. There's one more gift under the tree, and it's for Suzy." His mother beamed as she handed the last present to me.

The box was small, but not a ring box. City leaned back and stared at me to gauge my reaction. I looked around as I undid the ribbon It's a horrible feeling to be the one left out—to be the surprised and not the one doing the surprising.

Tucked inside was a small business card. I read it, but didn't know what it meant. "You gave me a business card?" I asked, confused.

"No, sugar. Read it. Turn it over."

Mrs. Perkins

Florida Real Estate Specialist

I flipped the card over and recognized Joey's handwriting.

Something to call "ours"

Merry Christmas, sugar

"I don't understand," I mumbled as I turned the card over again.

Joey grabbed my hand as he spoke. "I want to buy a house for us. I want you to pick out your dream home, or we can build on my land."

"Joey, we can't afford that, but it's a nice thought." I knew his gesture was sincere, even if it were a fairytale.

His mother started to giggle, and the entire family laughed. I didn't get the joke. "Tell her, Joseph," his mother said as she sat down next to his father.

"Suzy, we can afford it. I can afford it."

"How?" I felt like an idiot.

"Jesus Christ, son. Suzy, our family owns a vineyard in Italy. We've owned it for generations. Joseph doesn't flaunt his wealth, but he has the ability to buy five homes."

I looked from his father to Joey, who sat there with a grin. "Is he telling the truth?"

"Yes, sugar. We all own a portion of the vineyard. We run the tattoo shop because we don't want to sit on our ass all day. We wanted something that was entirely ours and separate from what we inherited."

"Why didn't you tell me?" I felt awkward having this discussion in front of his family, but I figured they knew his reasons.

He stroked my face. "I like my little farmhouse. It was enough for me. I also don't like people to know my business. Too many people want things when they know you have money. Sugar, you have to understand. I thought if I ever—and I didn't think I would—found someone that I loved, I had to know they loved me for me and not my money."

"I do love you for you, Joey." The words came out with ease, and even though I knew he'd lied to me for months, I could understand why. "I'm happy in my home, though. No need to buy another."

"Exactly—'your home,' sugar, not ours. I want something that we pick out together with room to grow. We're cramped, but happy. Anything you want is yours. All I ask is for a big garage for my motorcycles and a space for the guys to hang out."

His mom clapped her hands. "Get lots of bedrooms too. I want an army of grandbabies." Even though the idea of a horde of children made my body break out into a blotchy rash, a big house would be wise.

"Not helping, Ma."

Her laughter filled the room. "Sorry, a girl can dream, can't she?"

"So what do you say, sugar? Can we buy a home for us? It can be a fresh start, the beginning of an amazing journey. We'll take our time until we find the perfect place. I love you, Suzy McCarthy, and this is what I want for us."

I didn't really have anything to think about. My last wall had crumbled. Everything I had on my impossible checklist had come true, and Joey was the man I'd always wanted. His family waited for my reply, and the air felt heavy. "Yes, Joey. I'd love to find our home and look to the future. I love you too."

His kiss stole my breath, as it always did. I thought back to the words Sophia told me not long ago. Butterflies—I still felt butterflies every time I saw him. The nervous energy never left my body, and I felt the electricity when we touched. When it's right, you know it. He was the one. Mine.